# Worlds Apart

## *Barry Woodford Weedon*

# Sixth Sense

When he woke up, Harry Bollinger could see nothing but featureless whiteness, and hear nothing but his own breathing and his heartbeats. He lay on his back for a few moments with his eyes open, his scalp crawling with strangeness, before he dared to move a muscle.

Nothing but whiteness and silence.

Harry raised his head and looked at his body. With relief, he saw his familiar, casual one-piece suit and heavy country shoes. He could feel that he was lying on something soft and warm. Smooth as the surface of a liquid, but dry and elastic, it made no sound as his fingers explored it. It showed no shadows and no discernible edge. Even when, with disconcertingly creaking joints and rustling clothes, he knelt up, he could not see any limit to the white floor. There was no line of demarcation between it and the whiteness above. He could not really see the floor itself. The light came from all around, above and below, and was not reflecting off the floor, but passing through it. His hand, waved near the surface, cast no shadow.

*This must be a nightmare,* he thought, *so, if I want to wake up, I simply wake up. It always works.*

It did not work.

He lay, waiting, quite conscious, and nothing happened.

The pounding thumps of his heart began to slow down, as he realised that he was comfortable, free to move, and under no immediate threat. He might even be safe. But he felt lonely and afraid in the white void.

*What's going on?* he thought. *I was walking over Kama Bridge – yes – on the way to meet Sally and the children for a picnic lunch. Sun damned hot, nearly mid-day, birds flying about, plenty of insects, plenty of green shoots – a very well balanced Spring, I'd say. In fact we've been doing very nicely since we introduced global envirocontrol in 2059 – or was it earlier? Yes, about 2057, because I took my first vacation here in 2058. That's right – and the grand-cows and great-sheep look fine, too.*

*God, what a sight that grand-bull is...*

*And – well – what?*

*Nothing.*

*I woke up.*

*Here.*

*Just like that.*

Harry stood up, staggering a little, because of the lack of reference points. Under his feet, the smooth whiteness was no longer soft, and, as he stepped tentatively forward, his feet did not slip. His feet made faint pats, with no echoes.

He had no reason to walk, and nowhere to head for, but it felt better to be doing something.

On impulse, he looked at his watch. It indicated 11.31 18 SEP.

11.31 *Time for coffee...*

Then he realised – SEP!

He stopped walking, his mind reeling.

He was on a Spring vacation in Saharania. In March. Six months ago.

His watch must be wrong. He took off the watch and checked all functions.

Perfect.

It was a waterproof, anti-shock, anti-everything, self-charging model. Old-fashioned certainly – using its own internal timing and built-in date program – but highly reliable. The makers had gone to great lengths to make it user-friendly. It was easy to set, but absurdly difficult to set by mistake. Harry had never had to set it. It had always shown

3

the right time and date since his father had given it to him fifteen years ago. No-one else had ever touched it. He never took it off except – quite unnecessarily as he admitted – to wash.

Therefore it must have been running for about six months longer than his memory.

Harry felt his scalp crawl again, his knees buckled and he sat down, heavily. The white surface cushioned him softly and silently.

Sweat ran down his back. He mopped his forehead with his sleeve, breathing fast, heart pounding. He sat for some minutes, staring at his watch. The digits changed at what seemed a normal rate: 11.33... 11.34...

The virtual hands agreed. The sweep virtual second-hand virtually swept.

Gradually Harry calmed, almost hypnotised by the watch's routine... 11.41... 11.42... a suddenly precious link with ordinary, predictable living.

Had he had an accident? Could this be some new treatment for people with loss of memory? Alzheimer's?

The whiteness fitted a hospital atmosphere, and the padded floor would seem a reasonable precaution. Except that it was not padded. It was soft if you sat, and hard if you walked.

No surface Harry had heard of could do that.

Besides, surely, there ought to be, at least, minimal furniture and some sort of background noise.

Perhaps, if he shouted, someone would hear him?

He shouted, selfconsciously, "Help!" just once.

His voice died, as if in fog on a marsh. Harry listened.

Silence for three minutes. Then, a sweet, melodious chime.

Harry jumped convulsively, gathered himself, and looked all round. No indication of where the sound had come from. He waited tensely. His shout seemed to have brought a response, at least, and his puzzlement was now mixed with curiosity.

Harry crouched on the white, soft floor, feeling strongly that he was being watched. Silence stretched behind his rapid heartbeats. He found himself counting them automatically:..13, 14, 15...

Perhaps he had imagined that chime – a hallucination caused by sensory deprivation and loneliness? The chime had come from no particular direction, but he was fairly sure it had originated outside him. Anyway, it was not a threatening kind of sound. It was, you could say, deferential and polite – like the *bing-bong* before an airline announcement: 'Sorry to interrupt your train of thought, but you may want to hear what the announcer is going to say.'

The banality of the sound was soothing.

"Greetings!" said a voice, a fluty, feminine voice.

"Christ!" gasped Harry.

Still on his knees, he swung round, to find himself nose-to-nose with a strikingly good-looking young woman.

Embarrassed, he backed away, and discovered, to his horror, that only half of her was there. Her hands were clasped across her tummy – and, just below them, with startling sharpness, was the line where her cut-off body met the white floor.

Harry cautiously got to his feet and stumbled backwards a few paces, staring. The girl returned his stare with a slightly puzzled gaze, her head tilted a little, as though listening or thinking.

After some seconds, she began to rise bodily. As she did so, the remainder of her came up through the floor until she was standing with her bare feet on the surface.

She wore a shimmering, ankle-length dress, in a deep green colour. The style was currently popular, though on the formal side. Her fashionably matching green hair hung in one plait over her left shoulder. She looked both ravishing and cold.

5

Harry cleared his throat, trying to think of something to say. Nothing appropriate sprang to mind. There was a long pause, while he tried unsuccessfully to pick out something sensible from his racing thoughts.

Then the girl said, "We are unable to interpret your remark. We are aware of the major beliefs concerning the individual whose name you mentioned, and of his cultural significance. However, we cannot determine whether you are identifying me with him, under various possible misapprehensions – including my depicted sex – or whether you are calling upon him to protect you from some threat that you imagine. Please clarify."

Harry could not recall making any remark that might have provoked this unusual utterance. In fact, he had not quite followed the utterance at all, being preoccupied with speculations concerning the girl's trick of emerging from the floor.

He had gathered that she wanted him to explain something. "Er – what did you say?" he managed eventually.

The girl repeated what she had said, word for word.

"Oh!" said Harry, "You mean why 'Christ?' Well, I was – well – surprised. It just came out... I couldn't... I mean, suddenly face-to-face like that... " He stopped, since the girl was looking more and more puzzled.

Another pause, then, "Is it perhaps a custom of your culture to use the name Christ as a greeting in the case of sudden, unexpected encounters?"

"Good God, no!" said Harry, realising, as he said it, that he had probably caused another misunderstanding, and hastening to forestall it. "Erm – well – yes – I suppose we do. We use words like that, just as expressions – you know – to let off steam, if you know what I mean."

"Steam," said the girl, "is water in the vapour or gaseous phase. It has been used by numerous cultures as a working fluid in heat engines. In many such cultures, phrases equivalent to 'letting off steam' are applied metaphorically to denote releasing of emotional tension. Did you use this exclamation for that purpose, as we suppose from the context?"

"Yes," said Harry.

"We understand!" The girl smiled radiantly and warmly. "You may call me Jean."

"My name's Harry Bollinger," said Harry, instinctively putting out his hand.

The girl inclined her head, but kept her arms folded.

Harry drew back, feeling a bit silly.

"We offer an apology," said Jean in her rounded, woodwind tones, "for our imperfect understanding of your language and customs. Our observations have necessarily been of limited duration, and this is our first two-way communication with a member of your particular culture."

Her smile faded slightly. "We regret, too, the inaccurate control setting of our three-dimensional simulator, which, at the beginning of our conversation required vertical adjustment to render my lower extremities visible. Our observers have reported no equivalent device in your culture. Your holographic computer animations still fall short of true credibility. We presume that you have been mistaking illusion for reality, and that initially you were under the impression that the part you could see was the whole of me. We had no intention to deceive. We request forgiveness." Now she looked serious, and somewhat crestfallen.

Harry was enormously relieved to hear all this, but not less nervous. He was, however, greatly impressed.

By the early Twenty-first Century, computer animations had become fairly realistic. Then MegaSoft came out with TruDee, which justifiably claimed to 'Create the reality you imagine, *warts and all.*' Writers, choreographers and production companies had jumped at it. It gave them total control, not only what of was done, but also of who did it, and how they looked. Actors and ballet dancers suddenly discovered why they paid dues to their unions. So did their union officials. Thanks to ageing Human Rights legislation, computer-generated virtual reality had eventually been banned from public entertainment in most countries, except (of course) for commercial advertising. It could easily fool a sober, adult viewer.

Harry realised that the girl was waiting for him to speak. She now looked quite miserable. It was surprisingly hard to think of her as a mere illusion.

"That's all right," he said, "but may I ask something?"

"Yes," she replied, smiling again.

"Where are we? What is this white stuff we are standing on? Why can't we see where it finishes? And why have you brought me here?"

"We distinguish four questions if we have understood correctly. Please confirm."

"Well I'm afraid I wasn't counting, " said Harry, "but I expect it was four."

"We are at Mid. The white stuff is a plastics material, a polymer based on silicon, carbon, certain metallic elements, and halogens. It cannot be seen to finish because its configuration is unbounded. We have brought you here to be Examined."

Harry felt that the girl had switched from confusing verbosity to equally confusing conciseness. Maybe he should take the questions one by one. He found the word 'Examined' disturbing, and felt inclined to put off discussing it as long as possible. So he said, "Please explain where you said we are – 'Mid' I think you said?"

"Mid is a name. It refers to a city and to a planet. The city is, by the standards of most cultures, large. The planet is, by comparison with most inhabited planets, small. The city covers the planet entirely. Your culture does not have specific knowledge of this city-planet. We have coined the name in your language, as a near equivalent of the corresponding names in the languages of the Fraternal Galactic Federation, usually referred to as the FGF.

"Mid is the meeting place of Galacon, the Council of the FGF. The Council comprises representatives of every member-species of the FGF. Since members are distributed randomly across the inhabitable parts of the Galaxy, Mid is situated as near to the Galactic Centre as is consistent with safety from the influence of the Central Black Hole."

*Back to verbosity*, thought Harry.

However, he now knew where he was, if he could believe it.

*But it is*, he reasoned, *impossible.*

The validity of Einstein's special theory of relativity had been demonstrated by numerous experiments, and no-one had come up with even a theoretical alternative that cast serious doubt on the basic consequences. Faster-than-light travel was out of the question. Harry could not remember how far the Earth was from the Galactic centre. *A hundred thousand light years, was it? Half that? Less? Whatever it was, I couldn't have got there in six months.*

Questions concerning the white surface now seemed pretty trivial.

Whoever, or whatever, had captured him clearly had access to some pretty advanced technology – as the totalistically 3-D simulator was enough to prove. Perhaps they could travel at speeds near that of light, and had really brought him close to the centre of the Galaxy, regardless of the fact that he would never be able to return to his own time and people. If so, they must either have some compelling reason, or be indifferent to the fate of individuals they chose to 'examine'. And yet, they had offered him polite apologies quite gratuitously, as though he were a guest, rather than a prisoner.

Their attractive simulante and their readiness to answer his questions – however implausibly – suggested that they wanted him to respond favourably. But how could they expect this, when they had just told him, in effect, that his life had been sacrificed to their curiosity? He was beginning to feel angry, as well as afraid, but determined to keep his temper, learn what he could, and stay alive as long as possible.

Jean was waiting calmly for him to speak. To Harry, her smile seemed warm and open enough to make him doubt his depressing logic. He forced himself to remember that she was only an illusion, and found enough courage to say, "You claim that you have brought me to the centre of the Galaxy, and you intend to examine me in some way. Do you feel that you have a right to grab people, take them out of their ordinary lives and seal them up in plastics? And what do you mean by 'examine'?"

Her smile did not waver. She appeared to have missed the anger in Harry's tone. "We do not need a right to 'grab' people, since we do not grab them. We simply bring them for examination. They are here for only a short time, and return to their ordinary lives. We naturally regret any inconvenience."

Harry wondered if he could detect a note of irony in the words. The girl's expression was sincere enough, and, ironical or not, what she had said was, at face value, slightly reassuring. They apparently believed they could send him home in time to take up his normal life. Or perhaps they did not appreciate the need for continuity. Perhaps they thought that if they put him back where they had found him, he would simply go on from there irrespective of any time lapse – as a small boy expects a frog to do when he puts it back in a pond after a few miserable days in a jam jar.

The girl went on, while Harry listened with growing disbelief and unease, "Galacon examines specimens of all sentient species encountered by members of the FGF, to determine whether each such species is eligible for admission to the Federation. Energy considerations render it impracticable to examine more than one specimen of any given species, though, in the interest of justice, we make an exception in the case of the death of a specimen before the examination is complete enough for a definite conclusion and verdict.

"You, Ha Ribo Lin-Jer, have been selected as a typical specimen of your species. The examination takes the form of a conversation. At the end of the conversation we shall let you know our verdict."

These cool words, spoken in the simulante's lovely, musical voice, filled Harry with mingled nausea and terror. He could scarcely speak. His throat had tightened up, but he forced out, incredulously, "Are you telling me that you are going to – to ask me – questions – and use what you find out from *one* conversation to – judge – the whole of the human race?"

"Energy considerations make it necessary to use a single sample," smiled the simulante. "The procedure is considered fair, since the sample is selected at random, as far as possible. There is some bias, since we must ensure that the Specimen speaks a language that we can translate. This restricts the choice to representatives of groups who use electronic communications extensively, because only these can be systematically monitored. The bias is thus necessarily towards technologically oriented sections of the population, and is therefore considered not only inevitable but also acceptable."

"But just one. Out of billions," muttered Harry, "How can you be sure?"

"We do not understand the question. It seems incomplete or irrelevant. We fail to see the importance of the ratio between sample size and population. We are not trying to obtain statistics. How can we be sure of what?"

"Of – er – whatever you're are looking for..." Harry was feeling out of his depth.

"We can be sure, because what we are looking for is a recognisable characteristic, and if present in any member of a species, is within the awareness of all. Or most. At, at least, those acceptably typical.

"We consider that the Examination should start as soon as possible, and will explain the rules, procedure and circumstances as soon as we perceive a sufficient reduction in the symptoms of emotional tension you are displaying. Please let us know verbally if you would prefer us to begin the explanation as a possible means of allaying your apparent anxieties. It *is* usually a matter of considerable interest to Specimens, and tends to distract their attention from their less immediate worries"

*So they've noticed,* thought Harry. *Maybe what she's suggesting makes sense.*

If they were determined to 'examine' him, and there was no way of escaping it, then the sooner it was over with, the better. "All right, then – go ahead. I'm listening," he growled grudgingly.

"The purpose of the Examination, as we mentioned before, is to enable Galacon to determine whether your species, which you call Humanity or Man, is eligible for admission to the Fraternal Galactic Federation. Our observers have established that Man satisfies most of our criteria, by watching developments on your planet over a period of 8216 Earth years. Such observations do not include two-way communication. They are therefore necessarily confined to trivialities, such as, for example, the making of artefacts, the domination of other species, harnessing of natural forces, the use of con-specific slaves, and control of the environment.

"We perceive that Man, like approximately 83% of the species that we have previously Examined, is capable not only of consciously constructing, but also of mindlessly destroying. Again, we notice progress in technology, which enables increasingly economical use of materials and energy, and we see, simultaneously, a rapid growth in waste of materials, and in irreversible consumption of energy. Since Man's development of electronic communications, we have monitored – on the same channels, and sometimes even in the same voice – exhortations towards peace and justifications of war.

"None of these paradoxes is unusual or significant. What members of a species do to one another, or to their planetary resources, is no concern of ours. Our observations are designed to build up a case for Examination, which is established by the trivia we have mentioned, and then to obtain enough physiological and linguistic data to conduct the Examination itself. Do you have any questions?"

"Several," said Harry, conscious of a long line of questions jostling to be asked. "I've been wondering. Why have you been watching us for such a long time? Eight-thousand-something years seems a bit excessive. I should have thought you'd have picked up at least one of our languages ages ago. And – another thing – once you have mastered a language, surely you can find out all you want from listening to people's conversations. Not only that. You said that if any member of a species has the characteristic you are looking for, then all of them know about it. In that case, why don't you just ask me, straight out?"

The simulante's expression remained calm and inscrutable. "We watch every planet on which we detect life, for as long as necessary and no longer. 8216 Earth years is not out of the ordinary. To help you understand the necessity, an analogy may be useful. Imagine that you yourself were set the apparently simple task of determining which species of birds, if any, mate for life, but forbidden to observe birds except by watching videos captured at random locations. To get an idea of the difficulty we face, assume that you have no idea of what a bird is, beyond the fact that it is a living creature. Allow yourself complete knowledge of the anatomy and physiology and behaviour of insects, mammals, reptiles and amphibians, and you'll still find that the task takes you some time, we suggest.

"We do not visit the planets that we Observe. Our equipment is highly sensitive, capable of acquiring finely detailed data. We can track the movements of an *ant* if we wish. However, we can only see, but not hear. Consequently, since almost all intelligent communication on your planet, as on most planets we have encountered that are inhabited by intelligent beings, is by speech, or through written symbols for spoken words, we were unable to understand your languages, or even to confirm their existence until you had developed electronics, which we can easily monitor. After that, we were able to interpret your major oral and written languages within thirty Earth years.

"Listening to conversations, or watching the output of visual communications media, has gravely misled us in the past, when studying other species. We find out a great deal, of course, but cannot reliably detect the crucial Characteristic without a two-way talk with a Specimen. As you noticed, at the outset of our meeting we had trouble grasping the connotations of your uttered words. We knew, for example, the immense significance of the notions associated with Christ among members of your particular cultural group. However, given the reverence normally accorded to these notions, we have been unable to establish a working rule to identify contexts in which the name may be pronounced casually, as you pronounced it. We have concluded that even individuals who hold the notions in awe are inconsistent in their use of this name.

"During our monitoring we constantly wish that we could ask speakers what they really *mean* by words that we thought we had fully assimilated. In direct conversation we learn more rapidly."

Despite lingering suspicions, Harry found himself impressed. He was becoming increasingly convinced that the Fraternal Galactic Federation was a reality, not some elaborate trick of technically gifted and extremely rich human practical jokers.

Jean went on, "Apart from this, the relevant Characteristic cannot be assessed by evaluation of interaction between members of the same species. The inter-species context is essential. Also, the Characteristic must be demonstrated, not simply referred to by the Specimen. This is one reason why we cannot question you directly. The other reason is that if you knew what we were after, it would be easy to pretend. You might not normally be a liar, but, with your race's membership of the FGF at stake, the temptation would be great. If you have no further questions, we shall explain the circumstances and rules of your Examination."

Harry thought, *Wait a minute. Until now, nobody has ever heard of the Fraternal Galactic Thingy. We've done OK without it so far – so why worry?* He shook his head. "No further questions – at the moment."

Jean bowed gravely, then recited, "You will be examined in a plenary session of Galacon, currently convened. This implies that you will find yourself to be in the presence of representatives of every FGF species. Some of the species are of forms inimical to Man. You will not be in physical danger, but are advised to prepare yourself against emotional shock.

"This simulante will not be present during your Examination, since, if you could see it, you might draw inferences from its expression and behaviour. This might mislead both you and Galacon.

"The rules of Examination are as follows. The Specimen may not be intentionally damaged or misled. Any question may be uttered by the Specimen or by any member of Galacon. Neither the Specimen nor any member of Galacon is obliged to ask or to answer any question or to make any statement. Every utterance, facial expression, gesture or posture of the Specimen is subject to evaluation. Do you understand these rules?"

"Yes, I think so. Just like a British police caution. 'You have the right to remain silent, but if you say nothing or refuse to answer our questions, we'll take that as proof of guilt' or words to that effect."

The simulante frowned. "That may or may not be a valid simile. However, you should bear in mind that you will be *Examined* for something we value, not *tried* to establish your guilt. However, in one respect you are admittedly at a disadvantage. You do not know what we are looking for, and yet it is up to you *alone* to show that your species possesses it.

"To give you an opportunity of preparing yourself, we shall allot you five minutes. Your wristwatch is operative. Although its indications probably no longer correspond with local Earth time, the intervals between indicated minutes are correct. During your preparation period, you may find it useful to read the Hints for Specimens on the virtual screen behind you."

Harry turned round, but could see nothing but the all-enveloping whiteness. Puzzled, he looked back to where Jean had been, to find that she had vanished.

The light dimmed, leaving Harry in complete darkness. After a few moments, to his immense relief, a glow appeared to his left, faint at first but brightening. As he stared apprehensively, it resolved itself into clearly defined sets of yellow Gothic letters on a blue background.

At first, none of the words made sense. But after a few seconds he realised what was wrong. He knew just enough German to recognise it, but no more. "Hey!" he yelled, hoping that someone was listening, "This is in German. How do you expect me to read it?"

Nothing happened. Pulse racing, Harry stared at the screen, willing it to change. His precious five minutes was disappearing. It was most unfair that he should be deprived of reading hints that Specimens of other races had no doubt been able to benefit from.

After what felt like an age, the screen blanked momentarily, and new letters appeared. They were in orange, on a purple background.

Harry's relief swiftly changed to irritation. "Now it's upside-down!" he shouted, squatting and twisting round to read the message.

It started (inverted):       'WELCOME    TO    MID, SPECIMEN OF MAN'

During your Examination, act on the following Hints.

They may help, and can do no harm. They –

At the moment Harry reached this point, the screen blanked again, and the words appeared the right way up. There seemed to be far more than anyone could read in five minutes, even without the desperate stress that Harry was under. He glanced at the last Hint, to see how many there were. It was numbered '17' and said, 'Make yourself comfortable. We do.'

Harry went back to Hint Number 1 and read: 'Do not worry unduly.' *Unduly? How much is duly? O God...*

The list continued:

2. Listen carefully

3. You may consume nutriment if you have brought it

4. To save you the trouble of counting, Galacon has 83 member species

5. Do not leave your support-system, the boundary of which is marked by a white circle on the floor

6. You may loosen or remove clothing

7. Your thoughts are not being monitored during the Examination

8. The Examination may be terminated at any time at the request of the Specimen or by unanimous decision of Galacon or because of energy considerations

9. Following termination for any reason Galacon will give a final verdict as to Eligibility based on the proceedings prior to termination

10. Some of the members of Galacon may look horrible to you. Some look horrible to one another.

11. You may whistle or sing.

Harry's anxiety did not diminish as he tried to take in what he was reading. Some of the Hints seemed trivial, some irrelevant, and some of obvious importance. Perhaps they were all equally important to whoever had prepared them. He had got as far as the fourteenth Hint, which told him 'Cosmetics optical and acoustic aids prosthetic devices surgical appliances medical dressings and/or apparatus to assist in locomotion will not if normally worn or carried by the Specimen be mistaken as being intended to deceive Galacon', when his surroundings began to grow light and hubbub swelled around him.

As the virtual screen faded, Harry just caught '15. Natural functions, including...' before it flickered and died.

"This isn't fair!" he protested, looking round wildly. It was a mistake to look round. He was not prepared for what he saw. His mind recoiled.

He came to, lying on the soft floor. He kept his eyes shut and listened, trying to collect himself.

A debate was going on.

"... perfectly ordinary reaction, I tell you!" in a deep voice.

"But, with respect, I still maintain that Specimens should be allowed some minimal preconditioning. At least show them some 2-d simulos. After all, this kind of black-out is not unprecedented, and it would save Council energy if we..."

That was in a clear soprano, cut off in mid-sentence by a gruff bellowing roar. "It would save a lot more Council energy if you didn't keep repeating yourself! And if Specimens made proper use of the Hints provided! Good *energy* went into preparing those Hints, though I say so myself, and it's a shame to see it wasted."

When the roaring stopped, a mild, precise voice said, "All right, Member Grag. We all acknowledge your splendid contribution to the Hints. You never stop reminding us. However, I am inclined to the view so ably propounded by, if my memory serves me – now, let me see – was it Member Reepeequee or Member Trartyop? No, it was –" The even voice pattered on and on.

Harry had by now recovered sufficiently to realise that the discussion was related to his collapse. None of the Council members seemed surprised or concerned about his condition in particular, though they seemed to have plenty to say regarding such break-downs in general. He felt quite offended that no-one was doing anything to help him *After all*, he thought, *I might have had a heart attack, for all they know or care.*

His feeling of grievance gave him the nerve to open his eyes slightly. Trying not to let slip that he was conscious, he surreptitiously rolled on to his side, scanning only what he could see without turning his head.

He found himself looking up the curving side of a vast circular bowl, of which he was at the centre. Most of the bowl was in darkness, but scattered up and around its sides were pools of light, each of a slightly different colour, and each containing the representatives of one, to his eye, extraordinary species. Every delegation of representatives was surrounded by an intense white circle. Harry could see his own surrounding circle about ten feet in radius. It made the floor he lay on seem pale.

He forced himself to study the Council members within his limited field of vision. It occurred to him that it was not the species totally unlike Earth animals that he found the most repulsive, but the distorted parodies of familiar creatures. The hairy tripods had a certain dignity, and the pom-poms with fern-frond antennae were almost attractive. But the five-foot-long scaly slugs, the woolly centipedes with two-inch fangs, and the hairless, slack-skinned sickly-green gorillas gave Harry the embarrassed feeling he experienced whenever he saw a cripple or a hunchback. He was aware of being unjustifiably condescending, but could not rid himself of the conviction that nature had made a mistake in permitting such monsters – and his flesh crawled.

A hoarse voice intoned, "Such attempts at concealing consciousness are only to be expected. The Specimen believes itself immune to questioning or evaluation, and that it can observe at leisure."

*My God!* thought Harry, *they must know I'm awake.*

The voice husked on. "It is, of course, under close surveillance, and the situation is thus within our control. I therefore submit that there is no need to continue the present debate. Would you not agree, Man Specimen?"

Harry sat up and looked round, trying to find out which of the delegations contained the speaker with the croaking voice.

"It is not necessary for you to know which Member is addressing the Council, since, without more prolonged acquaintance with each of us, you would gain nothing in your ability to assess and evaluate any particular utterance, which is presumably the purpose of your attempt at identifying the source of remarks. However, it may interest you to know that, by long-standing tradition, in every plenary session of Galacon, a red or green light is made to appear above the delegation of the current speaker. If, as I surmise, your eyes are in what you call your front, then I am behind you. If you wish, you may inspect me, make any judgement you prefer, and answer my question or not."

Harry at last located the speaker's red light, and found that he was being spoken to by something like a large bottle wearing a grass skirt. He said, very slowly and carefully, "I am very sorry, but I am afraid I didn't quite understand what you asked me. Please would you mind repeating it?"

Uproar broke out. Every Member seemed to be shouting at once. "What did it say?" "Can't understand a word!" "The auto-translator's kaput. Someone kill the technician!" "Are you getting it direct, too, Member Venshoon?" "When will those idiots give us proper service?" "And I bet the Specimen can't hear us either. It's a disgusting waste of Council energy if you ask me..."

Eventually a huge voice bellowed, "All right! Members! Members! Please be calm. Quiet! NOW!"

The din subsided slightly, and the voice went on with lessened volume. "A switching fault – that's all. We can proceed with the Examination. I extend formal apologies for the interruption. Member Pren has the light. Please, silence for Member Pren."

Silence fell.

Evidently, the bottle in the grass skirt was Member Pren, since the light remained on over the same delegation. Harry hoped that Member Pren would not ask him to repeat what he had said before the interruption, since he had no longer any idea of what the question was, or of his reply.

Member Pren took his time. Harry found that it was becoming uncomfortable to look at him, as he stood, swaying slightly, in his grass skirt. A familiar and unwelcome feeling that he had not experienced since childhood was welling up within Harry. To distract himself he looked away from Member Pren and tried to organise his thoughts into a review of the Essential Qualities of Man. Perhaps he would recognise the right one if he could only… could only…

Pren's croak broke in, preventing any progress. "I shall not pursue my question. I shall, however, take this opportunity of reminding the Specimen of the importance of this Examination to its Species. And also of the Rule that requires the Specimen to exhibit he Characteristic for which it is being Examined."

The light over Pren's delegation went out.

Harry winced. *Was that supposed to be helpful? As if I needed reminding!*

"Is the Specimen suffering pain?" A kindly murmur came from one of the nearer delegations in a position to see Harry's face.

His wince had seemingly been misinterpreted. Not wishing to explain the true cause, Harry said tactfully, "Er – just a twinge. But I'm quite all right now, thank you."

Again uproar broke out. This time, however, many of the members were cheering. "It works! It works!"

"Well done, Trartyop. You"ve done a fine job on its language."

"Yes – well done. It"s coming through as clearly as my own thoughts!"

"Shows it can hear us, too."

"Never any real doubt –"

The cheering and chatter died down, and the speaker who had enquired about Harry's feelings spoke again, in its soft, friendly tone. "We are relieved to learn that your suffering was short-lived. We speculate as to whether its cause was physical or mental. Would you care to tell us which?"

*God – this one's sharp!* Harry thought. *He's going to get it out of me if I'm not damned careful.* He looked steadily at his questioner – a frog-shaped creature with long, silky fur – and tried unsuccessfully to think of a reply that would put it off the scent.

The Persian frog looked back with no expression that Harry could read.

Finally, Harry said, "Mental. It was something I was thinking. That's all."

The frog's mouth drew down at the corners. Furry lids half closed its eyes. It remarked smoothly, "We believe we understand... 'Mental'... 'Something I was thinking'... These expressions are often synonymous. Usually that kind of unnecessary repetition – when followed by the apparently innocent but again unnecessary assertion 'That's all' usually, I emphasise, can be taken as an indication that the speaker is trying to hide something. We should welcome your comments."

The frog's suave manner, and the cunning skill with which it had dissected Harry's words, turning each of his phrases into a link in an incriminating chain, reminded Harry of a lawyer in cross-examination. His heart was racing, but his brain was focusing more clearly, now that he faced a specific

22

challenge. He recalled that the Rules allowed him to refuse an answer, but he felt that to say nothing would create a poor impression. Also, he had spotted a weak point in the frog's reasoning. Perhaps by playing on this he would have a small chance of deflecting the creature's uncomfortably accurate probing.

It was worth a try. "But surely something mental is not the same as something you are thinking? You as good as admitted that, when you said that they were 'often' synonymous. Saying both things is not necessarily repeating oneself, is it? Otherwise you'd have said 'always', wouldn't you?"

The frog's eyes were almost shut by now, and Harry felt that his argument was not cutting much ice. He knew he was beginning to blush, and finished rather lamely, "Anyhow, I think you're taking rather a lot for granted."

The frog opened its eyes a trifle, and rocked gently back and forth on its folded legs. When it spoke, its voice was a purring caress. "Indeed your analysis is logical enough. It would be sufficient to refute my assertion, if I were making a statement in philosophy, for example, or in an exact science, or in logic itself. However, my deduction and conclusion were in a field where the strict rules of logic must be applied with caution – namely, psychology. It may interest you to know that we have found many aspects of psychology to be species-transcendent. In particular, it is never safe to take at face value any statement made under stress. Logical self-consistency within such statements is neither necessary nor sufficient evidence that the individual making them is telling the truth or even intending to do so.

"Apart from this, you tried to put me off by challenging my logic. If you really had nothing to hide, you would almost certainly have simply denied my conclusion, rather than criticised my reasoning. Furthermore, observation of many sentient species has revealed that sudden changes in surface colouration invariably mean something."

At this, Harry felt his face and neck reddening hotly again.

The silky purr continued. "Mostly these changes occur for one or more of a limited number of reasons. Having not hitherto personally observed your species, nor consulted its entry in our central database, I have been forced to interpret the change in your colouration by a process of elimination. The commonest reasons for the changes are: for camouflage; to denote or to respond to sexual excitement; and to show anger or embarrassment. I rule out camouflage, since your new colour makes you more conspicuous than your previous colour. The context seems unfavourable to sexual excitement. At risk of being criticised for leaping to conclusions I dare to suggest that you were, and are, angry or embarrassed or both. At the same risk I take this as confirmation that you were, and are, hiding something."

As the frog developed its theme, its voice had grown ever friendlier, and it had gradually opened its great amber eyes. Harry was fascinated and disconcerted. For a brief pause, he feared that it wanted him to reply. But then it half closed its eyes and went on, charmingly, "Now, let me ask you once more. When Member Pren finished speaking to you, you experienced a minor convulsion, did you not?"

"Yes – but – "

"And I then enquired as to whether you were in pain, to which you replied that you had felt a spasm?"

"As I said, it was just a twinge – "

"A *mental* twinge?"

"Well yes. You know how thoughts sometimes strike you … I"

"Perhaps. And yet, somehow I formed the impression that there might be a cause-and-effect relationship between what Member Pren said and your – *mental* twinge. Rightly or wrongly I surmised that, at the time when Member Pren saw fit to remind you of the importance of the Examination and of the requirement that you display a certain Characteristic, you were well aware of both. I supposed that you considered the reminder ill-judged and untimely. And that this caused you suffering, which induced a momentary facial distortion. Please tell me if I was on the right lines?" The frog's tone had become thoroughly ingratiating.

Harry was feeling very small, but clung to his determination not to be pushed into offending Pren. He knew he would have to concede something to the frog, but he would keep it to the minimum. "More or less..." he said.

"You were caused suffering, then?" murmured the frog.

"I suppose you could say so," said Harry wretchedly, "But it really wasn't much and it didn't last long."

"Thank you," breathed the frog, blinking slowly. Then, languidly, it turned away from Harry and faced towards Member Pren, who appeared to be resting, since the fat part of the bottle was horizontal, and only the neck was sticking up. Still in a low voice the frog went on. "The Man Specimen is fortunate. Apparently it has suffered less, and for a shorter time, than many of Member Pren's victims." Now the frog's voice lost its friendly tone, becoming hard and sneering. "Member Pren, what would you say if I accused you of attempting to inflict mental damage on a Specimen? I give you the Light."

The bottle jerked upright. Its grass skirt was clearly not an item of clothing but part of its body, since it now stood bristling out round the creature's middle, and had turned brilliant orange. It croaked thunderously, "I'd say you were a hideous, hairy hypocrite, you deformed, endoskeletal blob! I'd say your conceited whining was enough to burn out the neural tissue of every sentient being within a thousand light-years, let alone cause mental discomfort to a single flabby Specimen. I'd say you'd do well to remember the Rules of the FGF and your solemn oath as a Member of Galacon, you infamous, predatory, leggy sac of virulence, you slanderer! And furthermore, I'd say – "

Member Pren gave the impression that he was just getting into his stride. The raging croak steadily swelled in volume as the vituperation poured out. The frog turned its back on the angry bottle, sleeked down the fur on its chest with its front hands, and settled down, supporting its chin on its back hands. It murmured something as Pren paused for breath, and Harry caught the phrase "most satisfying colour-change..."

"Can't face me now? Are you afraid to look at me, Member Thrullint, you carrion-eating, self-opinionated..."

Harry stopped listening. To his ears the furious croaking was music. The words themselves did not matter, since they were aimed at the frog.

*Not me! Not me! Not me!* he thought, *the frog-thing wasn't after me! Oh God – what a relief! It was gunning for Pren all the time. No wonder it was trying to sound friendly. The crafty creep. What a pair! Bad as each other. Go on, Pren – give it hell. But it doesn't seem to mind – just lying there looking smug. Probably a sadist. Gets satisfaction from stirring things up. Thank God it wasn't after me.*

Relief was making Harry light-headed. At the back of his mind he knew he should take advantage of what could only be a temporary break in his ordeal, by going on with his review of human qualities. Instead, curiosity made him look round to see how the various delegations were reacting to Pren's tirade.

Again it was a mistake. This time it was not the horror and strangeness that constituted the danger. Tentacles and scales no longer bothered him with their threatening associations. The danger lay in the fact that everything he saw reinforced the insidious urge he had begun to feel when he first saw Member Pren. If he gave in to that urge, he was finished. Every member of Galacon would be insulted beyond forgiveness. Any hope of a verdict in favour of Man's admission to their federation would be lost irrevocably.

Pren's outraged croaking still resounded, but, from what Harry could see, his fellow Members were taking it quite calmly. Of those with discernible eyes, very few were apparently even watching the speaker.

Four lizards in a pool of bluish light were eating from a bowl, each helping to support the bowl with one hand, while delicately dipping for small morsels with the other. Five small tree-like creatures with branching legs reminiscent of mangroves stalked slowly round in single file, just within their white circle. A group of enormous mice lay on their backs in the middle of their circle, heads together, legs sticking up, tails radiating at precise angles, with the tips wagging in leisurely unison. The half-dozen furry frogs that accompanied the target of Pren's attack were all squatting in the same posture, facing in different directions, occasionally preening their hairy chests. Even Pren's colleagues were showing little interest. Three of them stood leaning together, and a fourth lay close by with its neck part resting on a cushion.

Harry thought, *So that's what the Hint meant when it said 'Make yourself comfortable. We do.'* He knew that he must stop looking round, since each oddity he discovered was undermining his self-control and building up the fatal urge. He shut his eyes and forced himself to concentrate. What single definable characteristic could qualify humanity for membership of this powerful, fantastically varied group of beings?

Intelligence? No – because apparently an interspecies situation was necessary for the characteristic to show itself. The same would apply to generosity, ability to organise, creativity and religious faith. Any of these could have been identified while the FGF was observing Man over all those thousands of years.

He found it impossible to systematise his thoughts. No orderly pattern of virtues would come to mind. The disastrous, welling sensation was becoming more insistent.

He tried to recall everything that had occurred since his arrival, hoping to find some clue as to what was expected of him – some thread running through what he had been told that might point in a definite direction. All he could think about, however was the series of curious events that he had witnessed: the simulante who had appeared cut in half, and the humble apology that followed; the faulty presentation of the Hints, and the Hints themselves (*'surgical appliances' for God's sake!*); the initial failure of the automatic translator. And, to add to these incidents, the contrast between the obvious intelligence of the Council Members and their childish squabbling. Furthermore, for a full meeting of a Galactic council to be run so unsystematically, however unimportant the Examination of yet another species might be to those who were already members, was astounding.

*Damn it – they're almost human,* he thought, almost bursting with the effort to control himself. He became aware of a change in the tone of Pren's croak.

Evidently the bottle, whose grass skirt had resumed its original straw colour, was winding up its speech. "Finally, and in conclusion, I totally reject Member Thrullint's insinuation that such a reminder can ever be ill-judged or untimely. And I informally propose that the Membership Committee consider in its next sitting whether a sincere apology from that Member would be sufficient to justify its continuing to represent its regrettable species in this great Council. I yield the Light."

In the pleasant hush that followed, over the soft murmur of conversations that must have been going on throughout Pren's speech, Harry overheard the nearby Thrullint half-whisper to a fellow frog. "This is the bit I like. You must watch. He always has a drink after a speech of any length. There now – see what I mean?"

Harry saw what Thrullint meant. Pren had moved over to the member of his delegation that lay with its neck on a cushion, apparently asleep. Pren bent down by curving and

28

extending his neck, and picked up the cushion, to the discomfiture of the bottle-creature which had been lying on it and which tried to get back to sleep without it. Pren had attached the cushion to the tip of his neck. He now erected his grass skirt so that it formed a sort of basket, in which he laid the cushion. He opened a slit in the side of the cushion and took out a bottle.

"Marvellous, isn't it?" breathed the furry frog Thrullint, admiringly.

The bottle Pren had extracted was almost exactly the same shape as Pren. Unlike Pren, however, it had no skirt, but it did have a label. Pren straightened up, lowering his skirt, with his smaller replica upside-down on the tip of his neck-part.

"There – you must agree that's a sight worth seeing!" whispered Thrullint, delighted. "But how he gets rid of it is even better. Watch now!"

Breathing heavily, Harry turned away, covering his face with his hands, desperately fighting for control. He could still hear the frog.

"Try to imagine," said Thrullint softly, "the mind of a creature that can construct a drinking vessel in its own likeness – let alone drink from it in a public place."

A splutter escaped Harry, and he converted it into a cough.

"Oh Thrullint," whispered a voice that Harry took to be that of the companion frog, "Thank you! I would not have missed that for planets!" The voice sounded deeply moved.

Convulsed, Harry stuck his forefingers in his ears, so as not to hear any more. *If they ask me,* he thought, *I'll tell them that this is how I always clean my ears.* He coughed until he felt reasonably sure of being able to breathe fairly evenly, and kept his back to the dangerously observant Thrullint, hoping that the frog's attention was still elsewhere. *If it sees me in this state, I'm done for,* he thought, *and even if I don't tell it myself, it's certain to guess what got me like this. And it'll have a lovely time explaining it to the Council.*

Unfortunately, the terror of discovery had very little effect. It was about half a minute before he dared to take his fingers out of his ears and open his eyes.

A new voice was speaking. "– such considerations are always interesting." The speaker's head, with huge eyes on flexible stalks, was carried on a swaying, slender neck, which emerged from a pool of bluish vapour in which the rest of the creature was invisible. It spoke softly and diffidently, shyly glancing sideways at Harry. "I think we should all welcome the Specimen's views."

Harry thought fast, faced with a choice between unattractive alternatives, either of which would risk offending the Council. He could exercise his right not to answer, as though he had heard the question – or he could ask for the question to be repeated, which might bring accusations of not listening properly. He could almost hear the frog's terrifyingly well-modulated voice. 'I see – so you admit that when you inserted your fingers in your ears – to clean them, as you allege – you were aware that the resulting impairment of your auditory sense would preclude your hearing anything that might be addressed to you. Please tell us, for what *precise* reason do you consider your action justified?' It would all lead up to Thrullint's great moment, when he revealed exactly why Harry had blocked his ears, and his fight for self-control would have been wasted.

The new problem had helped in one respect. It had tensed and distracted him. The dangerous feeling still lurked, but he no longer had to rub his mouth to conceal its effects. He had just realised that he had a third choice – to pretend that he simply did not understand the question – when a hoarse grunting broke out behind him, from a large, bear-like animal.

"I borrow the Light with respect, Member Furali – or is it you, Member Larndot? – can't see you properly in that fog you hide yourselves in. I can sympathise with the Specimen if it's refusing to answer. It can be a very delicate subject for some species. It is in mine, for example, especially among the younger and less experienced adults. Never can understand why you parthenogens always seem so obsessed with reproduction. Not as if you got any pleasure out of it yourselves. Anyway, most of it's covered in the Specimen's species's Full Classification. Trartyop's people did a very thorough treatment. So, unless you feel very strongly that it's germane to the present purpose, I suggest with deference that you do not pursue the matter. With gratitude I return the Light."

Harry wanted to cheer. He looked back at the pool of bluish mist. After a few seconds just a pair of eyes came up, and their owner said, rather sadly, "I didn't want to upset it. I only wanted it to – I thought – I thought, if it could only – I – I yield the Light – but – " The eyes submerged.

Once again Harry had been let off the hook. He felt sorry for the thing that lived in the fog. All it wanted, apparently, was a little chat about the facts of life. He recalled the incident when, at age sixteen, he had been invited by his father to go for a walk. "You know, Harry – the human body is a very beautiful thing," the Old Man had said, quite out of the blue, "The female body – and – and your *own* body too. And if there's ever anything you'd like to know, well, I want you to ask – d'you understand?" *Yes – that was Dad's contribution to my sex-education – a bit little and a bit late. I suppose he must have wondered, sometimes, why I would never go for a walk with him for years after that.*

To get away from this dangerous train of thought, Harry made yet another attempt to identify the elusive *something* that the creatures around him claimed to be seeking. *But they've hardly asked me anything. How can they expect to find anything out about me, when they do nearly all the talking themselves?*

Perhaps he should just make a speech. Just talk about the good qualities you find in people, and hope to touch on the one they are looking for. He felt he ought to be giving Humanity a chance, instead of just sitting there in the lengthening silence. What if the delegates were to ask no more questions?

The thought of trying to make a speech appalled him. Where could you start? And how should you set about it?

You could stand up and say, "I'd like to make a speech on behalf of Humanity!" And maybe one of them would say, "Well – proceed. You have the Light!" And then you would forget everything you had managed to think up, because your mind would go completely blank, and there you'd stand, feeling like an idiot.

And then it struck Harry that this might be exactly what they were after. The more he thought about it, the more excitingly plausible it seemed. Now he had seen it, he could kick himself for not having spotted it earlier. There had been plenty of obvious clues. All those technical hitches, for example. In a system as advanced as the FGF, they could only have been deliberate. Everything fitted beautifully – the simulante's briefing, the rather incongruous Hints – the lack of direction in the Examination itself – the whole set-up was designed to give him every chance to make a fool of himself. And what quality could be more universally acceptable than the ability to make silly mistakes?

Armed with this insight, Harry felt for the first time that he had a reasonable hope of success. Making a speech would be as good an opportunity as any, but if it didn't work out, no doubt there would be others.

He would have to be careful, of course. From what he had seen, the delegates took themselves pretty seriously. It would be fatal if they thought he was trying to make fools of them. Above all, he must keep himself under control. He hoped fervently that there would be no more incidents like the bottle affair. Even to think of Member Pren was perilous.

Harry steeled himself and stood up. Although he knew he had been under close scrutiny all along, he felt that this action was drawing attention to himself. He suspected suddenly that his fly was unzipped, but dared not check it in front of everyone. He did not know what to do with his hands. Before he could fold his arms for safety, his right hand, unbidden, checked his zip for him, filling him with mixed relief and embarrassment.

He cleared his throat, certain that his voice was going to let him down. It did. "Members of Galacon," he squeaked huskily, and stopped. Disconcertingly, there came a faint click from above him, and he looked up to find a bright green light shining overhead.

"I should like to make a speech," Harry husked, and stopped again.

"That is your privilege. You have the Light." croaked the pompous voice of Member Pren.

*It would have to be you!* thought Harry. Then he forgot all he had managed to think up, his mind went completely blank, and there he stood, feeling like an idiot.

It occurred to him that things had gone just as he had anticipated, and yet somehow not quite according to plan. He was making a fool of himself all right, but the only response from the Council Members so far was a polite hush.

"Oh God! What am I doing? What can I say?" To his horror, Harry realised that he had spoken his thoughts aloud. He was conscious of sweat trickling from his armpits. Trying to cover up for his involuntary utterance, he stumbled on. "I mean – there's so much I could – if only I knew where to – Oh God, it's no use, is it?"

There was respectful silence for some seconds, broken by an apologetic grunt from the bear who had recently saved Harry from prurient questioning. "I most deferentially borrow the Light, Man Specimen, and anxiously await your forgiveness of my interrupting your devotions, but I feel that I may be able to supply some answers – possibly even useful answers – to the questions you have addressed to the Deity. If I have your permission to proceed, you have only to nod."

Harry nodded. He could not have spoken anyway. Previously, the kindly bear had over-estimated his reticence concerning sex. Now it was over-estimating his piety. He found it necessary to cough and rub his mouth for a second or two.

The bear continued. "You have offered to make a speech. You are entirely free to do so. You may say anything you wish. But I feel obliged to point out that it's probably no use at all. Quite a few Specimens try it, but it never works. And in any case, we can't allow you to risk mentally damaging yourself by too much over-exposure. You might become seriously embarrassed. The Rules, you know. 'The Specimen may not be deliberately damaged or misled.' Have to be scrupulous. Go by the spirit, not just the letter."

As it made this last remark, the bear pointedly glared in the direction of Member Pren, whose grass skirt went pinkish.

The mighty animal continued. "I've seen records going back to the earliest Examinations. Very informal. No proper Rules. No Hints. Gradually evolved. Even in my time there have been improvements. I remember some cases though – quite near things, really. Had an invertebrate recently. Transparent skin – see right through it – all its organs visible, you realise…"

Harry relaxed gradually as the bear expanded on its theme. He felt relieved that the Members were not, after all, waiting for him to make a fool of himself, but baffled by the collapse of his theory. *Oh well,* he thought, *better just wait and see what happens – and try to keep a straight face.*

"Watery liquid pouring out of it, all over." The bear seemed to be relishing his anecdote. "Skin was wrinkling up, and the creature was getting noticeably smaller. And making a most wretched bubbling sound. Trartyop managed to save it. – recognised the symptoms – very thorough Observer, you know – not much he misses. He said they tend to *ooze* when they get embarrassed, but he'd never seen one as bad as this. Said darkness might help. It did, too. We watched it on the night-vision scanner. Sat there for a while in its pool of vital fluid, then flattened itself out and soaked it all back in. Uncanny. Recovered completely, but too close for comfort altogether. Happened so fast, you realise...

"Then there was that amphibian from out near the Galactic rim somewhere – went rigid. Oh yes – that other one we found over in your region, Man Specimen. Rows and rows of stubby legs sticking out through holes in a kind of carapace. Head poking through a hole at the top. Pulled them all in, even the head, and shut up all the holes with little lids. They all tried making speeches. Never worked. There really ought to be a Hint about it. Must bring it up at the next Procedural Committee. In fact, you know, when you come to think of it..."

A very sad voice cut in, stopping the bear in mid-sentence. "Terribly sorry to butt in, old fellow, but do you mind if I take the Light?"

"Er – not at all, not at all, Member Trartyop. I yield the Light, of course – er – willingly!" The bear sounded quite relieved.

"Thank you, Member Havar," said the miserable voice, whose owner Harry located far up the side of the bowl under a red light – a strangely man-like figure that he had not noticed before. "As Co-ordinator in Session, I have the unwelcome duty to inform Galacon that our Computer Chairman has just told me that we have an energy limitation. We shall be forced to Terminate in not more than 62 standard micros time. For the benefit of the Specimen, a micro is a relatively short measure of time. In order of decimal magnitude it is the same as an Earth minute. However, the Specimen is advised not to worry unduly."

Amid the groans that greeted this announcement Harry worked out that a micro could be anything from just over six seconds to just under ten minutes. He therefore had between six minutes and ten hours in which to convince the Council of

Humanity's fitness to join their federation. He wondered how knowing this could be of any possible benefit.

He was becoming increasingly certain that if Humanity's chances really depended solely on him, then the whole business was a waste of time. He tried to keep in mind the importance of the occasion, but this only made matters worse. It seemed to reawaken and strengthen that terrible, urgent feeling that had afflicted him in similarly grave and formal circumstances as a boy. He forced himself not to pay attention to that urge: *not now – please not now! Oh no – not here – not now... Oh God, let me control myself. They'll never forgive me if I –*

And now the speaker with the melancholy voice had murmured, "I suppose it's about time that I had a closer look at the Specimen. I request mobile Support." It was moving slowly down the curve of the bowl. The white circle surrounding the delegation was moving too, so that both its tall, thin man-like members were approaching side-by-side.

As they drew closer, Harry saw that they were wearing what looked like giant dish-cloths, draped round their sloping shoulders. The grey, coarse cloths hung to below their knees, and the hems dipped into liquid, which lay in ring-shaped troughs slung around their legs. The dish-cloths soaked up the liquid, and the waddling figures steamed gently.

*The idea must be to keep them cool,* thought Harry, *but surely it would make more sense to run their life-support system at a lower temperature?*

When they were close enough for Harry to see their faces clearly, Harry know that he had reached the end of his control.

They were nearly bald, with wispy grey hair. Both wore long, straggly beards, one brown and the other deep red. Their cheeks were wrinkled, and they had bags under their dark, sad eyes. They kept their muscular arms folded as they walked, unable to step out because of the troughs and skirts, and they held their heads slightly bowed, in a manner reminiscent of monks.

About twenty yards from Harry, the one with the brown beard moved slightly ahead of his colleague and said, in tones of deepest misery, "My name's Farson-Smith – Aubrey Farson-Smith. Allow me to introduce Senior Observer Trartyop." The red-bearded delegate came forward and bowed.

It was not so much the double-barrelled name, or the mournful demeanour of the solemn pair, that took away the remnants of Harry's self-control, as their little red shoes with turned-up toes.

At first he only shook silently.

Then he gave way to giggles.

Then he broke down completely, and his roaring, howling laughter filled the tremendous bowl of Galacon.

Tears streamed from Harry's eyes. His knees buckled, and he threw himself on the comfortable floor and rolled about. He was as unable to stop as he had been on two ghastly occasions as a boy in the church choir.

He gave up trying to fight it after a while, and abandoned himself to the wild, overwhelming belly-laugh, only dimly aware of the terrific sound swelling from the delegations around him, and of the frenzied waving of tentacles, limbs, antennae and pseudopodia.

Gradually the enormity of his failure dawned on him, and he began to calm down a little. As the general excitement died away, he came to what he considered was the only decision that could save some face on behalf of Humanity.

Harry stood up, and silence fell. He took a few deep breaths, still shaking intermittently from residual mirth, and blurted out, "I can't go on. Please stop the Examination!"

A chime, like the one he had heard before, sounded over the murmuring that followed Harry's words, and a rich female voice similar to that of the simulante Jean said quietly, "To avoid deceiving the Specimen, we point out that the voice now speaking is synthetic, and emanates from the Computer Chairman. Also, for the benefit of the Specimen, I mention that, by long tradition of Galacon, in every Examination, a computer acts as Chairman in the interest of strict impartiality.

"As Chairman, it is my duty to ensure that you recognise the implications of opting for immediate Termination. Namely, that Galacon must give its verdict on the basis solely of the proceedings up to Termination, may take into account that you have chosen this option, and will – by long tradition – reach its verdict in closed session, from which you, the Specimen, will be excluded. You will be informed of the verdict as soon as it is reached. There is no higher council in the Fraternal Galactic Federation, and therefore there can be no appeal. Do you understand?"

"Yes," choked Harry

"Do you wish to change your mind?"

Harry was filled with doubt now, but could not rid himself of a picture of little red shoes with turn-up toes, and knew that it was hopeless to continue. He had laughed at one of the most distinguished and respected Members of the Council. Every delegate had been driven frantic at the effrontery. No need for the frog's probing skill to interpret his behaviour. With an effort, he said, "No, thank you. I'll stick to my decision."

Instantly, whiteness surrounded him. Whiteness and dead silence.

Harry sat down.

After a few seconds the beautiful voice of the simulante Jean spoke from behind him. "Hello again, Harry Bollinger. I understand that you requested Termination."

Grateful to hear her, but without looking round, Harry said, "Yes. It's all over now. I made an idiot of myself, I'm afraid. How long do they normally take to reach a verdict?"

"Usually it's quite quick, when the Specimen opts for Termination."

Harry sat despondently, with his arms round his knees. As he thought back, trying to sort things out, trying to find some excuse for having let down his race, it struck him that he had never had a chance. *How many normal 21ˢᵗ Century adults could have kept a straight face in all the circumstances?* The thought helped a little, but he still felt pretty wretched.

"Do you like my dress?"

For the first time, Harry raised his eyes to the slim, graceful figure that stood before him. His heart jumped at what he saw. Her dress was now a deep red-bronze, matching her shining hair. It was sleeveless, and the neckline plunged to the waist – front and back, as Harry say when she pirouetted. Her skin was slightly tanned and very smooth. The skirt was full but startlingly short. She wore no jewelry. Her feet were bare.

She looked concerned. "From your facial expression I think you are surprised at my appearance. I cannot tell if you are also pleased. Are you also pleased?"

Harry shrugged. "Pleased? Well – yes – I suppose so." *It's better than a kick in the face, but what's a fake woman's appearance got to do with anything?* " I mean, - I didn't think… I suppose I thought I'd be on my own."

"Would you prefer me to go?"

"No – you're very welcome. Please stay." *Might as well have some decent scenery while I'm waiting for the chop.*

"Then I shall stay. Would you like to talk, or just think?"

"I suppose I'd like to talk. But I've got rather a lot on my mind. I don't know what to talk about. Unless – unless you can tell me what they were looking for?"

"You refer to the critical Characteristic for which you were Examined?"

"Yes – that." Harry braced himself.

"I am not informed of that, I am afraid. I am here to give you pleasantly distracting company. I have been warned that you may be feeling tense and not happy. That is why I chose this dress. It is of a kind worn by females of your species at happy gatherings, is it not?"

Harry's spirits were sinking. The girl was chattering like a geisha. *Apt simile,* he thought, *decorative but unreal.* He suddenly thought of his wife – a total contrast to this tall, elegant, empty-headed creation. Black hair, big brown friendly eyes, and a decent-sized pair of breasts. *Dear God, what can have happened to her in all this time? And the kids… Six bloody months! Christ, I hope they're all right…*

Harry hardly noticed the chime, or the brief buzz of voices as the whiteness faded and he was in the vast bowl again.

The sad voice of Senior Observer Trartyop roused him to half-hearted attention. "Specimen Human known as Harry Bollinger, you have represented your species in an Examination conducted by Galacon in plenary session. You have exercised your right under the Rules and Hints of Examination, to call for Termination. Accordingly, the Council has reached its verdict in closed session, as is customary in such instances."

Harry dearly wished that the literally steaming old twit would put him out of his misery. *Come on – get to the point!*

Senior Observer Trartyop evidently had no such merciful intention. "Before informing you of the verdict, long tradition demands that the Co-ordinator in Session explain the considerations that led to this verdict. After the verdict has been pronounced, I shall, in my capacity as Observer, together with certain of my fellow Members, be available to answer any questions you may wish put, subject, of course, to energy considerations. Until then, since your Examination is concluded, and since Central energy is not unlimited, we ask that you remain silent. We have disconnected your channel from the global auto-translator, so that we should not be able to hear if you do speak, but we do want you to understand, so that you will not spend the rest of your life in speculation. If you comprehend what I have said, kindly nod."

Almost past caring, Harry nodded.

"You may recall," said Trartyop dismally, "That at first sight of this Council you fainted. This established, we presumed that you are not insensitive to the more obvious implications of what your senses tell you. Very soon after that, following a doubtfully helpful remark from Member Pren, you stubbornly tried to evade the astute questioning of Member Thrullint, and yielded only under the most extreme pressure. From the circumstances, we could readily deduce that you were refusing to answer so as not to offend Member Pren. This proved, we again assumed that you have a proper and commendable respect for the Members of this Council. – especially as you were clearly trying simultaneously not to offend Member Thrullint.

"Subsequently, and during a space of time immediately after Member Pren had finished his rebuttal of the charge laid against him by Member Thrullint, you appeared to be struggling to conceal an emotion. We were unable to make a definite diagnosis of what was causing the disturbance of your composure at that stage, even while the disturbance recurred at intervals during the proceedings that followed. The correct diagnosis became clear only when I approached you, and my esteemed colleague Member Farson-Smith introduced me."

Trartyop's voice had reached depths of desolate misery, corresponding with Harry's feelings. The Member's delegation was back in its distant position, and Harry could not see his face clearly, but he fancied he caught the glint of a tear on the speaker's wrinkled cheek. In spite of his own trouble, he felt sorry for the unfortunate Trartyop, who was clearly not enjoying his task at all.

After a brief pause Trartyop resumed, speaking with solemn intensity. "We know that you were aware of the importance of the Examination to your Species. You had acknowledged that you understood the fact that there could be only one chance – unless you were to die during the Examination. And yet, in the presence of representatives of every sentient species of every planet in the Fraternal Galactic Federation, here assembled in full Session, you exhibited – plainly and unmistakably – paroxysmal symptoms of mirth, manifestly directed at one of the representatives.

"Taking all these considerations and circumstances into account, only one verdict is possible, and the voting Members were therefore unanimous. I formally request the customary silence of Galacon, so that I may, without fear of distortion or misapprehension, pronounce, proclaim and record this, our verdict."

Like a terrible drum, Harry's heart pounded in his ears. Just as he had often tried to will a golf opponent into missing an eighteen inch putt, he now desperately tried to will Trartyop into making a slip of the tongue. His apathy had vanished as the sombre voice had built up the case, and now that the last moments had arrived, he felt the full, sickening significance of the fiasco. He concentrated all his strength on his absurd, hopeless mental endeavour, so that he missed the meaning of Trartyop's words.

With infinite pathos, speaking very slowly and distinctly, Member Trartyop said, "Harry Bollinger, Specimen of Man, the Galactic Council unanimously declares its formal and final verdict that your Species is eligible for admission to the Fraternal Galactic Federation. Plenary Session is closed."

A mighty tumult erupted. Every delegate joined in the roaring, whistling, clapping, clashing, scraping, clattering and stamping, hooting, howling and booming. The bowl magnified the clamour and focused it on Harry.

Harry sat slumped over his knees in mingled humiliation and resentment. He despised the way the delegates were so enthusiastically triumphing over the defeat of a single being. But, as the volume moderated slightly, he began to pick out coherent words and phrases: "Damn fine Specimen…" "Well done the Thing – I mean the Human!" "Oh no – its 50 you owe me. I distinctly recall your offering five-to-one against the Specimen!" – this last remark in the silky tone of the nearby Thrullint. And in the growl of the kindly bear-being "Unanimous, too – quite unusual, really – credit to its Species. But we really ought to put in a Hint about..."

At first the remarks meant nothing to Harry. Then he could not believe that they were genuinely friendly. But the unmistakable croak of Member Pren clinched it. "Pity it's another squishy vertebrate. We could do with a few more decent exoskeletals. But at least it's not entirely covered in nauseating fur, so I suppose it's not as bad as it might be..."

There was more, but Harry had stopped listening to Pren. He was trying to piece together how things had suddenly gone right. He stood up and smiled vaguely round. The noise redoubled. He felt happy and proud, but until he could ask some questions, he would have no clear idea of what he should be proud about.

The sweet chime began to sound repeatedly. The din subsided to a tolerable level of excited chatter, over which the feminine voice of the computer said, "Members! Members! Your attention please. I have recorded a fair and proper Examination. With the energy limitation we must, in courtesy to our guest, allow what time we can for clarification of any questions it may wish to raise. Plenary Session being closed, Members with no further business will be helping to conserve FGF Central energy by leaving at the earliest opportunity.

"Meanwhile, I record Galacon's sincere congratulations to the guest Harry Bollinger and to his Species, and confirm that it is our hope that Humanity will in due course enrich our Federation by joining us. Goodbye now!"

Almost immediately, there was a chorus of farewells, and most of the bowl became dark. A scattered handful of delegations in their brightly lit circles moved down and formed a small group in front of Harry.. He was pleased to see the kindly bear among them, and equally pleased that Pren had not stayed. He was not so sure about Thrullint, and felt distinctly sheepish towards Trartyop.

As the last of the group were moving into position, Thrullint spoke. "I have no official reason for remaining, and will depart forthwith. I have waited until one particular – er – colleague – left, since for personal reasons I did not want him to hear what I have to say. I want to congratulate you on your conduct during the Examination, and to apologise for causing you discomfort by my interrogation. My fellow Members here gathered will explain my motivation if you wish. I am glad that you appear to have suffered no lasting injury."

"That's quite all right," said Harry, rather touched. "I'm – "

The delegation of furry frogs vanished instantaneously. Harry found himself staring at one of the bears, who had until then been obscured by Thrullint. This flabbergasted Harry, who had assumed that, when delegates left, they simply turned off their lights and went away in some ordinary manner. The moment he thought about it, however, he realised that this could not be the case. The delegates could not move off in the dark, since they needed their white circles to show the limits of their support-systems. The implication was sickening. Harry appealed to the bear, "Surely you can't all be simulos!"

The bear sounded puzzled. "Sorry, little fellow, I take it that you are addressing me, since you are looking my way, but I can't tell whether what you uttered was a question or an assertion. Either way, I don't understand it. Would you mind explaining, please?"

*If he's bluffing, he's a mighty fine actor,* thought Harry, *but anyway, I'd better play safe...* "Member Thrullint suddenly just disappeared, with his whole delegation. And all the others who left – well – it seems to me that they simply vanished too." As the horrible suspicion developed, Harry found that the beginning of anger gave him the courage to think aloud. "And yet the Rules say the Specimen must not be deceived. Or is the whole thing a trick – Galacon – everything – is it just a hoax of some kind after all?"

There was a tense hush. The bear gazed at Harry for some moments, then looked round at the delegations on either side, then slowly turned to look at Harry and growled softly, "It appears that there has been a most regrettable failure of communication. Did you not read the Hints?"

"Well yes – but – well I didn't have time to read all of them. They were in German to start with, then upside down. I was half-way through one about 'natural functions' when the Examination started."

All the delegates glanced at one another, with exclamations of surprise and dismay, and then they all stared at Harry as though seeing him for the first time.

The bear said, incredulously, "Then you didn't read Hints 15 and 16?"

"Well, no. I saw the last one, number 17, wasn't it? And then I started at number 1. I got up to 13 or 14 – but –"

"Then your performance is all the more remarkable!" growled the bear. "You believed you were physically here on Mid, thousands of light-minis from your home planet, surrounded by real live aliens also physically present, and yet – having recovered from the initial shock – you not only stood up to Examination without mentally disintegrating, but also demonstrated the crucial characteristic!

"Only a small proportion of species possess even a smidgen of what we call the Sixth Sense. And it has never been supposed that the sense could be so strong as to show itself in such adverse circumstances. Most remarkable!" Amid approving murmurs from all sides, the bear growled on. "Better explain about those Hints you missed. You see, number 15 states quite clearly 'Because of energy considerations, all proceedings of Galacon are conducted in sub-photonic total-scan' and number 16 says 'If you do not understand, ask!' But you didn't ask. Why didn't you complain about not having enough time to read all the Hints?"

"I started to," said Harry, "but it was then that I must have fainted. And when I came to, everything seemed to happen so fast, what with Member Pren and Member Thrullint asking questions, and that trouble with the translating equipment. But what does that mean – 'sub-photonic' something? And why do you all keep on about 'energy considerations'?"

"Ah! So you tried to protest. Yes – I thought I heard you utter something. But the auto-translator was out of action – yes – of course – that explains it." The bear sounded relieved. I think Senior Observer Trartyop is best qualified to – er – would you mind, Trarty, old fellow?"

Trartyop was refilling his cooling-trough from what looked like an animal-skin bag. "Sorry to keep you waiting, Specimen Harry Bollinger – I shall not be very long." He sounded every bit as morose as before, and his bearing was equally woebegone.

It occurred to Harry that Trartyop's voice and body-language were probably misleading. Signs of sadness that a human showed might, in Trartyop's species, indicate pleasure and friendliness. If so, Senior Observer Trartyop's ability to interpret the expressions and gestures of other species was all the more impressive.

Steaming satisfactorily again, the tall, thin man-like being sighed, "Moons of Blue-Earth! That's better... Now then – ah yes – Total-scan, energy considerations and so forth... Ooh, the lovely coolth! Forgive me – that's my first replenishment today..."

He sighed again, dreamily, and went on. "Much as I wish otherwise, I'm no expert in sub-photonics – I merely use it in my Observation work. All I can tell you is that it exploits a form of radiation that propagates many times faster than light. For example, it takes less than a millisecond for sounds that I utter here to be translated into your language, converted to sub-photonic radiation, travel all the way to you, and be converted back to sounds that you can hear and understand. With me so far?"

"Well, I suppose so – but –"

"Good. And what makes it so useful for my Observational purposes is that a sub-photonic scanner can provide information about the internal structure and processes, as well as the external appearance, of solid objects – including living organisms. Hence the term 'Total-scan'. Your physical body is inside a scanner hidden in a region of Earth named Saharania, a former desert now devoted to agriculture, still sparsely populated and therefore suited to our purpose. All the delegates to Galacon are in similar scanners on their own planets. The support systems allow us to meet as though face-to-face. And with the auto-translator system, the whole set-up is quite convenient."

Harry was past being surprised by, or even interested in, the technical details. He felt that he had been deceived. It did not much matter whether it was by carelessness or by deliberate intention. "But your simulante – the one that briefed me in the first place – she told me we were here – I mean on Mid. Wasn't that deception?"

"Sadly, I recognise that – technically – it was. Not intentional, but no less regrettable for all that. You asked 'Where are we?' and she told you 'Mid'. Yes?"

"Yes!"

"Ah – as I thought. If you had said 'Where am I?' as most specimens do, she'd have got it right. But it was the monitoring Controller's fault. Should have spotted the slip and rectified it. We've treated you very badly, and I can only apologise."

Mollified, Harry replied, "That's quite all right. With all the glitches one after the other – the simulante cut in half, the Hints being upside down, the auto-translator not working and so on – I was beginning to think everything was aimed at disturbing me. I mean, in a society as advanced as yours, surely such mistakes must be deliberate."

Trartyop shook his head. "Would that it were so. Unfortunately the only valid generalisation concerning the reliability of systems produced by advanced cultures is what we know as Gumdeeli's Maxim: 'The more you can make, the more you can make mistakes!' And energy considerations are a severe limitation…"

"Energy considerations. Would you mind explaining?"

"Not at all. By the time a species becomes eligible to join the FGF, it has almost invariably used up most of the available resources of its planet. Life becomes almost exclusively concentrated on culture, rather than artefact-production. Absence of useable commodities and manufactured goods makes ideas and aesthetics seem more interesting and important. In culture-oriented societies, the supreme purpose of technology is communication. Every spare unit of readily convertible energy is devoted to electronics and sub-photonics.

"Solar power and fusion are valuable stop-gaps, but eventually even these degenerate because of the lack of spare parts to maintain and repair them. So you can see why energy considerations are so important."

Harry said thoughtfully, "I see. I suppose that's why you want new species to join the federation – so they cam contribute to the energy reserves?"

"By the Six Moons of Blue-Earth!" howled Trartyop, tears pouring from his eyes. "Forgive me – I shouldn't cry at you. But that struck me as very droll. No, that's emphatically not why we welcome new member species. Far from it.

"Just look at me! Elected representative of an ancient species with a recorded history spanning the equivalent of a hundred thousand of your Earth years – and what do you see? A creature in a tattered, hand-woven garment, shoes made from the dried gourd of a fruit-tree, walking about in a crude cooling ring that he can afford to refill twice a day. That's what you see.

"And in all of Galacon, do you recall many artefacts? Pren's bottle you might have noticed. And Genimo's wooden Stilletto of Office. And the odd item of clothing. Not much else – and not a scrap of metal. We have no weapons and no means of acquiring them. Infant races, full of energy and arrogance, wouldn't wish to join us and give up what they regard as valuable for our Federation. And if they were somehow, to give us all the energy we would need to regain the material standards of such a race, we would be putting the clock back fifty thousand years!

"Oh no – we don't want your energy. But – erm – that reminds me of a rather delicate matter. Your wrist-watch – er – have you noticed anything about it?"

"Yes I have. I've been meaning to ask you about that."

Trartyop was clearly uncomfortable – even smiling slightly. He spoke firmly and fast. "Your watch has an electrical storage cell of – by our standards – considerable capacity, together with suitable electromotive force. Our field operators are not always able to resist the temptation of such a convenient power source. In this case, having anaesthetised you and erected the total-scanner, they dismantled the watch and used its cell to set up the primary scanning field. We are most regretful, but are unable to return the electricity for technical reasons. Also, unfortunately, the field operator concerned found it difficult to restore all the indicated outputs to their original settings. We shall credit Humanity with the borrowed electricity pending your admission to the FGF. Do you forgive us?"

It was Harry's turn to be amused. "You may have the electricity as a present," he smiled, "But, you know – I still don't understand why you want new species in the FGF. And I didn't understand when you explained why you think we are eligible for membership. What is the 'critical characteristic' – what you call the sixth sense?"

"Great moons and beards! – you know we have an energy limitation – only a few micros left – and you wait till now to ask that? Well now – to put it briefly – it's the sense of humour. Not *a* sense of humour. Many species have a sense of fun, of the ridiculous, of the ironical or of the comic. Very few have what we recognise as *the* sense of humour.

"*The* sense of humour springs from an instinct for the fitness of things, from a sort of pride in one's species, and a sort of self-respect. It recognises and responds to the simultaneous value and worthlessness of all entities, sentient or otherwise, and it is powerful enough to make a Blue-Earther cry, or a human laugh, in the face of humiliation, disaster or death.

"Now that your Examination has confirmed that your species possesses it, we know that it will be worth the energy required to maintain our watch until you are ready to join our federation. Meanwhile we can do nothing to help you, and would not do so if we could. Nothing destroys people more surely than well-meaning but unnecessary help. Judging by your present rate of progress, you should be ready in a slightly less than average space of time – say, one or two thousand of your years.

"Of course, your species may not live that long. The sense of humour is not a survival-characteristic, though it helps to make survival interesting. But if you do eventually join us, you should establish sound multi-species relationships and make a valuable contribution to our collective wisdom – and, with luck, our amusement. Do you understand now?"

Harry nodded reflectively. "Yes – I think I'm beginning to understand now…"

"Then farewell, Harry Bollinger!" Trartyop stood very straight and rigid. "Farewell and prosper greatly, you and Humanity. You have the good wishes of every Member of the Fraternal Galactic Federation."

"But – " Harry started, then remembered the energy limitation, and changed his mind. He went on, a little chokily, "Well – goodbye – and thank you for – everything – and – goodbye!"

As he spoke, the delegates faded into blackness, murmuring "Farewell, farewell Harry Bollinger!"

Harry's senses reeled, and he felt himself falling. The grunt of a big-pig roused Harry. Though he was in shade, the brilliant African sunlight dazzled him.

He felt, suddenly and overwhelmingly, that he had made good friends, only to lose them. Trartyop, and the bear – even the suave and disconcerting frog Thrullint.

*Might have been a dream. No sign of their scanner. Wouldn't expect to see anything, I suppose... Oh God, I hope it wasn't a dream. No-one'll ever believe me, of course, but I'd like to be certain myself.*

*One thing – can't imagine what I was doing, going to sleep like that. I was on my way to meet Sally. I wasn't sleepy. I was damned hungry – still am, by God!*

*Maybe that's all the proof I'll ever get.*

Harry got up and walked on down the path. Grand-cows turned to look at him as he passed. The laughing voices of children, and of a woman, were coming nearer.

Harry stopped suddenly, and looked at his watch.

He shook his head and walked on again, chuckling.

# Close Encounters of Another Kind

In the stealthed observation unit high in the night sky over the sprawling city's lights, Skump the Underthing looked down, waiting nervously for permission to proceed. The new Master, Gogwuldukk, settled into the prime viewing couch, and raised a pincer. "You have synchronised with Planet Tribe-Home?"

"Yes, Master. Synchronisation verified."

"And this – this alarming –  erm – whatever it is – was recorded recently?"

"Yes, Master. Within the last ten macros. From the usual transmitter, near the city pronounced *Loss Anjellies* on the seacoast of the region named *Califor* –"

"Spare me the details. But we can be quite certain that it is not fiction, not mere entertainment?"

"O Master, we can be certain only that it was transmitted on a designated news channel at a time when only news is expected."

"Good. Proceed."

*The video recording is excellent, and, to Skump's relief, the translation is instantaneous and smooth. A blonde woman's face fills the screen. The translator renders both meaning and tone of her speech in realistically vernacular o'Tribese.  Her voice is stridently indignant. "Inside their ship everything was all white. Everything kept going blurry. I must've passed out."*

*She looks from side to side as if seeking reassurance that someone believes her. "Anyhow, when I came to, we were in this kind-of, like, operating theatre. They had us both naked, tied down. On these sort-of padded tables. With our legs spread. Me on my back, Jeff on his front. And they..." Her mouth grimaces.*

*The media-man's voice-over  is quiet, eager. "They – ah – examined you? Or...do you mean they..."*

"Yeah – I mean – they...you know... Several of them... One after the other. Both of us..."

Close-up of a man's face. Sub-title: 'Jeff Bridges, 28'. The man's eyes are shut tight. His nose wrinkles. He is blushing.

The media-man emits an oily sound. "And – just how did it feel? Was it very different than – you know what I mean – different than...usual?"

The man's close-up frown deepens.

The blonde speaks. The picture switches back to her. She is making an effort, concentrating. "Different? Not really. How different can a todger be?"

Reaction-shot of the media-man looking rueful, thinking fast. He chuckles uneasily. This is prime-time TV. Family viewing. "Well I guess that means we and the aliens have something in common." He grows serious, earnest. "But they did more, didn't they? Some kind of – experiments?"

"We don't rightly know what they did. We weren't properly awake while they were... doing – what they did first. And then they must have really knocked us out. 'Cos we eventually woke up, and they'd gone and left us. Out there in the desert. No sign of their spacecraft. Not a trace... Well, there was this round circular patch where the bushes were flattened. But it wasn't burnt or anything."

"I see. But you definitely were physically harmed, weren't you?"

Now the blonde gets his point. She nods vigorously. "Sure we were physically harmed. And mentally. I tell you, I felt real sore. So did Jeff. Not so much – you know – where you'd expect – but our tummies. We've both got these scars. They must have examined our insides and sewn us up again real neat. The doctor says they're just scratches. They'll heal up in no time, but... You show them yours, Jeff."

As the man pulled up his shirt, Gogwuldukk the Master reached out a jabber and switched off the video recording. "And you say this is typical – that there have been other such accounts of Contact-sightings?"

Skump the Underthing grovelled with practised precision. "At least eight reported in their news media,

53

Master, to my certainty, in the last local year, in this immediate area. Plus twenty-three accounts of sightings without Contact. It is –"

"The sightings without Contact are of little concern. What of our other Watches – on the other continents – have *they* reported accounts of sightings *with* Contact?"

Skump's crest fell visibly at the implied suspicion that it might be less competent than its colleagues. Its answering murgle was almost too quiet to hear. "No, your Mastery, not so far."

"Not so far," echoed Gogwuldukk. "Not *so far*. Are you insinuating that there is more than one Visiting party Out of Control on this planet?"

Skump cringed. "No, glorious Master-Master. But the natives have given accounts of some very strange happenings at many locations."

"For instance?" Gogwuldukk failed to keep the tone of curiosity out of its murgle.

"For instance... Well, in the Watch 3, 4 and 5 areas there are reports of phenomena they call Crop Circles. Strange patterns that appear overnight in the vegetation of fields. And around all Watches natives have told of lights that moved in formation too rapidly to be their own flying machines. These people are no fools, Master of Mastery. Their scientists and defence experts investigate all such reports. Many of them turn out to be mistaken, but there is a hard core of sightings that defy explanation. Unless..."

"Unless...Hmm...I commend you, Skump. You did right to call for help."

The Underthing's antennae groomed each other and flared slightly. It did not yet dare to utter the slightest grunt without being asked a question, but gazed at the Master in gratitude.

Gogwuldukk pretended to ignore the Underthing's pleasing adoration, and mused on. "If there is an Out of Control party operating around here, you could not be expected to pin them down unaided. What does surprise me, however, is this: if their Shielding is good enough to escape detection by our instruments, how is it that they let themselves be seen by natives?"

"Could it be deliberate, Master? Could they be..."

"Renegades? Yes – by the thundering backside of Gamarsh! You could be right. Renegades! Tell me something, Skump – having only just arrived I have not yet attained your level of fluency in the local native language, and the translator misses nuances. The light-coloured being on the video did not seem to describe what the Contactors actually *did*. Was there any hint that it was of a copulatory nature?"

"I have no doubt whatsoever that it was, Masterly One."

"And am I right in thinking that copulatory activity is, among these beings, universally regarded as normatively pleasurable?"

"Normatively, yes, Master – but –"

"Then that's it! Renegades. They aim at opening full socio-economic relationships in defiance of every communitised principle. Their first step is to demonstrate that the most highly valued pleasure can be shared between or among members of the two species, despite differences in appearance..."

"But – " glopped Skump, lowering its outer mandibles placatingly. "That's what worries me. None of the natives' accounts mention anything *like* our appearance. No antennae – no external mandibles, no tentacles. They all describe the aliens that abducted them as being more or less *humanoid*. Big heads, short bodies, only four major external appendages, two for walking on and the other two for – other purposes."

"Other purposes? You mean signalling? Feeding? Manipulation? With graspers?"

"Yes, Master."

"*Graspers* like *ours*?"

"Yes, Master.""Grodddbble! That settles it for me. They disguise everything else, so as to look as much like natives as is practical. The one thing they can't disguise, while still being able to operate effectively, is their graspers. So they leave them visible, and use them for sex-play, for which nothing could be better suited. And then – Bratarchis is your progenitor's sibling! With that barrier down, all else follows: first play, then sport, then exchanges of the performance arts, then joint scientific research, and finally – what they are *really* after – trade! They'll make a packet out of this planet for their own sole benefit if we don't stop them."

Secretly Skump had reservations. It could not believe that the aliens Contacting these natives were o'Tribe. For one thing, it could not imagine how or where Gogwuldukk supposed they could hide their tentacles. They *must* be of some *other* race with true-space technology. But even to raise such a possibility would risk worse than the Master's scorn. If this Master should be a Basicalist, as so many seemed to be nowadays, an o'Tribe could be brain-pincered for lesser heresy than that. Besides, when they located the illegal Contactors, the question of species would answer itself.

So the Underthing wisely kept quiet. Suddenly, with a shubbling jolt, it realised that the Master had asked a question and was expecting an answer. Fortunately, Gogwuldukk's expression was kindly. In point of fact it was the expression of an o'Tribe properly admiring the bushiness of another's antennae, the curve and placement of the tentacles, the plump but firm sitting-portion. Scarcely daring to believe its senses, Skump spread its crest in apology and asked for clarification.

"Clarification? Certainly, friend Skump. I asked if this vessel of yours stocked any recreational fluids. I brought some vine-juice from Back Home. I thought, perhaps, a *cocktail*?"

'*Friend* Skump!' In the resulting gush of pleasure and excitement, all Skump's tentacles turned extra-attractive dark green. Gogwuldukk moved towards it, glorpling softly. Tentacles mingled.

Later, they lay contentedly on the navigation couch, sipping a cocktail of vine-juice and local native liquor, watching the stars come out as the light faded.

"Which one's Back Home?" murgled Gogwuldukk. "Can we see it from here?"

Skump showed it how to locate their home-star, using pointers in what the natives called the Big Dipper.

"Beautiful," Gogwuldukk smeefed. "But duty calls." Reluctantly, it untangled its tentacles and erected itself on its podia.

Skump smeefed too, heaved itself off the couch and activated the ship's propulsion units. "Random search pattern, O Gogwuldukk?"

"Might as well. Got to start somewhere."

Success came thirty-eight patient nights later. From a height of five thousand metres their sensors captured a pattern that caused the neurocomputer to screech triumphantly.

"Can you get it on visual?" murgled Gogwuldukk.

"Trying, Gog-Master. Yes – here we are. By Gamarsh – it's a true-space craft all right. Grounded but fully functioning. Look at the peripheral lights – never seen that pattern before, mind you, but..."

Gogwuldukk grorgled, almost choking. The sound made Skump's skin tingle with fright, like the sound of the ship-fire warning. "You didn't hear me say this, Skump, my ship-mate, but *that ship isn't o'Tribe*. This is worse than I thought. Go in. No – hold it! There's a road running right by it. Are you sure we are fully stealthed?"

Skump sneffled indulgently. Ship-working was its lifelong speciality. As though it would sail around at this height without full precautions. It slapped its sitting-portion with an open grasper, and acknowledged in the murgle-tone of an old-time sea-pirate Back Home: "Aye-aye, Master-Master – fully stealthed! And with your permission I'll take us down as close as I can without them catching nary a whiff of us."

Gogwuldukk extended a claw and pincered the Underthing good-naturedly.

Skump settled the o'Tribe machine on a small hillock about fifty metres away from the silvery, circular, flattened dome-shape, and shut down the propulsors. No indication that they had been detected came from the strange ship, and no sign of movement except for the lights chasing incessantly round and round its circumference. Through the uproar of bats and crickets clicking and scraping, a sound foreign to the desert came to the discerning antennae – a steady purring, accompanied by a faint hiss.

"What's that steady purring?" murgled Gogwuldukk.

"You mean the steady purring accompanied by a faint hiss?" Skump murgled back.

"That's the one I mean," confirmed the Master. "Mind you, I didn't realise there was a choice. Is there?"

"Not really. Just thought I'd better check."

"Well?"

Skump wished it could turn the lights on, so Gogwuldukk could see what an apologetic shade of yellow it had turned its antennae. Screwing up its courage, it came straight out with: "Well, it sounds like a diesel motor to me. Running a low-pressure compressor. With a bit of a leak."

The pause before Gogwuldukk replied lasted long enough for Skump's antennae to turn purest panic-white. By the time the Master finally spoke, the Underthing had completed its preparations for the next phase of its existence, which it confidently expected to spend amid the merciful tentacles of Gamarsh. As a result, it could not believe its antennae when Gogwuldukk slowly murgled: "I think you're right, Skumpy. That's just what it is. But people with true-space technology don't need diesel motors. And their low-pressure air systems don't leak. So what in the name of the Eighteen Acolytes is going on? What do the sensors say?"

Skump pulled itself into shape, and prodded several controls with expert rapidity. "I'll give the micro-radar a try. Start on the centre of the ship. That's it..."

The screen came to life. Both o'Tribes gaspluttered.

The ship was an empty shell. Less than a shell. A mere skin.

With a grasper that shook slightly, Skump swept the focus and direction throughout the volume occupied by the great dome. Nothing. Looking right through, beyond the far side, the micro-radar showed clear pictures of two vehicles, parked where they were hidden from the road: a very large 4 x 4 all-terrain pick-up and an even larger mobile home.

Realisation dawned on both o'Tribes simultaneously. Together they out-murgled, "It's a fake!"

Then "O Gamarsh," breegled Gogwuldukk. "O generative organs of the ur-Tribe! We are in Trouble."

Acoustic instruments confirmed that the diesel sound was coming from the all-terrain vehicle, and the hiss was from a small hole in the silvery balloon-fabric that represented the hull of the 'spacecraft'. The idling 'propulsor-lights' were ordinary tungsten-filament bulbs lit up in repetitive sequence.

Gogwuldukk's crest contracted down to a vestigial lump. Its antennae in-folded. It smeefed very quietly to itself. Skump found itself filled with an unfamiliar emotion: anger. It hated to see its beloved Master worried. It was amazed to hear itself murgle boldly, risking rebuke: "We have tools. We have weapons. We could..."

Being just as deeply bonded as the Underthing, Gogwuldukk detected its new mate's touching concern, and felt no Masterly urge to slap it down. Instead, it lay a soothing, *gathering* tentacle round Skump, and murgled softly: "Gbgblgbl-now... hold your riding-beasts, Skumpy. Whatever happens, the Prime Directive is still the Prime Directive. Besides, we don't know for sure that this – arrangement – is behind the natives' reports of Contact. We must wait."

While they waited, Skump passed the time devising ingenious punishments for the idiots that originated the Prime Directive. *How can it* never *be permissible to 'interfere'? What's so wonderful about the local natives' culture that means it never needs help? And if help is needed, what makes it wrong to give it? Back Home every o'Tribe has a duty to fight injustice. The laws of physics apply everywhere; why don't the laws of behaviour? Prime Directive? Prime drone-fly dung!* But it did not confide these thoughts to Gogwuldukk. A Master could not be expected to sympathise with such unorthodoxies.

While they waited, Gogwuldukk passed the time trying to work out how they could break the Prime Directive without damaging Skump emotionally. *All the Underthing's brave talk of tools and weapons means only that it wants to do something positive. One reminder of the Prime Directive and it went silent. Gamarsh alone knows what would happen to Skump's faith in me as a Master, if I proposed so much as merely bending our deepest moral law...* Rather than risk their lovely new relationship, it gave no hint of these thoughts to Skump. An Underthing could not be expected to understand that exceptional circumstances justify exceptional measures. "All we can do is wait and watch, friend Skump. Using the micro-radar, of course."

Some time after midnight, distant headlights appeared on the highway. Shortly, peculiar figures emerged from the mobile home and moved towards the road. They wore suits of shiny material and carried extra heads under their upper appendages.

When the headlights reached a point about five hundred metres from the 'space-ship', there came a loud click, and the air began to throb with a deep and terrible humming. At a hundred metres, an array of floodlights engulfed the car in brilliance. It weaved briefly, skidded, and came to rest just off the road.

A profound Voice spoke words of Reassurance and Command. "Fear not, earthmen! We come in peace. Remain calm. You are safe. Stay where you are."

At the o'Tribe ship's controls, Skump had already managed to damp out most of the awful recorded hum. It focused a directional pick-up on the brightly lit car, catching the driver's reaction: "You got it, buddy! We ain't goin' nowhere!"

Now a blinding-white mist arose all round the car, deepening.

"O-my-Gaaad – my Gaaaad – my Gaaaaad!" came the passenger's voice, shrill, demented.

The mist crept higher, and started to cover the car windows. "O Shiiiit!" they heard the driver moan. "Let's get out of here." He gunned the engine, spinning the wheels, but the mist had swallowed the car, so he could not see to drive. He stopped the car, engine idling.

In a little while, the voices were calm and dreamlike.

"Are we dead?" murmured the passenger? "Is this heaven?"

And the driver said, "Don't know, honey – but it sure feels good to me."

Figures appeared from both sides of the car. The extra heads turned out to have been helmets. Silhouetted for a moment, the figures disappeared into the mist. The faint sound of the car engine ceases. The faint red glows from its lights disappeared.

The figures re-emerged, supporting the man and woman, who staggered, but made it far enough to get a good close-up view of the space-ship before they collapse altogether. The figures then carried them into the mobile home.

At the un-curtained window, fully cloaked, Gogwuldukk and Skump watched, but did not altogether understand, the activities in the 'operating theatre'.

When it was all over, the driver and passenger were left lying by the roadside beside their car, with their clothes scattered around them. The other humans had removed their grotesque outfits. They deflated and folded up their 'UFO', which they dumped into the all-terrain vehicle and covered with canvas.

Briefly, the humans stood in a bunch, looking round, checking. The eastern skyline was becoming discernible. One of them said, "Thanks, you guys. That went real smooth."

Others said,"Sure did!" and, "That chick – not bad!" and, "Not to mention the fellah!" There was laughter.

One of them said, "Just look at the poor suckers. Us aliens have all the fun!" and another answered, "Ah – bullshit. They love it. And they get to be on TV – we don't!" More laughter.

They all got into their vehicles, waved at each other shouting, "So long!" and, "Till next time!" and drove off.

Carefully not looking at Gogwuldukk, Skump coverered the inert bodies, as best it could, with pieces of their clothing. The Master showed no sign of noticing what the Underthing was up to.

Back in the ship, both o'Tribes felt too nauseous to talk. They tried to get some sleep until the sun got too bright.

When at last it felt that it could speak without fear of vomiting, Gogwuldukk murgled softly "You awake, Skump?"

"Yes. I don't think I've been asleep. I can't get it out of my mind."

"Nor can I. We have witnessed some kind of sickness in action. Some maladjustment that enables some humans to get pleasure from sexual activity with unwilling or unconscious fellow beings. I can almost understand that part. But tell me, Skump – you've Watched this culture for...a long time. Why did these specimens eventually cut their victims' abdomens? Is this some magic ritual or some religious observance – the acting out of a myth, perhaps?"

Skump scorfled ironically. "Acting out of a myth. You guessed it. The myth of the Visiting Aliens. Technologically far above humanity – morally far below. Treating people as experimental animals."

"I think I see. So the cuts are fakery too. No more than just part of the deception – like the bug-eyed monster-heads and the bright lights...Hrhbrrhhhbrrr!" Gogwuldukk shook its crest in sadness. "What a perversion of resources and energy."

Skump joined its new mate in crest-shaking. "Indeed. Strangely, in spite of all the years I've Watched these people I am still no nearer understanding why some of them do some things. The pretence of cutting open abdomens for dissection I can explain as being consistent with the rest of the deception. But I cannot fathom why any single being – let alone a group as large as we saw – should want to carry out such a deception. You have studied widely, Master Gogwuldukk. Can you explain it?"

"I'm afraid I can, Skump Underthing. My hypothesis is this. Their mind-sickness is complicated. It makes them *enjoy* exercising power over helpless victims. It makes them *enjoy* sexual acts not full-shared. It makes them proud to be successful *deceivers*. But it does not make them stupid or careless. At some time, fellow natives have honestly and sincerely given accounts of being abducted by aliens. I imagine that most people in their culture see such tales as nonsense, but some have doubts. The sick ones exploit this."

"But surely," Skump broke in, "Surely, if most people believe aliens to be purely imaginary, then there's no point pretending to be aliens. People who don't believe aren't going to let themselves be taken in, are they?"

"That's just it. It doesn't matter what the victims believe *beforehand*. They all get a dose of the mind-altering drug in that white vapour. Afterwards, those who hear their story and don't believe in alien abductions simply regard the victims as deluded and totally unreliable. And those that do believe go on blaming *aliens*. So nobody even bothers to look for *humans*. So that bunch we saw can go on doing it indefinitely."

"And *we* get the blame. I see now – that's what you meant when you said 'we are in trouble'. But, by Gamarsh, there must be something we can do."

"I wish there were, Skumpy. Look – pretend we've never heard of the Prime Directive. Even then, there's nothing we can do. We can't simply wipe the deceivers out, just because what they are doing gives us aliens a bad name. It wouldn't be justice. Not unless we first wiped out all the humans doing even *worse* things to one another. And I bet there are enough of those to keep us busy, if I know anything at all about sentient beings. Are you with me so far?"

"Hrhblblll..."

"Hrhblblll indeed. And short of wiping them out, what else could we do that would be effective? Nothing. Damaging or destroying their equipment wouldn't work. They'd simply replace it."

"But couldn't we plant some evidence? Give the local law enforcers a helping grasper?"

"Were you listening just now? The law enforcers aren't even *suspicious*. They think the victims are either mentally challenged and therefore to be pitied; or publicity-seekers and therefore to be ignored."

"All right. I accept. There's nothing we can do." Skump looked the picture of dejection. Antennae matted. Crest tiny, almost black. Mandibles entirely covered. It sounded even sadder as it added "And that means your mission's finished. You've diagnosed the problem. You've decided what can be done. Which happens to be nothing, but it counts as a decision. So you'll be leaving now..."

Gogwuldukk could not reply. It too looked the picture of dejection. Its thoughts too were as black as its crest: *Trouble is, everything Skump says is true. Action decided – mission complete. That's the rule. Oh, by the dung-heap of Gamarsh itself, this is not one of my better days!*

Around the invisible craft the desert was waking up. Small furry creatures sniffed the warming air. Lizards appeared, flattening themselves on rocks to capture warmth from the early sunshine. Above the still-dark horizon a large bird wheeled, and to the o'Tribes' sensitive antennae came its high scream.

Skump murgled wistfully. "This time of day reminds me of Back Home. I wish... I suppose..."

"Huuuuuhhh?" grortled Gogwuldukk slowly, "Huuuuuuuuh? My dearest Underthing – you've done it again. Take us Up. I want to be able to see stars all around us. No – don't ask questions – just do it."

Skump rapidly ran through pre-flight checks. Then, having prodded in commands to resume default Watch Station, it jabbed the auto-exec button. The craft lifted silently.

On-Station, Skump turned from the instruments to find Gogwuldukk erect, with green tentacles. It stood slowly to face the Master, feeling weak with excitement.

Gogwuldukk intoned, "Give me your grasper. There now – that's fine. Now, Skump – is it your wish that my spawn and yours together be brought to First-Swim in the Great Pool Back Home?"

"Oh Gogwuldukk," breegled Skump in ecstasy, "Master of my dreams, you know it! And is it your wish that *my* spawn and *yours* together be brought to First-Swim in the Great Pool Back Home?"

"Verily and so mote it be!" murgled Gogwuldukk, its crest rising in scarlet splendour.

"So mote it be!" over-murgled the crimson-crested Skump. Then added with sudden doubt: "But does being be-wished really make everything all right? Will I really be able to come Back Home with you – for certain? "

The Master kept its crest stoutly erect. "Nothing in life is certain, dearest Skump. Nothing except my love and admiration for you."

At this the Underthing's antennae curled into ringlets of joy.

"But we can hope," the Master continued in stately tones. "As you know, the law provides that being be-wished gives us the right to petition for Homeward Transfer. Let us not delay. Send the Words of Publication now, Skumpy Underthing."

Skump found its voice. "What words shall I use, Master? Shall it be in the local native language so as not to attract attention, or..."

"Not at all!" up-murgled Gogwuldukk in fullest dignity. "Nothing but the traditional Words would be good enough for our be-wishing. Publish and be damned, to coin a phrase! But use the local character-codes as usual, just in case"

"Aye-aye, Master. I have the traditional message composed. Let us both together press the 'send' key."

*At 07.10 local time the SETI satellite omniscan AI monitor chirps. Dave Clements, weary at the end of a long night at the observatory, reads the message it displays. He scratches his head. What the AI is convinced is a 'valid' message reads:* 'SKLOGGEL BRISKS KIK POK PEFF GOGWULDUKK SKUMP'

*Dave is about to call his research supervisor when he notices the directional read-out. "Oh, Jeez. It's from* below *the satellite. Bunch of frigging kids again. Why do the little bastards bother?" Shaking his head, he tags the message as yet another hoax.*

Later, in the evening of the same day, stationary over the huge city that the natives call Los Angeles, the o'Tribe ship's sensors are locked on to hundreds of channels of TV and radio, recording every second for deep analysis by research students Back Home. The neurocomputer tries unceasingly to absorb and analyse every aspect of the local culture, in the hope of guiding investigations into the most promising lines of xenopsychological enquiry.

"I won't be sorry to leave all this to someone else," murgles Skump. "Every time I hear one of them speak or see one of their faces in close-up it reminds me of – you know what. And I feel sick. Do you really think the Deciders will let us come Back Home?"

"We can only hope so, Underthing truefriend."

Gogwuldukk and Skump watch the lights come on as evening spreads across the conurbation. At their height, the sun is still way above the curving horizon. They hold graspers, sipping a cocktail, waiting for darkness.

# Snapshot of a Spaceman

## Earth

It was quiet in the Officers' Mess ante-room – just a couple of pretty Wren officers on the window-seat, and old Colonel Williams by the crackling fire. Lieutenant-Commander James Roberts came in from the bar, walking very carefully, carrying a large whisky.

The Colonel's voice was like friendly gravel. "Ah – Commander Roberts – James, isn't it? Not watching the big show on the holovision? Goes over you Navy chaps' heads, does it – this interstellar bally-hoo?"

James smiled in spite of himself. "No, well, not really – I mean, I've seen quite a few parades in my time, sir. And – er – I'm only ex-Navy really. I'm with the RSS now."

"RSS? Huh! I notice you're still wearing the old Royal Navy tie. Don't blame you. RSS – Royal Space Service – new-fangled outfit. No traditions – no past. D'ye see any future in it – what? Suppose you must. Wouldn't have joined it otherwise. Hm. Anyway, come and sit down like a civilised fellow – keep an old soldier company, don't y'know?"

This was what James dreaded most of all – having to sit down in public. He'd been practising the manoeuvre for seven solid weeks, but still couldn't be sure how it would turn out. Sweat broke out on his forehead, but he made it across the room and steadily bent down to put his drink on the low mahogany table by the great leather chair. Then he swivelled with his back to the chair and lowered his bottom towards it.

Relief! He needn't have worried. He was sitting perfectly normally, and his right leg had not disgraced him after all.

He became aware of the Colonel's puzzled voice: "I say – didn't mean to offend you, old chap. RSS – jolly good bunch of types – must admit. Not really upset are you, what – eh?"

Relief! thought James. I actually sat down like a normal human being. Bio-electronics spot-on. The Colonel's a lovely old buffer: talks like a twentieth century movie-maker's idea of a typical British soldier – marvellous. Oh boy – what a relief just to sit down without a hitch!

James picked up his whisky, feeling warm and expansive. He glanced meaningfully at the Colonel's pint tankard, and – beginning to say, "Your very good health, sir" – went to cross his legs.

His right foot caught the table hard, and his right leg straightened. The Colonel's beer tumbled and splashed.

From the pretty Wrens at the window came a giggle, quickly suppressed.

"I say," said the Colonel, "I thought we'd got that myo-electric leg job properly sorted out by now. It is a Mark 3A they've given you, isn't it?"

So he's known all along. Those Wrens probably knew all along, too... James found himself relaxing despite himself. His right leg had done its worst, and these strangers simply accepted it. They treated it as amusing, or as a technical problem. They were not embarrassed.

"Yes, sir – a Mark 3A. It's got the latest neural network as well as the superchip. But I'm afraid it's not quite house-trained yet. I'm very sorry about your beer."

"Think nothing of it, old fellow. But d'you think you could persuade your prosthetic contraption to co-operate in getting me another pint? My legs may be Nature's own, but a hundred-and-fifty-three's no age to be charging around carting booze like some young subaltern – what?"

The bar was deserted. The duty steward must have left his post for the holovision lounge. You couldn't blame him for that. Few people on Earth would willingly be missing tonight's show – the first public appearance of the crew of Seeker-4 Plato. The first Starship crew to come back alive.

Seeker-4 had returned nine months previously. Lt-Cdr James Roberts was senior pilot on the dismantling team, whose job was to take the Starship apart and shuttle the critical pieces down to Edwards or Woomera on their way to examination and assessment.

On Seekers 2 and 3, James had been a junior pilot flying space tugs. This time he commanded No. 1 Shuttle. The first, most critical task had been to ferry down the refrigeration unit with the crew still in deep sleep.

He remembered the tension as the tugs brought the unit alongside, the worried voices on the communications net. The shuttle control cabin was facing the sun, and James had to keep the visors in position, so he couldn't see much directly. The TV monitors never seemed to be showing what he wanted to see, so he suited up and went aft to watch from the cargo bay.

The refrigeration unit was built into a standard living module with view-ports, brightly lit inside for the medical team, who were already at work. James knew what to expect when he peeped in. Sure enough, the Seeker 4 survivors looked exactly like the dead from the previous missions: free-floating in those weird plastic bags. Brown, pink and yellow bodies. Each body tangled in shiny tubes and wires inside a smooth amniotic bubble, with a complex umbilical cord snaking away to a life-support machine.

God, they look skinny!

But they were alive. The instruments said so.

James, quite shaken, had chinned his helmet transmitter switch. "Shuttle commander to Retrieval Control – over."

"Retrieval Control. Boris Stalnov here. Hello, James. What's the trouble?"

"No trouble, er – not exactly. I'm just taking a look at my passengers. I didn't realise how – how thin they'd be. How did it happen? And weren't they supposed to wake up months ago?"

"Yes, James. That is correct. Towards the end of final deceleration. They were to have at least eight weeks of activity under pseudo-gravity. They were to eat normal food and to exercise. They did not do so. It is a problem. It is your problem, in fact. To get them safely through re-entry will be difficult. They are fragile, I think."

"Fragile is right. But why didn't the computer wake them up? It must have been running normally all this time, or they would all have been dead by now."

"We do not know. It says it cannot recall that waking them up was ever part of the plan. It admits that it may have suffered some memory damage. But it insists that its self-healing routines are working properly, and that it has perfect control of its functions. Would you like to talk to it yourself? It can hear you; it is monitoring the net. Perhaps you can get some sense out of it with your English charm."

"Scottish," James corrected automatically, "And you know very well what I think of so-called 'intelligent' computers."

"Yes – you told me often. You British are not always eager to welcome progress, I think."

"Progress? We were better off with the old computers. We knew where we stood; 'Garbage in – garbage out'. Now we put in the distilled wisdom of three hundred years – and we still get garbage out. Look at this idiot machine they put in charge of a Starship. It hasn't the common sense to wake up the crew. Talk about 'machine intelligence.' – programmed lunacy more like."

"James. I apologise. I should resist the temptation to tease you. And of course I agree with you. I tell you something, James. That machine is giving a press conference in one hour. I have told it not to discuss the true condition of those men and women you have seen. I hope it has sense enough for that."

"My god – I see what you mean. But you said one hour. You haven't got the media people here already, have you?"

"No, no – do not alarm yourself so much. It will be a remote-control holo set-up. Strictly fake. Mobile units – but under our command, naturally – the usual cover-story – 'for safety reasons'."

"But they'll want pictures of the – the –"

"The crew – yes. They will have their pictures. It is taken care of. Faces only – very pale and peaceful. Nothing too – what is the right word? – 'disconcerting'. Nothing too disconcerting. But by then you must be gone. Only the holo must be here."

"But, Boris – we're programmed for a normal re-entry. Not for match-stick men!"

"James, you must change the program. Or over-ride it. That machine of yours has wings. You must make it fly. You have the skill. I remind you that you landed a Shuttle manually when the computers were damaged by fire. You can do it. All you must do is to fly slowly and steadily, not so?"

It was impossible, of course. A nightmare. Listening to the skin over-temperature alarm. Fighting the urge to put on a touch more 'g'. Fighting the trained instincts that wanted him to save his ship – and to hell with the half-dead bodies in the back. Impossible – but somehow they all survived.

A huge white hover-transporter was waiting by the end of the runway. It gingerly hauled the refrigeration unit inboard and gently screamed off into the desert.

There were no more news conferences after that first one, which the computer handled like a professional – never quite lying, but giving nothing away.

Weeks went by. The World Space Agency denied rumours that the Seeker 4 crew were dead. The dismantling programme was completed slightly ahead of schedule. When James had seen the last of the radioactive main engine components shielded up and safely on their way back to the manufacturers, he went on leave.

And lost his right leg.

He was in no mood to watch tonight's celebrations. He felt strangely more bitter than ever. Six months ago he had been a superbly fit specimen looking after a bunch of skeletons. Now the skeletons had been fattened up into heroes, and he was half a cripple.

Lieutenant-Commander James Roberts – the Man Who Can Sit Down! Two arms, one leg, and a somewhat unruly prosthesis.

Better get the Colonel his beer before he turns a hundred-and-fifty-four! The bar steward doesn't seem to be coming back. Lift the bar-flap. Smoothly into action. Pull the traditional handle and listen to the traditional sound of English ale sloshing into pewter.

"Rotten service round here!"

The Wren's voice startled James pleasantly. The woman held out two schooner sherry glasses, in beautifully made artificial hands. "We're drinking Harvey's Bank sherry, if you'd be so kind as to give us a refill."

"Delighted, madam," James heard himself say, "Your taste in sherry does you great credit. Perhaps I might have the honour of paying?"

"Does the duty barman normally regard paying for drinks as an honour? Or could it be that the handsome RSS officer is making a none-too-subtle pass? No thank you, sir – put it on my mess-bill as usual. How did it happen – your leg – if you don't mind my asking? Line of duty, was it?"

"No – no such luck. I was in a taxi on my way to Edinburgh Airport. Tanker truck jack-knifed. Taxi went into it. Fireball. I was blown clear, apparently. No burns – not like the other poor..."

"Yes – I remember – it was on the news. It must have been terrifying."

"Not really. One moment we were going along. Next thing I knew I woke up with my right leg itching. Went to scratch it and found there was nothing there."

"Terribly bad luck. Your new one's ever so good though. You're doing very well with it."

"Thanks. It still itches most of the time. I have to stop myself trying to scratch it. Still – it's better than having it hurting, like most phantom limbs do, so they tell me."

James found it strange that he could find himself pouring sherry and talking about his leg. Until then he had sneaked about the hospital avoiding people – obsessed with the grotesqueness of knowing that beyond his right hip he stopped, and a cunning machine began.

He set the sherry glasses on the bar. "Do you happen to know how much this stuff costs? I can't seem to find the bar-list."

"They're eight new euros fifty since the revaluation." The Wren's beautiful hands picked up the glasses, one after the other. She noticed James watching, fascinated, and smiled. "They are rather nice hands, aren't they? It shouldn't be long before all that's real skin, and then you won't be able to tell the difference by looking. But I must say, it never used to be my hands that I relied on to get me noticed!"

James grinned. This felt like old times – like before Edinburgh. "I see. So that's the secret. All a man has to do is to become a one-legged barman, and he gets lovely women fishing for compliments! That'll be seventeen neuros for two large Bank sherries. Your name, madam?"

"Jennifer Ramsden."

James scribbled the details. "Thank you, madam.", and slid the old-fashioned book and pen across for her to sign. "I see we have something else in common – same initials. My name's –"

"James Roberts. I overheard the Colonel. He doesn't exactly whisper, does he? Look – I must be getting back. My little friend'll be wondering where I've got to. Don't forget to sign for the old boy's beer."

And off she went. My god – talk about the quick brush-off! Just when I thought we were getting somewhere. And what's that 'little friend' bit supposed to mean? Does she want me to understand she prefers women?

Irritated but quite intrigued, James poured himself another large whisky to save time later, signed for the drinks, and went back to the Colonel.

Both the Wrens had left the ante-room.

"Birds have flown," growled the Colonel. "Pity. Brightened the place up – what? Went to watch the big show, shouldn't wonder. You know what I think about all this inter-stellar business? Absolute and utter folly! What do you think? You're a Space Service chap. Do you think it's all worth it?"

"Well – I –" James hesitated, not sure if he was ready to admit his real feelings – not sure if he could remember how he felt before the accident. "You see, before – what happened to – this leg... Well, I'd always assumed that – eventually – I'd –"

"Go off in one of those confounded Starship abortions, frozen stiff like a holo-V dinner? You're a bloody fool, sir! What good do you suppose you'd ever have accomplished?"

"Well, I reckon finding life out there would be something. I know the odds aren't all that – well –"

"Odds?" the Colonel barked. "Odds? What odds? There aren't any odds. Listen to me, my young friend. Those pep talks they give you when they're after volunteers – they're just a load of codswallop – bloody balderdash."

He took a pull at his beer and held up a hand to prevent James from interrupting. James wondered how many the old man had had already. "All right – I'm just an old bio-mechanics has-been. People go around knocking lumps off themselves – I give them replacement lumps. I don't do miracles. I can't do miracles. I work with Mother Nature. That's the only way I know. Of course, I cheat the old girl where I can get away with it – but really I'm using Nature's own tricks against her, to help her in the end, if you follow me. How else could we have developed beta-beta cloning – eh? And, without that, how could we have given that girl those hands back? Noticed her hands, have you? Lovely job, though I say so myself. She'll have it all back eventually. Some lack of feeling, mind you – well, probably almost total lack unless she's really one of the lucky ones – but she'll have movement, control, and certainly no permanent disfigurement. Not bad, considering..." The Colonel looked into his beer and frowned. "Where was I? Got carried away – what?"

"You were saying that the odds –"

"Ah yes. Now you just take it from me, sir. Nine subjective years in coma will cripple any man. Zero gravity'll make it worse. I'll admit you can slow the process down by cooling, so as to lower the metabolic rate. And you can spin the craft to simulate gravity, for what good that'll do. But you're still going to lose not only flesh but bone. And you're going to get nerve damage too, if I'm any judge."

He stared at his half-raised beer-mug. "I've read all the scientific papers. I've viewed Krotovsky's holos. I used to go to all the conferences, till they stopped inviting me. Damn fools. Just because I'm not working in that field myself any more. Well – that was their excuse, but I'm pretty sure it was because I kept telling them they were kidding themselves."

James waited, uncertain as to whether the Colonel expected him to comment.

The fierce, low growl resumed. "This whole so-called Seeker Project should be scrapped, if you ask me. Four of the blasted things is enough. Twenty-four of our finest young men and women written off in a noble cause – ought to satisfy us – don't you think?"

The Colonel took a long pull at his beer.

James was puzzled. "Twenty-four? I thought we'd lost only three crews. That's eighteen, surely?"

"Huh!" The Colonel leaned forward, bristling. "Wondered if you'd fallen for that. Mind if I ask you something man-to-man? Something you don't have to answer?"

"No, sir. I don't think I quite follow what you're getting at, though."

"Hm – well, we'll soon see about that. I know all about you, young man. You're the flyer. You're the chappie who brought those poor buggers down with no bones broken, so that the world can enjoy tonight's orgy of self congratulation. What I want to ask you is this. Did you see them in the fridge?"

"Yes – I –"

"You did. Hm... So – you're in it too, are you?"

"In what, sir?"

"In the bloody conspiracy of silence. It's all right – you needn't worry – I'm in it myself. Yes – I thought that must be why you aren't watching that farce on the holo."

"I'm afraid I still don't quite understand what you're driving at, sir. I saw them – yes. I also saw the dead ones from the other two Seekers that came back. Knowing that these people were alive made it easier to take this time. That's all. I don't know what you mean by 'conspiracy of silence'; these things aren't the sort of thing I usually talk about."

"Or think about, apparently. You've got your own worries, I suppose – give you that. Still – you saw them. Would you like to guess how much our heroes weigh tonight? Don't bother I'll tell you. They average fifty kilogrammes apiece. Hundred-and-ten pounds. Nine months of scientific feeding and exercise, and they're up to fifty kay-gee. Physically crippled. Those cars they're riding in have special seats – did you know that? More like acceleration couches. I shouldn't be saying all this, damn it. Keep it under your hat – there's a good fellow."

James shook his head. "But surely it's not all that bad, is it? Those people who got trapped on Callisto were worse than that, weren't they? They were just skin and bone – but they recovered completely, didn't they?"

"Yes – they were all right. All they did was starve. They didn't lose half their brain cells, did they? They didn't have to be trained like chimpanzees to sit up and smile and wave to the crowd – not like tonight's superstars!"

James was silent. This was new to him.

The Colonel held his shocked gaze for a moment, then looked away. "You know," he rumbled quietly, "somehow it wouldn't seem so bad if those people hadn't been such perfect human specimens to start with. For god's sake – if they're going to bring them back crippled, why not send them out cripples in the first place. Damn it – most of the chappies here'd give their right arms... Sorry – poor choice of phrase, that. What I mean is that if you offered any one of the patients in this place a chance to go off in one of those maniac contrivances, he'd jump at it. You would – you said so yourself."

"I don't know that I'd actually jump at it, sir," said James grimly.

"Ah – there I go again. Putting my foot in it. Forgive me. But you'd go like a shot, if you got the opportunity – wouldn't you?"

"Well – yes – of course I would. But a fat chance I've got of being asked to volunteer. I doubt they'll ever let me fly again. I know other people have done it – flown with artificial limbs – but not in space. And not when there are hordes of whole people lining up for the job."

The Colonel said nothing. He appeared to be deep in thought. After a while, he looked up at James. "Sorry, old boy. Did you say something?"

"Well – yes. But it doesn't matter – nothing important."

"Oh. Well I think I'm on to something. Yes – damn it! You people would be perfect for the job. No – not perfect. Better than perfect... You'd have the psychological advantage of being able to cope with being crippled. Better adjusted... You've got less to lose... And less mass, too, when you come to think of it! Yes – and it would give you people something useful to do with yourselves, instead of rotting away at desk jobs... D'ye know, Mr Roberts, I've got a good mind to write a memo to the Powers That Be. Might do some good. There's nothing we can do for the poor devils on tonight's little caper, but if we can't stop the whole damn project, we might at least make someone think... It's a sad business, Mr Roberts. A tragic business. I say – get me another beer, would you? You're a good fellow. I'm feeling my age tonight."

As James left the ante-room he heard a sound like a trumpeting elephant: the Colonel blowing his nose.

The crowd from the holovision lounge jostled out excitedly chatting, and swept James towards the bar.

"Damn fine show!"

"Got to hand it to these Yanks – they do these things in style."

"Well – it was better than watching funerals like last time. But I reckon we English can still show them a thing or two when it comes to real ceremonial."

"Oh – rubbish! You Guards chappies are too damn regimental. Now – for my money –"

James looked out for the Wrens, but they didn't seem to be around.

The next morning he went down for an early breakfast and had more luck. Jennifer Ramsden was helping herself to coffee at the side-table. She was in civilian clothes – roll-neck sweater and skirt. No-one else had arrived.

"Good morning, madam," said James tentatively.

"Good morning, Mr Roberts. I've got the best table – over there in the window. Join me, if you like."

A bit brusque, but not unfriendly.

James shovelled sausages, eggs and bacon on to a plate, and sat beside Jennifer, facing out to the sunlit lawns and autumn-coloured trees.

"Beautiful place, Headley." He spoke without thinking.

Jennifer turned and looked sideways at him. "You're incredibly observant, Commander. How long have you been here at Headley?"

"Five months, but –"

"Only five months? Good heavens! Amazing that you should have spotted the scenery already. The trained eyes of a spacer – most impressive. You are a spacer, aren't you, Mr Roberts? I know you're in the RSS, but you're a real spacer, aren't you – not just ground staff, or whatever?"

"Yes – I'm a pilot – was... But – look, er –"

"Jennifer."

"Look, Jennifer – aren't you being rather –"

"Unfair? Aggressive? An awful tease? Yes I am, aren't I? But I'm really quite nice with it." She smiled at him briefly, with bleak eyes, and then gazed out of the window.

James was bewildered by the woman's tension. He was suddenly too excited to eat.

After a while, Jennifer looked down at her steaming black coffee. She glanced at James, and deliberately stirred the coffee with her right index finger. She sucked the finger, looked at James, and repeated the process with her left index finger.

She said quietly, "There I go again – showing off my superiority. Don't you wish you could do that – stir scalding-hot coffee with your fingers?"

She put her hands in her lap and sat rigidly with her eyes closed. James felt that he was beginning to understand something. He stared, and admired her face – the small crease at the corner of her eye – the stray wisp of soft blonde hair. He waited.

With her eyes still shut, Jennifer spoke sharply. "Don't stare. I can feel you staring. I'm not a freak!" Then she grinned at him defiantly. "Just a bit out of touch, that's all. 'Out of touch' – get it, Mr Roberts? And you can blame old Colonel Williams for that particular pun."

James found himself grinning back, but he still couldn't speak.

"Garrulous type, aren't you, Mr Roberts? Won't let me get a word in edgeways. Better change the subject. Let's see, now. What can we talk about? I know – last night – why weren't you watching your distinguished colleagues in their hour of triumph? Professional jealousy, was it? That was my excuse, anyway – what was yours?"

"Something like that, I suppose. You said 'professional jealousy'; what do you –"

"I was – was – an engineer, Mr Roberts; propulsion systems. In the Navy, I worked on guided weapons motors, mostly. I was seconded to the RSS for the Seeker project. Planetary probes – landers – all the chemical stuff. I drifted into the thermonuclear side – plasmadynamics – anything with thrust. People said I was temperamentally suited to it, being the pushy type. Hah-hah; that was a joke, Mr Roberts. Kindly stop frowning; you look like a bulldog with piles. That's better! Where was I? What was your question?"

"You were saying you were an engineer."

"That's right. Past tense. Now I'm only half an engineer. The inside half. The outside's just for show – like these hands."

"How do you mean? They look marvellous. You seem to be able to do – everything."

"Everything? Oh yes – absolutely. Everything except practically anything a human being might want to do with hands. Shut your eyes – go on – I'm not going to tickle you."

James did as he was told, feeling foolish.

"Right – now touch your fingertips together. Easy, isn't it? I can't do that. Keep your eyes shut. Now touch your nose. That's right. I can sometimes do that with my left hand – never with my right. They had to take the whole arm off. You hadn't realised that, had you?"

"No – I –"

He looked at her. She looked back.

"Want to know what else I can't do? Apart from not being able to type properly, or drive a vehicle safely, or swing from branch to branch of a young oak tree? Shall I tell you the worst thing – apart from not being able to go anywhere without my little friend?"

"If you really want to. I'm not sure I –"

"It's all right, Mr Roberts. I'll put it so that it doesn't shock your delicate Scottish sensibilities. The worst is a whole lot of things, but one of them's enough to get the message across. I can't feel it when I run my fingers through my hair. I couldn't feel it if I ran my fingers through anyone's hair, Mr Roberts."

He briefly met her brimming eyes, and looked down, then out of the window. His feelings were turmoil. Idiotic clichés kept repeating in his head: 'This is so sudden, madam!'; 'I bet you say that to all the boys!'; 'What have I done to deserve all this?'

He tried to feel certain that she was merely feeling sorry for herself – that she had picked his shoulder to cry on simply because he was the first man down to breakfast – that this intensity of attraction could only be one-sided.

After a while, Jennifer slipped away without saying anything more. Her coffee still steamed. James watched it, with an overwhelming sense of inadequacy.

The feeling of inadequacy was never to leave him entirely, throughout their life together.

---

## Warmworld

The little farmer looked out through the fringe of spade-leaves that shaded the entrance to his burrow. The strong light of late evening poured across the red-brown, gently undulating land – light streaming into the leaves, so that their branching veins showed sharply black against the glowing scarlet membranes.

Hanba was only eight-square years old, but should have known better than to worry about the pormin-crop, and he knew it. Even so, he felt as anxious as he had always felt during every Hotfast since he had been Assigned to the farm. He longed for the reassurance of the first black porminet spears, and riffled his breathing-plates uneasily, gazing at the silent brown clearspace, until the light began to fade and the spade-leaves dimmed from scarlet to faintest yellow against the violet sky.

When stars appeared, Hanba stirred, and crawled out through the rustling leafy screen. He luxuriously spread his antennae to catch the drifting scents in the night-wind: the richness from his silicate silo; the metallic tang from the clearspace soil; and – just discernible, but causing him to riffle with excitement – the odour of young porminets from a nearby farm where harvest was coming early.

He turned away from the dying dayset and looked far over the flat country behind his burrow to the jagged Teeth. Their lower slopes were already dark, but the last light of the Daystar on their peaks gleamed in crystal fire, and Hanba's hearts glowed at the sight, as always. His progeny would almost certainly be up there among the peaks while daylight remained – sliding down smooth ice, soaring in the swirling up-draughts, or hover-watching for wild creatures scrambling back to crevices and burrows for the night.

Two-and-eight progeny this brood, he thought with some pride. My third brood and my best so far. Six in the first brood, six in the second, and now two-and-eight. Two survivors from the first, one from the second – and all good friends of mine still. Good  friends and good vrarnin. This brood should do well, too – a bit tameless, but trusty on the whole. Might even get four through...

Hanba checked himself from following that line of thought. He was determined that, if ever he were to Upgrade, it would be by his own personal merit, and not through anything as chancy as a high survival ratio. Besides, although he liked his offspring and enjoyed being a progenitor – in contrast to many vrarnin, who considered the whole business of brooding to be a tiresome chore – he felt no vocation to be a Fullbrooder.

For one thing, he leaned towards monogamy, and had mate-paired with only five vrarnine in his life. He had formed a deep closeness with his present pairmate, Aciele. The thought of losing contact with her was not pleasant.

For another thing, Hanba was convinced that he had a vocation to be a Describer. The conviction had grown over a period of half eight-square years. Ever since he could remember, he had thrilled to hear Descriptions. At first it had been the Events described that had stirred him, but gradually he had become fascinated by the styles and techniques of Describers, by their power to move the emotions of vrarnin and enrich their thoughts; and finally the urge and desire to Describe had germinated within him.

Like a pormin spore, Hanba's vocation lay dormant in poor soil, waiting for water and silicaceous fertiliser. The water and fertiliser his talent needed would take the form of an Event. Not just any event, but one that would be worth Describing – something that would make every vrarnin and vrarnine take a fresh view on life.

If he could Upgrade to Fulldescriber, he would be free to leave his farm and wander the Warmworld – or stay where he wished. He could visit Aciele when he liked, or even take her with him if she wanted to come. He need not grow any more pormin if he did not want to. Probably keep a small clearspace to dig and spread for recreation...

Evendreams – just evendreams, he thought, gazing across his dark, quiet clearspace. It must be an eight-cube harvests since anything interesting happened within a dayflight of here. In the whole of Warmworld there can't be more new Describers each year than a vrarnin has legs... How many others with the gift are waiting like me – tied to their Assignments, on farms, in brooderies and goodsbarns and makeplaces, at waymeets and control centres?

If only something would happen. Not just because I want to Describe, but so that there can be new things to know – a sense of going somewhere...

Around Hanba's mind a dangerous thought began to gather, like a shadow: in the darkness, terrible menace moving. Attractive as well as frightening... He forced himself not to think of it. Not now – not yet...

Anyway – first moonrise beginning – those progeny should be back by now.

It was the distant churrs and squeals picked up by middle-aged Hanba's still-sensitive hearbeard that reminded him of his brood. When he was sure he could hear them, he began the methodical preflight routine of exercises his progenitor had taught him: "Now – don't shirk. You must check every muscle – not only your beaters and your trimmers. You never know when you might get cramp, and have to improvise with your legs to keep control.

"And breathe – breathe – breathe – till your hearts slow down. That's the way to be sure you're fully oxygenated. Then check your senses: can you smell, hear, see, orientate? Wave those antennae – spread that hearbeard – blink those eyes – look near – look far – turn – turn again – Locate! And now sing the Rhyme."

That Rhyme. As the brood had grown older they had come to hate having to sing it out loud; 'Oh, Progy – need we? It's only an old broodery-rhyme!'

'Yes you do need. And don't look down on broodery-rhymes. They may be poor verse, but they make sense. So – come on now, Allbrood – all together.'

Then the ragged chorus, getting louder and faster towards the end:

'If you cannot find your way
You'll never see another day.
Well before you start your flight –
Make sure every muscle's tight.
Riffle every breathing plate,
Check your senses and Locate.
If you do not want to die,
Do all this before you fly. Can we go now, Progy?'

Hanba had taught his own broods the same old rhyme. The Psychology-keepers said you always tended to bring up

85

broods in the same way as your own progenitor, which was probably why Fullbrooding ran in bloodlines. His present brood were getting past the age where they would sing without protest. Still, he had lost only a few of his offspring through careless flying, so it couldn't be doing them any harm.

By the time he had Located, and stood with his wings outspread, flexing his slightly athletic beaters, the incoming vrarninets were within wingbeat of the farmstead. They had stopped churring, and Hanba could tell that they were flying as quietly as they could. They knew he would be away at the Hollow that evening, and might have left already. If they could manage it, they would land undetected, Locate, and sneak off on a nightflight in first-moon.

"Allbrood!" Hanba called. "I can hear you. Come on, now – it's time you were in burrow and resty."

Groans, churrs and squeaks came from the swooping brood. "Oh, Progy – can't we just stay up in first-moon? We promise to be back before stardark."

"No you can't. You know you're all tired. The days are long in Hotfast. Whatever time you go resty, you'll be up with the Daystar and flying far. And if you're tired..."

Hanba paused, listening carefully, suspicious. After a moment he said quietly, "Allbrood – what's the count?"

"One-and-eight, Progy," came the chorus.

"Which – and what happened to him?" said Hanba wearily.

"Prosperity," said the brood together, as though they had rehearsed it – which they undoubtedly had. "He and Fortune were playing Daredrops and Prosperity dropped on a pinnacle. We couldn't get him off. We tried, Progy – honestly we did – but it was stuck right through him – "

One of them added, "Anyway, he said it didn't hurt, Progy. He said he felt fine."

They were flying in a tight circle round Hanba now.

"Of course it didn't hurt, Duty, you silly broodling," muttered Hanba roughly. "It was too serious to hurt. Couldn't you see that? When did it happen?"

"About midlight," said Duty.

"About midlight – midlight! And you wait until now to tell me! Why didn't you come for help straight away?"

"Well – Prosperity said he felt all right – and Chance saw a true-snake out of burrow, so we – we sort of forgot. You know how it is, Progy."

"Yes – I know how it is," Hanba snarl-churred angrily. "And only this evening I was thinking you were quite a trusty brood. I must be as stupid as you."

The vrarninets swirled in their circle, chastened, hardly daring to beat their wings. Presently, Hanba went on more calmly. "Next time any of you has an accident of any kind – by hitting something, by flightfailure, by getting lost, by being eaten or stung or burnt or frozen or starved or overthirsted or anything else at all serious – next time and every time – all of you must do what you can to help. And if you don't succeed in completely rescuing the damaged vrarninet, you must leave two with the damaged one, and the rest must come and tell me. If you forget again, as you did today, I shall close your burrow for good, and let you fend for yourselves. Do you understand?"

"Yes, Progy."

"All right, now – down to burrow and no more nonsense. If you're not resty when I get back from eventalk, I'll seal you in from the outside."

"Yes, Progy. Sorry, Progy. Fairest night, Progy!"

"Fairest night, Allbrood!"

The swishing circle broke into a swift string of graceful grey forms, white wings flashing in the gleam of rising Littlebright, and the vrarninets swept down to the broodburrow, alighting on the run and jostling in with whispers and churrs.

Hanba watched them fondly until the last disappeared with a wing-wave and a timid whisper of "Fairest night, Progy!"

"Fairest night, little rascal!" said Hanba, churring softly to himself. Amity last – as usual. Got a soft spot for little Amity – hope he comes through.

Instead of flying off immediately, Hanba pushed through his elegant spade-leaf screen and crawled to the store-room to fetch his camera. He checked that it was set 'exposure wide-ranged to visual spectrum plus', put it in his thoracic pouch, and emerged again. He paused to assure himself that the water supply to the spade-leaf vine was wicking properly, went quickly through his preflight routine once more, and flew, climbing powerfully until he was high enough to glide to the Hollow.

The twin moons were almost directly behind him as he flew, so that far ahead he could see his racing shadows – the sharp, dark one caused by Littlebright partly overlapping the vague blur cast by Greydim, the bigger but less dazzling partner.

Hanba felt heavy on his wings – disappointed and somewhat angry. Poor little Prosperity... Right through him. Still – it wouldn't hurt – must have severed all his pain networks. Hope it cut out his survival-urge system, too; it would be pitiful to think of him frightened as he watched the scavengers coming for him. They'll have started to eat him as soon as the brood left. At that time of day they'd have seen him from dayflights around.

No good blaming the brood too severely. These things can't be helped. And if they'd called me and I'd saved him from the scavengers, he'd have only gone to our local rot-bacteria instead...

Strange thing, our vrarnin make-up. Pain sensors to warn us that we are damaged – but the moment we are badly injured they go out of action. You'd think that the more you were damaged the more you would hurt – like with illness.

The sicker you are, the more you ache – so why not the same with injury? I must ask the Biology-keeper some time. Tonight, perhaps. Yes – I think it's old Taruano tonight – good.

And I've never heard a convincing explanation for the sheer stupid tamelessness of the young. All that skill and daring they seem to have to prove to one another. In a calm, stable old race like ours, such behaviour's downright anachronistic. And when they come Through they turn into ordinary adults just like the rest of us. I know I must have done all those wild things myself when I was a vrarninet – but why? What drove me? Damned if I can remember.

And yet – if I'm really honest with myself – have I truly forgotten, or do I merely pretend because of convention? Is tamelessness still there in me – waiting? Is that what makes me want things to happen – to be different?

No – not exactly to be different; the old things are still good. No – what I want is simply something more than we have. Something more to learn? Yes – and some new form of understanding...

The shadow in Hanba's mind waited. But he dared not look into it, yet.

Perhaps I can ask the Fullkeeper a few things tonight – get my ideas straight. But I don't want him to suspect the way I'm thinking, do I? So – how should I ask?

Let's see. 'Is tamelessness – or traces of it – part of all of us, or is it only in the young?' No – that would be too obvious. What about 'Why are the young tameless?' No – that wouldn't get a relevant answer; the old vrarnin would just deliver his usual lecture on the need for progenitive discipline: 'tameless young are the result of slack progenitors' – that old garbage.

'Why do the young start life with such an urge to develop skill and courage?' Stock answer, I suppose: 'it's to maintain the strength of the species, so that, if ever anything threatens us, we'll still be able to respond to it and defend ourselves.' Then I could ask: 'But if the adults no longer possess those qualities – and none of us seem to – then who will do the defending – helpless vrarninets?' Yes – that should make old Taruano think. He might even come up with something interesting.

And I could go on to ask what he imagines might threaten us, as all the biology-keepers seem to think might happen one day. And yet the same keepers tell us that it's a long time – eight-to-the-sixth years or so – since we reached optimal equilibrium with all the other species on Warmworld. Keepers talk a lot of pormin-husks when they don't really know the answers...

The moonlight was bright enough by now to have caused most of the stars to vanish, and to show Hanba the blue-green of maturing porminets in the low-lying clearspace over which he was gliding. He was tempted to dive and examine the quality of his neighbour's crop; having made a delayed start, but could not spare the time. He contented himself by remembering the old saying 'Early is curly – late is straight.' It gave him some consolation – but the sight of his own first shoots would have been better.

The scarlet ellipse of the spade-leaf vines surrounding the Hollow appeared beyond a low ridge. Hanba banked gently to his right, beat his wings three times to correct his height, and aimed himself at the tall antenna-fern where he and Aciele always met before eventalk.

He could see other vrarnin and vrarnine converging on the Hollow, the vrarnin gliding smoothly and beating only to correct, in contrast to the vrarnine, whose smaller wings did not generate lift so efficiently, and who therefore flew with a dipping gait – beat-and-glide, beat-and-glide.

Hanba recognised Aciele's individualistic jinking flight – beating to the left, gliding to the right – long before they were close enough to pick out her beautiful pormin-green antennae with their sensuously out-curving tips. As usual, they reached their meeting place together – it was one of the many small symptoms of their closeness – and mingled antennae, churring with pleasure, before alighting.

"Steadfast, little closeness!"

"Steadfast, Hanba, my Littlebright! Do you prosper?"

"Well enough – though my pormins seem very late, and I lost a vrarninet only today. And you?"

"I hope for harvest soon; my porminets are on the turn already, and quite straight so far. But – oh, Hanba – my brood... How can they be so tameless? I only have three left now – and I've tried so hard!"

"Only three, closeness? But you had three-and-eight, didn't you?"

Aciele was twitter-churring miserably. "Three-and-eight – yes. But since we last met, Attentiveness picked up a true-snake, Generosity forgot her breakfast and overthirsted, and the other six picked up vrarninets, forgot my advice and died of premature pregnancy. Oh Hanba – am I such a bad progenitrix? Isn't there something I can do to stop them wasting themselves?"

"Perhaps the Psychology-keepers can help?" suggested Hanba without much conviction. "But I think you're no different from most of us – perhaps a bit too tender for your own good, but not by any means a poor progenitrix. You've had survivors from every brood, haven't you? Anyway, brightness – eventalk is starting; we must go down."

Eventalk that night was starting with a song, a popular song in a style which pleased Aciele but made Hanba want to fold his hearbeard. In fact, he half-furled it in self-defence until Aciele tweaked it, whispering, "Don't be so rude! Claste's bound to notice you, as an old pairmate. And – besides – I like it anyhow. I think she's dreamed a lovely song. Listen to the words; they're very stirring in my opinion."

Dutifully, Hanba forced himself to listen, glad to have missed most of it.

"Their wings shone white in Littlebright as they took flight," Claste howled in an old-fashioned thorax-voice; "We saw them fly away to die – and wondered – why!"

The singer dramatically extended the last words in an unbelievably drawn-out diminuendo. As the last squeak faded, leg-joints were clicked in applause – mostly polite from the vrarnin, and mostly enthusiastic from the vrarnine.

"I bet I know why they flew away," whispered Hanba very quietly. "I bet it was to get away from old scavengers like her!"

Aciele pincered him violently. "Old scavengers indeed. Old scavenger yourself. You were close enough to pairmate with her not so very long ago. And you ought to show more respect for our great vocal traditions!"

"Great vocal pormin-husks and body-rot! She's only just dreamed that drivel out. How can you call that a tradition?"

"You know very well what I mean. It's the sentiment expressed that's traditional."

"If by 'traditional' you mean 'worn out and irrelevant', then I'll concede that her sentiment is traditional. Otherwise –"

"Oh, Hanba – how your cynicism disgusts me! Aren't you at all proud of our past? Doesn't the Search mean anything to you? Sometimes I wonder whether we're really close, when you talk like this."

"It's not cynicism to despise false sentimentality." Hanba spoke more loudly, beginning to be irritated. "Of course we should be proud of our past. Of course the Search is of great significance to every vrarnin worthily brooded. But the past is dead – and the Search was a failure. Glorious, yes – but still a failure. Those horrible confections of Claste – and the others you so admire – they all invite us to celebrate great happenings and wonderful deeds that led nowhere!"

Every vrarnin at evenmeet was looking at Hanba now. Aciele tried to soothe him by gently stroking his thorax and fanning him with her breathing plates. When he failed to respond, she undid any good effect by whispering, "Closeness – your hearbeard's dishevelled!"

Hanba riffled heavily, stifled a snarl-churr, and went on. "And another thing: where do all these so-called traditions take us? These recallings of obsolete virtues – courage, tenacity, ingenuity, risk-taking, exploring, adventurousness, and so on. Do they inspire us? Do we recognise them in ourselves?"

Many of his listeners churred uncomfortably, partly amused at his vehemence, partly embarrassed at his questions.

Hanba took offence. "I ask in seriousness – what use have we for these qualities today? And where do we find them? Only in the youngnames of vrarninets! Daring, Skill, Judgment, Flair – once they were active exhortations to the young from adults who practised such virtues; now they are pormin-chaff – mere reminders of vanished life!"

Hanba paused to riffle. There were murmurs of approval from the younger vrarnin and vrarnine: "His point is sound."; "Yes – Hanba displays eloquence, and is worth hearing."

He continued, riding an updraught of excitement. "And where would we apply them – these splendid virtues – if they were still alive? What opportunities arise in our existence? Have we a Search? Do we try to create one? Are our traditions worth no more than the platitudes of the Morality-keepers? If a new Search were declared, how many can honestly claim that they would volunteer?"

Many of the audience began to applaud, but an old vrarnine cut them off with a scornful churr. "You Actionaries are all the same. You think you have achieved something, when you have merely seen the significance of the youngnames. Or – rather – you think you have seen their significance – but even that you misinterpret. They are aimed not at the young but at the old – can't you understand that? Have you not noticed that the behaviour of the young exhibits all the energetic characteristics you choose to praise as an orator – and no doubt condemn as a progenitor?

"Vrarnin Hanba – you make accusations of false sentiment against the lovers of our Searchsongs. You suggest that we should all show the old virtues on our lives. Do you happen to recall your own youngname? I do. It was Equity; not one of the spectacular change-virtues of which you have so suddenly become an advocate, but one that can still be practised in what you call our 'existence'. Does the thought disconcert you? It should – because I will ask you your own question: can you honestly say that you would volunteer for a new Search? Would you yourself be willing to leave your burrow and face mortal danger, for nothing but a faint hope?"

Though he was pincered into fury by the way the aged Fullbrooder had seemingly cut the water-wick of his argument, Hanba could think of no entirely suitable counter. He temporised, with what dignity he could command. "I do not choose to answer, Vrarnine Djienli; my question was rhetorical."

Djienli sneered, "Can't answer his own question! Seems his rhetoric has suffered flightfailure – along with all his high-soaring virtues." She and her cronies cackle-churred in triumph.

Aciele couldn't stand this. "That's most unfair! Stop it!" she shrieked. "Leave him alone – he didn't attack you – you negative, egg-bound old broodery!"

At this there were appreciative leg-clicks from most of the younger vrarnin and vrarnine, since all those who lived locally had suffered under the Fullbrooder's sharp mandibles at one time or another.

Hanba himself was silent. He was pleased that Aciele had come to his support; but more that this, he was grateful for the interruption, which gave him the chance to bring his emotions under control and his thoughts into a more orderly and less scattered formation.

Djienli and Aciele joined in fierce verbal battle, much to the enjoyment of the assembled vrarnin. Eventalk at the Hollow was generally a lively affair, but this was something out of the ordinary, and would provide burrowdreams to while away resty-times until the next full moons.

"Upstart broodling!" roared Djienli. "How dare you to speak to me before I address you? Is this the way you train your young? Is this the sort of example you set? No wonder only sterile idlers survive from your scanty broods!"

"Flopwinged, decrepit, shapeless, senseless makeplace of low-grade vrarninets!" countered Aciele. "What do you know about training? What sort of example do you set – you graceless void?" She had wanted to say something of the kind for a long time but had never dared.

Djienli half-spread her wings haughtily. "I set a damned-sight better example than you do – you with your fancy antennae – like – like the curly pormins round your dirty burrow-site!"

"Oh yes? Well I don't doubt that your burrow's clean enough; you bring all the dirt with you. In fact, I'm surprised that you talk of dirt as though you disapproved of it – you who never cleanse your mandibles! Even from here my antennae are choked with the stench..."

The two vrarnine injected enough venom to make up for any lack of finesse, and the exchange continued amid growingly enthusiastic applause at each slash and pincer-thrust.

Hanba was trying to work out just why Djienli's attack had riled him to such an extent. She had made it seem that he was suggesting it was time for a full-scale revival of the change-virtues; whereas all he was trying to do was to draw attention to the hypocrisy of those who praised the virtues in song, but would hate to have an opportunity of practising them. He had had no intention of expressing genuinely Actionary sentiments, and no wish to claim that he was any

95

more ready to accept novelty or to seek challenges than the next vrarnin.

And yet – where so I really stand? he thought. Am I an Actionary in my hearts? Surely not; I accept my Assignment, keep burrow, raise broods, share harvest... I live the life of a conventional vrarnin.

Admittedly, I want to Upgrade – but so do most people. And I'm willing to farm pormin until my Event comes along, without going around stirring up good people's lives for the sake of a change.

But if I'm not an Actionary, why did I get so strangely excited just now, when I was talking about the change virtues? And why did it hurt so much when Djienli made out that I was hypocritical in mentioning them? Maybe because she's right; perhaps I do feel that we need a new Search. Perhaps we cling to our comfortable Equilibrium simply for want of anything better to do...

After all, when we gave up the Search, what else was left to work for? I wonder if I should... No – not yet – not yet...

Hanba hadn't been paying much attention to the quarrelling vrarnine. His eye was suddenly caught by the splendid spectacle of Aciele in full fury. He sidled away to improve his angle of view, surreptitiously taking out his camera. Squatting, he framed his pairmate in the view-finder so that the dark green feathery spirals of her angrily-rolled antennae were backed by the violet of the sky, and squeezed the shutter-release just as her mandibles gleamed in the light of Littlebright.

Magnificent, he thought. One of my best, it must be – with the yellow from the infrared to add warmth, too... Hanba, old vrarnin – you've done it again!

His modest reflections were cut short by a shrill squawk from Djienli, who had spotted him taking the photograph. "Look at Hanba! Would you believe it? Look what you picked yourself as a pairmate! Leaves you to fight his battles for him – that's bad enough, coming from a puffed-up little Virtue-keeper – but then he takes snapshots of you with your hearbeard all over the place and dust on your wings! Will you pincer his antennae off, or shall I do it?"

Hanba hastily thrust his camera in his pouch and braced himself for flight, thinking fast, trying to look innocent by spreading his hearbeard. "Surely you don't think I would do a thing like that?" he said firmly and indignantly. He was pleased to see that Aciele's disdainful expression softened slightly, as though she wanted to believe him. To clinch the point, he went on, "I mean – the light's all wrong – I couldn't possibly..."

Aciele exploded with sharp peals of churrs, and rushed at him. He leapt backwards, twisted, and flew violently, pulling several muscles painfully.

Aciele managed to control herself sufficiently to gasp out, "Come back, you idiot – I'm not going to pincer you!" and burst into further helpless churring.

Most of the other vrarnine were also churring, but the majority of the vrarnin looked as puzzled as Hanba felt.

"When will you learn something about vrarnine?" said Aciele, as Hanba landed, somewhat shamefaced. "I didn't believe you for a moment. You know I can always tell when you're lying; you never spread your hearbeard like that when you're telling the truth. But – really, closeness – fancy telling a vrarnine that the only reason you didn't take her picture with her hearbeard all mussed up and her wings dusty was because the light was wrong! Surely you can see that's about the worst thing you could have said, even if it was true – in fact, especially if it was true!"

Hanba felt like a broodling whose progenitor has caught him nibbling porminet shoots but has let him off with a warning. Aciele looked up at him fondly, and put her pincer-legs round his thorax. As he bent to kiss her, his strained muscles protested, but he concealed the twinge tactfully so as not to spoil the moment.

Good-natured jeering broke out. "What a beautiful mate-pair they'd make!"

"Not in the light – please!"

"Just like a couple of first hymenals – makes me feel young again just to look at them!"

The Duty Convenor called for order. "When you've all quite finished, do you think we might get on with eventalk?"

He was greeted with groans, ironical leg-clicks and cries of "About time too!" and "Good grief – it's old Sosto – he's here after all. Glad you could make it, Vrarnin Sosto – welcome to evenmeet!"

"Very witty, I'm sure. Churr churr. There – now we've all churred. Does that satisfy you, Virenba? Can I take it that I have your permission to proceed? I can? Good.

"Right, then – the next item is Artefacts. Anyone need anything? Wings, please – not shouts!"

Four vrarnin spread one wing. Sosto called, "You first, Intiolu."

"I need a new fling-disc for my spreader. The rim's so worn down that the range is only about ten wing-beats."

"Can we manage that, Kerihona?"

"No reason why not," said the makeplace director. "I think we have one in stock. But if not, we can fabricate one within a quartermoon."

"Any objections? No? All right, Intiolu – you get a new disc. By the way, if you'd rather not trust that rickety old transporter of yours, I can lend you mine to pick it up in. Who's next – Vrarnine Ligtani – what do you need?"

"Well – I'd like a camera of the type Hanba has. My old Vista 454 is hopelessly unreliable."

"Kerihona?"

"What type is Hanba's?"

"It's a Varichroma 33-777," said Hanba.

"Thought so. Stereo-reflex, auto-zoom, the whole lot – beautiful job. But we can't make the lenses here – or the electronic shutter; have to get the more intricate bits from

Down-Overway-the-Hill makeplace. It'd take at least three months. Couldn't you get by with something simpler, Ligtani? A Vista 676, perhaps – we can make them here."

"I suppose I could, at a pincer," said Ligtani doubtfully, "but I really want to be able to take photographs like Hanba's. Will a Vista 676 do that?"

Hanba bristled. "It's not the camera that – ow!"

Aciele's pincers were sharp and well directed. She whispered, "Seal mandibles, halfwit. I know what you were going to say: 'it's not the camera, it's the photographer that makes the pictures'. You're always saying it. Do you want to upset Ligtani?"

"Of course not," whispered Hanba. "I was just trying to help her to understand that she doesn't need anything more elaborate than a Vista; there was no need to pincer me like that."

"Liar! You know very well..."

Convenor Sosto broke in, speaking with the patient irony of a Fullkeeper who has noticed vrarninets chattering at learnmeet. "Vrarnin Hanba – do you think that perhaps we should all be allowed to benefit from your expert opinion in this matter, or do you wish to instruct only your pairmate? You started to tell us something, no doubt of great value. Our hearbeards are spread in eager anticipation – so would you mind continuing?"

Just you wait until it's my turn to be Convenor, thought Hanba. Smoothly, he replied, "Before I was seized with a slight muscular spasm in the dorsal region – for which Vrarnine Aciele has now successfully treated me – I was about to remark that the Varichroma series of cameras is not considered entirely suitable for the kind of work Vrarnine Ligtani has in mind; namely rapidly taken shots of vrarninets, giving an effect of – er – spontaneity."

Hanba had been helped towards his choice of the word 'spontaneity' rather than 'carelessness' by very gentle pincer-pressure. Having avoided this particular down-draught, he resumed didactically; "The Varichroma range is designed for semi-Fullphotographic use. Indeed many Fullphotographers carry one because of its combination of lightness and versatility. The camera is complex, and though it is largely automatic – with automatic focusing, picture-balance optimisation and so on, it requires a number of manual settings in order to achieve the best results, particularly in terms of tonal range.

"The Vista, on the other hand, is noted for its convenience and simplicity. It is especially good for snap – er – snap-action photographs. And the lenses in the 676 are really rather fine. Why not try a new Vista, Ligtani?"

"But Hanba," said Ligtani sweetly, "If the Vista's so good, then why don't you use one when you're taking action shots?"

"Well – you see, I need the Varichroma for night work, microphotos, in-burrow stuff, and so on. It would be – er – confusing to keep changing from one camera to another all the time. So I – er – make do with the one that I have to have in any case – if you follow me..."

"I think I see," said Ligtani. "What you really mean is that a Varichroma would be wasted on me, but you're trying hard to be tactful. And I think you're very kind – not like some vrarnin." She side-glanced at her pairmate, who pretended not to notice. "Anyway, if Hanba says the Vista's all right, I'm sure I can manage with it."

"Good," said Sosto. "Any objections to Ligtani getting a Vista 676? None? Good – that's settled then. Next – Piki? I hope you don't want a Varichroma camera too!"

"No thanks – just a husking-knife."

"No objections, I take it – all right, Kerihona? You're easily satisfied, Piki. So – Rugdo – what so you need? Something big, by the look of your antennae!"

"Afraid so, Sosto. I think it's time I had a reconditioned harvester. Mine's so slow and unreliable now – it fails to keep up with the pormins. Three days I've been harvesting this year, and each day I've lost about three per eight-square of the ripeners. By the time I was into the last of them, they weren't fresh enough for scavengers to eat. Beriu's finished his harvest, so he's lending me his machine for the rest of my cropping, but next year..."

"Looks bad, right enough, Rugdo. Beyond our discretion here, too – have to put it up to Burrow-under-Dale control centre, I think. Anyone here know the procedure?"

A very old vrarnine with drab brown antennae and sparse hearbeard wheezed, "Yes – that's it, youngvrarn' Sosto – the clever folk have to talk over big machines like harvesters and such. Last time we Downhollow folk had to trouble them must be – let me see now – eightsquare years ago – the time the makeplace cutting-laser had to be replaced... I talked to the clever folk myself – I was makeplace director here then, you know – had no trouble convincing them; the laser was terribly old. How old's your harvester, Rugdo?"

"Getting on for three eightsquare harvests according to the Assignment records."

"Certainly an old one," said Sosto. "No wonder it's slow. I'm surprised you don't have to push it..."

"Mine's older than that," put it a rather pretty young vrarnine. "It's exactly three eightsquare three-eights-three this harvest; three-three-three!"

"Amazing! Does it still work – or do you have to borrow all the time?"

"It still works fine. But my soil's much lighter than Rugdo's – much lower heavy-metals content – mostly aluminium and titanium oxides, you know, whereas he's mainly on copper and iron."

"Yes – that probably makes all the difference. So you won't be needing a new harvester yourself yet awhile, will you?"

"Oh no – should be good for another eightsquare harvests yet."

"Fine. Anyway, we'd better have a special meeting to discuss Rugdo's machine and work out how to put the case for replacement. Who will we need? Rugdo – Kerihona of course – me, I suppose – and can we call on you, Vrarnine Pielo?"

"Yes – delighted to be of some use in my old age. But I can't fly any more, you understand; you'll have to come here."

"Thank you, Vrarnine Pielo. I'm sure we shall need all the help you can give us. Then we'll meet here in a moon and a day, if that suits all of you. That should mean all our harvests are complete, and it will give an opportunity for anyone who has thought up any suggestions to bring them up at eventalk the night before. Settled? Good – then that concludes Artefacts.

"Next we would normally have Assignments, but we don't seem to have any to discuss tonight... Oh – I'm so sorry, Saruba! We have yours to confirm, don't we? Saruba requests formal confirmation of his Assignment as Fullfarmer to Under-Downhollow Farm. Will anyone speak for him?"

There was an embarrassing silence, during which the young Saruba tried not to look concerned. Normally, confirmation was a formality, requiring only a word or two from someone who could attest to the quality of the Assigned vrarnin's work – in this case the porminery master, who received all the crops and knew the pormins from every farm as a progenitor knows his vrarninets.

After a few heartbeats, Sosto said, "Is Palidu here?" and everyone looked round at neighbours.

A vrarnine's voice called, "There he is – up under the spade-leaves – he's gone resty again. He hates it when we discuss machinery and such like. I'll wake him up."

An expectant pause was succeeded by yells: "Help! Crawlers! I'm being... Oh – it's you, closeness. Is it time to go, then?"

Sosto silenced the churrs. "Vrarnin Palidu, we are sorry to intrude into your concentrated thoughts on Vrarnin Saruba's pormins. We should hate to suggest that you utter a snap judgment on the question as to whether they are of sufficient quality to merit confirmation of Saruba's Assignment. However, we feel that you may have made up your mind by now, and that you might be ready and willing to say a few words on the subject; Saruba's pormins - are they good enough?"

By the time that Sosto had cleared his breathing plates and emptied his lung of this speech, Palidu was almost awake. "Saruba... Saruba - new vrarnin at Under-Downhollow, isn't he?"

"If you count eight harvests as new - yes." said Sosto heavily.

Palidu liked to keep his listeners in suspense, and had a jealously guarded reputation as an eccentric. He eyed Sosto, furling and unfurling his hearbeard dramatically for some moments. Then he turned and gazed upon the unfortunate Saruba as though he had never before seen anything quite like him. Next, he placed all his feet in a precisely regular octagon, set his body vertical, rolled his antennae tightly, furled his hearbeard completely, shut his eyes, and stood in an attitude of profound thought, riffling very slowly.

At last, amid riffles of relief and a few stifled churrs, he spoke. "Under-Downhollow pormins... Yes - yes - I think so. Not very good when old Palfo had the place - too feeble to tend them, he became. But recently - yes - recently - during the last eight harvests - pretty straight - adequately ripe - better than most, I'd say. Yes - yes - Saruba, is it? Yes - he'll do."

Sosto thought: stingy, mis-brooded old hoarder-snake! "Thank you, Palidu," he said. "Your praise is most generous and much appreciated. Please return to your deliberations with our unanimous gratitude."

Palidu crawled off with great dignity.

"Anyone to speak against Saruba?" No. Good. Vrarnin Saruba - you are confirmed as Fullfarmer to Under-Downhollow."

There was energetic applause. Saruba wing-waved.

"We come now to Keepertalk," announced Sosto. "Tonight we are privileged to have with us Fullkeeper Taruano, who will be discussing Biology. Fullkeeper Taruano, you have our hearbeards."

Amid respectful silence, an aged vrarnin with stained, brownish wings emerged from the crowd and half-crawled to the centre of the Hollow, flapping feebly to assist his shaky legs. His voice was surprisingly firm and deep.

"Vrarnin and Vrarnine, I see it as my main duty to help you to an understanding of the science which it is my life's work to keep – namely Biology. We recognise four-and-three-eights sciences to be kept, and – since there are seven-and-eight moons in a year, I come to speak to you only about once in two years. Therefore, to enable you to build up a clear and undistorted picture, such as can constitute understanding, I must needs, in my thematic statements, confine myself to sketching in the framework on which your own reflections and conversations can hang the flesh, particularly if you talk things over with your local keeper..."

"He'll have us all resty if he goes on like he usually does," whispered Aciele.

"Shh, closeness! I like to hear him; he usually rewards those who manage to stay awake," said Hanba, spreading his hearbeard to emphasise his concentration.

"... and, as some of you may recall," Taruano was saying, "I pointed out on that occasion that all the elements and activities of a farming community such as yours have biological analogues. I went on to discuss biological systems in general, and suggested that Biology is the science which – more than any other – integrates and draws together not only the other sciences but our entire social structure.

"And tonight I shall briefly speak of Equilibrium – the concept which underlies all of our post-Search Vrarninist philosophy. We all tend to take the results of Equilibrium for granted. I shall say enough to show that this is a truly dangerous attitude. Equilibrium, and the benefits it brings, had to be fought for. The fight must go on without pause – or be lost.

"What are the benefits of Equilibrium? Security of living; stable communities; and continual peace. A quality of existence that was regarded as idealistic and impractical by all but a few far-sighted individuals in the pre-Search era.

"Your Prehistory keepers have shown you pictures of this area as it looked in those terrible times, now mercifully long past. Artefacts of all kinds cluttering up the scene – some of them constructed for trivial purposes, some for no known purpose at all. Makeplaces everywhere – above the ground as well as below it – turning out the artefacts. And under the haze of effluvia from the makeplaces, the wretched, almost uncountable multitudes of our people – many of them rendered virtually flightless by the damaged atmosphere in which they spent their lives.

"Today, in contrast, all is purposeful. All is integrated into our natural system. No artefact is made without need – whether for work or for recreation. Nothing is destroyed until it has become useless, and then everything than can be recovered is recycled. Each individual vrarnin and vrarnine can find a role to play on our society, and can Upgrade as ability grows. Every species on Warmworld occupies an appropriate place in the balance of nature, without the need for artificial interference on our part.

"And yet, as I said just now, all this must be fought for, or it will be lost. Why? Because there are – even after all the generations that have passed since the Search ended – vrarnin who want to undo all that has been accomp-lished, by seeking to improve radically on what we have achieved. I refer to the so-called Actionaries.

"Actionism is the last enemy of our race – and the most dangerous we have ever encountered.

"Ignorant or unthinking vrarnin often regard scavengers and crawlers as our enemies, because they will eat

105

us if they catch us unwary or damaged. This is a stupid attitude. Scavengers and crawlers are not our enemies; they are simply dangerous friends. They are useful to us because they can eat anything they can catch. This happens to include vrarnin, but only those who are careless. If we get eaten, that is our fault – not that of our friends who eat us.

"The digestion of a scavenger breaks down flesh into its constituents and returns potential nutriment to the soil eightsquare times as fast as rot-bacteria can do the job. This not only keeps the countryside pleasantly free of decaying bodies but also maintains the cycle of nature at a healthy speed. Not even those who fear and detest scavengers would suggest that we eradicate them just because they are ugly, fierce and inconvenient; everyone can see that they play a vital part in maintaining the balance of nature.

"The danger of Actionary suggestions is that they ask us to upset the balance of nature – and the danger is all the more deadly because it is hidden. No Actionary would be foolish enough to advocate eradication of scavengers. Actionary proposals are always positive and well-intentioned, so that even thinking, intelligent vrarnin sometimes respond to them. Actionaries do not tell us to take away from one side of the balance – by, for example, killing off a group of species; they ask us to add to the other side of the balance – by increasing our own competitive advantages.

"You have all heard Actionary suggestions, and no doubt you have treated the more obvious ones with the contempt they deserve. Some examples are subtler: 'Let us time our flying-races, so that we can compare the results from one year to the next'; 'Let us try growing pormin further from the equator, so as to increase the variety of Assignment farms available'; 'Let us invite Fullbrooders to explain their methods of bringing up vrarninets to the whole community at evenmeet, so as to increase our average survival ratio."

"There is hidden danger in all these attractive suggestions. Just to take one of them, for illustration: suppose that we were to increase the average survival ratio of vrarninets. This has often been advocated for vrarninitarian reasons. Nobody enjoys the loss of broodlings of which he has become fond, or whose appearance is aesthetically satisfying. Equally often, the motive has been to improve the quality of adult life; since, if more of our young came through to adulthood, we should be freed from the duty of continual brooding which is concomitant with our first Assignments. This in turn would mean that we would have a better chance of Upgrading, and could Upgrade earlier in life.

"It is argued with some logic that we all have an obligation to achieve as high a survival ratio as we can, and that we instil – by precept and example – the principles by which we ourselves were enabled to survive and come through to adulthood. We even make a high survival ratio a qualification for Upgrading. Therefore, the argument runs, why not systematise the methods of upbringing, and disseminate them throughout our population?

"Firstly, we should notice that a high survival ratio is a qualification for Upgrading only to Fullbrooder. Since most of us would hate to have only brooding as our lifetime activity, this is not the incentive it might appear to be at a surface glance. Thus there is no contradiction within the present system in this respect.

"Secondly, let us examine the consequences of more efficient brood-training. We would need less broods. Adults would Upgrade earlier in life, and consequently escape altogether from having to brood. There would be a reduction in the brooding population. It would be an extraordinary coincidence if this reduction exactly compensated for the increase in survival ratio. Almost certainly the total number of vrarnin would fall.

"At the same time, the unusually tameless vrarninets who at present die because of their carelessness would stand a better chance of coming through, because of their more intensive and better-directed training. This would alter the distribution of personal characteristics in the general population, and alter it in the direction of instability. There would be a tendency towards increasing Actionism, and a reduction in the proportion of vrarnin able and willing to resist Actionary proposals. At the same time, our contribution to the food supply of scavengers and crawlers would diminish. This might well cause these animals to turn to other food sources, thereby reducing the numbers of the species forming those food sources.

"It is thus difficult to assess the full consequences of even minor changes in vrarnin behaviour, but easy to see that the effects will be far-reaching, long-lasting, and almost certainly irreversible.

"This is the most important reason why we keep the sciences rather than practising them. Sociopsychology gives the reason as a loss of motivation, a reaction against any kind of exploration, consequent on our admission of failure in the Search. Prehistory tells us that Keeping is the outcome of tendencies that could be discerned long before the Search was even begun; that the storage of knowledge had, over the generations, become a greater problem than its acquisition – so that more and more vrarnin with an ability to appreciate science had to devote their energies to learning what had already been discovered and passing it on, rather than adding to the store. Techno-economy suggests that, quite simply, a point was reached where obtaining new knowledge was no longer worth the effort. There are nearly as many explanations for Keeping as there are sciences to Keep.

"Only the need for Equilibrium provides both an explanation and a positive motivation for Keeping. To maintain Equilibrium, we must neither lose nor gain a single item of scientific knowledge.

"I do not wish to give the impression that I deplore the desire for improvement. Nor would I claim that vrarnin society is as perfect as it could be. I do, however, suggest that physical change and alteration of our behaviour patterns –

such as the Actionaries desire – are not the way to improvement, but the flightpath to disaster.

"Improvement must come from within, and take place inside the individual vrarnin. We must all strive to absorb knowledge, the knowledge that our Keepers hold in trust for us. And we must – having assimilated what our Keepers can tell us – build up – each in his own hearts – a true and strong acceptance of the wonderful system which our foreprogenitors have handed down to us.

"This will not be easy. The temptations to Actionism are many and powerful. Even some of our Describers are not free from the taint. In the interest of self-aggrandisement they stir up their audiences not towards understanding and acceptance of the Events they are privileged to have witnessed, but towards emotional surges and a desire for great deeds. The Searchsongs are the right place for this type of emotional manipulation of the gathered vrarnin; everyone – or almost everyone – recognises that they are meant only to entertain, and that their calls to action are not to be taken seriously.

"I am an old vrarnin now. This may be the last time I shall be able to speak to you, vrarnin and vrarnine of Downhollow. All my life I have continued to study my chosen science more and more deeply. I have tried to give you the same understanding of the overall picture as I myself have come to behold. I shall, as usual, try to answer your questions after the music session. But – whatever you fail to understand – whatever you do not know – never lose faith in the wisdom of our foreprogenitors, those glorious generations who saw that the failure of the Search was not the end of our species's achievements but the beginning. At the end of the Search, we vrarnin did not despair; we checked our senses, Located, and flew – towards the rich, wonderful destination that is the life we live today.

"And so I end with these admonishments: learn and understand; admire acceptance; despise Actionism!"

The echoes of the fine old voice died away, and silence filled the Hollow. Then leg-clicking swelled into a moderate ovation. Fullkeeper Taruano's antennae curled outwards with pride and pleasure. He stood tall, spread his wings and turned slowly round to acknowledge the appreciation of each section of the audience, then resumed his inconspicuous position in the crowd.

Hanba clicked politely, watching the expressions of the vrarnin around him. As far as he could see, everyone's antennae were wide and straight, and every hearbeard was spread. Some of the people had been stirred so strongly that they stood up with outspread wings.

It seemed that Hanba alone had found the Fullkeeper's farewell address disappointing. To him the words had brought no comfort or inspiration. He had heard them as a message of desolate emptiness. Until this night he had assumed that there was a purpose in life. He had assumed, without questioning the assumption, that the knowledge held by the Fullkeepers was intended to be used for the improvement of every aspect of life – and that such improvement was the purpose not only of the knowledge but of life itself.

Now, for the first time, Hanba truly realised that there were vrarnin who would be content if they knew that in eight generations – or in eightsquare – life on Warmworld would be no different from the life they had led themselves. And to judge by the reaction to Taruano's speech these people must be in a majority.

The discovery filled Hanba with an intense feeling of dislocation and loneliness, in an emotional surge like those he had sometimes experienced when, listening to a Describer, he had been struck by an insight. Incoherent, shifting thoughts conflicted confusingly: beauty of Equilibrium – youngnames and change-virtues – peace and tamelessness... Do we want a new Search? More to the point – do we need one? Am I an Actionary?

Why do vrarnine understand vrarnin so much better than vrarnin understand vrarnine? Would it help if pairmates were to live together in the same burrow? Is that an Actionary suggestion – or has it been tried?

What would it be like if vrarnin could have vrarnine broodlings, and vice-versa? Why has nature made this impossible – evolutionary advantage, or accident? Is evolution an accident?

Does Equilibrium mean the end of evolution? If so – do we really need Keepers for the sciences?

When was the Varichroma developed? It must have been since the end of the Search, surely – and in any case, the Vista 676 only came out – what was it? – about five years ago. Is camera development Actionary?

Oh – Hanba – what an idiot – what a picture you missed just now; all those white wings spread, and Littlebright at exactly the right angle, too... Lovely it would have been. May not get another chance like that for years... Damn.

Irritation at the lost opportunity brought Hanba's emotions into perspective. The feeling of dislocation left him; the major issues, though unresolved, receded into the background of his mind.

He became aware that Aciele was speaking to him. "Come on, now, my brightness – you really ought to listen – it's very beautiful – so open your hearbeard, do!"

She had put her mouth close to his hearbeard to make sure he could hear her; with sudden lightness and affection he kissed the top of her head and mingled his antennae with hers.

Little closeness, he thought – you're a perfectly good reason for living, if nothing else is...

To give time for the people to prepare their questions for the Fullkeeper, it was the custom at Downhollow for the string choir to play an intermezzo. This evening they were performing a superb chorus by Valienji, whose progeny

Valienba was Fullmaster of the choir. It was Valienba's invention of the sticky-stick that had enabled the gourds to produce a singing tone, as opposed to the churring sound given by the traditional serrated sticks. This had transformed the strings from mere clowns into instruments of expressive delicacy, ranking equally with the winds and percussion in the modern orchestra.

"The style is Valienji's," whispered Hanba, "But I don't recognise the piece. What is it called, closeness?"

"It's Vali'ji's latest – that's why you don't know it. He calls it 'Chorus Number Six for Allstrings', but he has let it be known that he will not mind if it is known as the Daydawn Chorus; he tried to express the atmosphere of dawn light brightening and growing..." Noticing that Hanba was not listening to her, Aciele stopped whispering and, like him, spread her hearbeard and gave herself up to the clear, soaring music.

Perfection, thought Hanba. Not a note superfluous. Every resonance and toneflight finely located. Only Valienji could have conceived it, and only 'ba could execute it with such sensitivity... And before them, no-one could have composed it or played it at all; winds could not generate this emotional intensity, and without the sticky-stick... Like trying to take my kind of night photographs without fullrange film. Those Vali's are aesthetic Actionaries!

We'd have missed all this if Taruano's ideas were applied to music... What are we missing by applying them to the sciences?

Disquiet and conflict surged again in Hanba, making him riffle rapidly. Aciele, nestling against his thorax, murmured, "I can hear your hearts, my brightness – they're fluttering like broodlings trying to fly. It moves me, too – that toneflight the highgourds are repeating now – so tender and hopeful..."

Rather than detract from her enjoyment by admitting the true nature of his disturbed feelings, Hanba replied by gently kissing her and respread his hearbeard to show that he was listening intently. The music caught him again.

In the rapt Hollow only the musicians moved.

The chorus ended in a splendid resonance, as strong and pervasive as morning light. It seemed to ring in the minds of the listeners long after the players had lowered their gourds.

No-one clicked.

As though it had been agreed in advance, every vrarnin and vrarnine rose and stood with outspread wings.

Valienba and his choir remained humbly seated, showing by their in-curled antennae that they were overcome by this unprecedented tribute.

Eventually Sosto spoke, very quietly, and for once without irony. "We shall remember this night. Our silence has been more eloquent than my speaking could be. Choir of Downhollow, we thank you for playing fine music beautifully."

Valienba and his colleagues acknowledged Sosto's speech in the traditional manner, by raising their gourds above their heads; but for some time none of them uncurled his antennae.

After another silent pause, Sosto said, "Vrarnin and vrarnine, my hearts are full. I know that many of you must feel as I do – that it would not be fitting to continue with questions now. If nobody disagrees, I propose to end eventalk here."

In a rustle of folding wings and quiet riffling the people relaxed. Sosto almost whispered: "Fairest night and calm rest to you all."

Gradually the vrarnin drifted out of the Hollow, up through the spade-leaf circle to the fountain-bowls, where they sipped the achingly cold spring-water before flying. Aciele and Hanba had no difficulty in finding drinking-room at the bowl by the great antenna-fern, since many left without the usual formality of a drink. The company were subdued, and there was only desultory conversation.

When he and Aciele had sipped, Hanba took her aside and said softly, "Sosto is right, of course – the music was wonderful; but I have so many questions I would have liked to ask Taruano. Now all I want to do is to go resty as soon as I can. Do you mind if I leave straight away?"

"No, closeness – I don't mind at all," murmured Aciele. "I feel entirely at peace. But I can't understand what's disturbing you. You seem to think that Taruano's arguments were flying on weak wings, whereas to me what he said made perfect sense."

"Oh – I don't know what it is myself, my Aciele. Perhaps it's just a mood... Anyway – you won't think me rude if I – if we don't –"

"No – of course not, little brightness. I feel too content to worry about missing that for once. And – besides – I think I may be harvesting tomorrow, so I could do with an early night. Preflight?"

"Thank you, closeness – yes – preflight now."

They carefully ran through the preflight routine together, kissed, whispered closely, and flew.

Aciele's use of the phrase 'flying on weak wings' had reminded Hanba that he had strained some of his muscles earlier, in avoiding her mock-attack. Otherwise, he would have postponed his departure at least until they had discussed plans for their next meeting. As for pairplay – well, it was a pity to miss that, but with strained muscles...

His back had seemed all right during preflight. However, he didn't want to get back to burrow after stardark, in case a crawler was visiting his burrow-site, which would mean prolonging his flying time. Crawlers stayed in their lairs until the darkness after first moonset; so he should have no trouble provided that he could make it back to burrow in firstmoon. With the early start, this might just be possible.

Nursing his protesting muscles, Hanba flew as fast as he dared.

He was too late for comfort, although by the time the last glow of moonlight died he was near enough to home to find his way by the light of the stars.

As he glided low across his home clearspace, Hanba spotted a very large crawler – over two wingbeats long, he judged – moving in the direction of his burrows. The creature detected him immediately, and reared up with fierce hunger. Instinctively Hanba beat violently to gain height, even though he was well out of reach. The stab of pain emphasised his foolishness in over-reacting. He collected himself, aimed for the faint yellow luminescence of his spade-leaf screen, and dived swiftly to his burrow.

He had secured the door-seal and turned on the lights when he felt the ground tremble as the baffled crawler slithered to a halt.

Safe inside, Hanba folded his wings as comfortably as he could, and tried to ease his aching muscles. His hearts were thumping and his mind was full of terrified admiration for the strong, savage beast outside his door-seal. He wondered where it would find food that night, and whether it had to feed every night to stay alive. No-one seemed to know the answers to questions like that.

Hanba put his camera away, sipped water from the fountain-bowl, checked the isotopic generator and the air-conditioning plant, went to the couch-room, turned out the lights, and composed himself to go resty.

Restiness did not come easily or quickly. Beneath the turmoil of his conscious thoughts, which he knew were capable of rational resolution – given time – a profound change had occurred in Hanba's emotional make-up. Whatever was told to him, by his own logic or by the Fullkeepers, he would never again lose an uneasy sense of dissatisfaction and longing.

And although, over the months, he regained his ability to go resty at will, the memory of this particular evening would haunt the edges of his mind as soon as he came to his couch.

---

### NGRS-323: orbit

Captain James Roberts, commanding Cripple-Cruiser Magellan – officially Seeker 12 – was a typical example of the results of Colonel Williams's memo to the Powers That Be.

The rest of his crew were equally typical. All but the navigation officer and the propulsion systems engineer had two arms; but none of the six had more than three whole limbs.

The Williams Memorandum started pithily: 'If we're going to bring back cripples, why not send out cripples?' and set forth a convincing case. The press had got hold of a leaked copy, and a tabloid had headlined the story 'For Cripple Cruisers Why Not Cripple Crews?'.

Initially, the public reaction was shock and disgust at the heartlessness of the question. Breasts were beaten. Banners were marched up and down with. People named Williams availed themselves of the deed-poll provisions.

Eventually someone took up a suggestion of the callous Colonel; they asked the few qualified cripples what they thought of the idea. The response of one Dr Yuri Lermentov – now physician and biologist in Magellan was typical: "Of course I accept. How can I object? What is that idiom? Oh yes – I have not a leg to stand on!" His questioner was uncomfortably unsure how to take this, in view of the literal truth of Dr Lermentov's assertion.

James Roberts stood leaning against the computer display panel in the Magellan's main room, which doubled as wardroom and bridge. His thoughts were, as usual, cynical and touched with bitterness. Science, he was thinking. Bloody science. What's the use of all these wonderful gadgets if none of the bastards works properly? No wonder we never get anywhere, or find anything when we do; the blasted gadgets don't work.

Eighteen days out of Sleep – down to reasonable velocity – ready to go into orbit round a splendid-looking planet with all the signs of oxygen-based life – ready to make history – and the blasted bloody gadgets don't work. Can't get a drink, for Christ's sake! God – I feel useless... What's the use? The only real personal contribution I can make to this idiotic mission – apart from just being here and nominally in charge – and the bleeding bloody thing won't work when we need it...

The immediate object of the captain's fury was a fairly simple mechanism. on which the mission's two engineers, Jonathan Ling and Jennifer Roberts, were working. In the tradition of the Royal Navy, James Roberts had insisted that if he were to command this ship, she would carry what he called 'decent drink'. Glass bottles were out of the question, and James would have no truck with plastics, which he claimed would be bound to taint their contents after a few subjective years. The minimum-mass solution had been found to be a dispenser that – it was claimed – could produce practically any alcoholic beverage known to mankind, and weighed next to nothing.

Like much of the equipment in the ship, the dispenser was now unserviceable.

James Roberts had had plenty of time to assess priorities, and he was no fool. The engineers had tried to repair everything else during the past eighteen days, and had achieved some remarkable successes. Until now, the captain had not considered the time ripe for a drink – but when the jury-rigged analysers confirmed that they had located a planet with an oxygen-rich atmosphere, he had ordered 'Splice the mainbrace!'

Jennifer had said, "Shall I do the honours, sir?" and pressed the buttons for a large Scotch and soda, exactly what James wanted.

Pure water had trickled into the drinking-tube.

After ten agonising minutes watching the engineers tinkering with the machine, James said, "Are you getting anywhere?"

"Think so..." said Jonathan, without looking round. "Say, Jenny – how about bypassing the blender-timer relays – try running it manually? I feel sure –"

"You mean, just short them out, like this? And... Good god – it's working! Here comes your Scotch, captain. Sorry there's no soda – only water."

"Marvellous," said her husband heavily. He took the transparent tube from her and waited politely while she and Jonathan extracted drinks for all the others. 'Sir', 'Captain' he thought. Christ – that little joke's wearing thin. Surely the whole crew must see through it by now – see how she despises me. Come to think of it, they must all have some idea of how I despise myself. They all reckon I'm useless – useless and worthless. In this, the captain was about right, as he usually was when his thoughts were blackest.

Like the others, James Roberts was unable to accept transplants, other than skin grafts. His body rejected replacement internal organs, even those cultured from his own cells. The reasons for this unusual condition were not understood.

Jenny's hands had re-grown their skin and kept it, but the nerves and muscles had failed to regenerate properly. Advances in micro-feedback cybernetics had given her just enough control to resume her career.

Unlike the other crew-members, the captain was a non-specialist. All he had ever been properly trained to do was to fly. He had flown every kind of craft from hovertrucks to Solar orbital ships, with slightly above average proficiency, until the accident that took off his leg.

It was fifteen years since he and Jenny had met at the rehabilitation hospital at Headley. More than fifteen years if you counted the time they had spent in the Big Sleep coming to this planetary system. But fifteen years you could seriously consider. For a time they had given each other support, and a chance of self-respect. Even love – for a time.

James had become an administrator, nominally still in the General Duties Branch; but in practice deskbound, competent and colourless. Jennifer went on with her career as a propulsion specialist. Wherever she was posted, the Space Service found James an administrative job, so that they were never separated for long, which was good for their marriage from one point of view. On the other hand, it was somewhat humiliating for James to be the cog that could always be spared from any given place and fitted in at the next – following his expert wife around.

After the tragedies and near-tragedies of the early Seeker missions, the project had become less risky. Improvements in the propulsion systems cut down subjective time for a given radius of exploration. Cryogenic techniques also improved, reducing tissue damage, though never eliminating it.

By Seeker 6 a successful crew formula had been established, a formula that kept whole people more-or-less whole. The formula was simple enough: a non-specialist captain commanding scientists and engineers. With no technical axe to grind, the captain had been able to run a balanced operation. Also, the crew was composed of equal numbers of men and women in sexually compatible pairs, two of them married couples. The mission had been technically satisfactory; it had returned to Earth on schedule with every member of the crew functioning normally, all clinically sane, most of them cheerful.

Subsequent Seeker missions had also been technically satisfactory. None of them had found life, however – let alone intelligent life – and hope was waning. The cost of sending out

119

a single Starship remained immense, and had a measurable effect on the average standard of living of humanity. Seeker 12 might well be the last; not even the most fanatical supporter of the project advocated continuing beyond Seeker 15.

Most thinking people felt that if nothing was found by then, it would be the end of the road for humanity – at least the end of the road to technical and scientific perfection; possibly the end of the human ambition to improve. If something was found, however...

"Vodka for you, Yuri?" said Jenny. "Yes – here you are."

"Thanks a lot." Biologist-Medic Dr Yuri Lermentov was a small, friendly man with no legs. The lander had been designed specially to take him, since finding life was the main object of the mission. He was extremely excited now that the great goal seemed close. "Fancy," he said, "My first vodka in thirty-five years – and me a grown-up Russian!"

The others laughed.

"Call yourself grown up?" bantered Bernadette N'Gama, Yuri's partner, the ship's navigation officer. "You're just a great big boy. You only came on this trip so you could have a ride in your own personal rocket ship. And what's this about thirty-five years? You're only twenty-four years old as far as I'm concerned. You didn't do any growing up during the Big Sleep."

Yuri pretended to be hurt. "All right – you extensive black beast – so I'm young in outlook. But to call me a boy is going too far. You only dare to say it because until we are in free fall you know you can escape from me on those long legs of yours."

"Is there something wrong with my legs now? You never complained –"

James interrupted. "Ladies and gentlemen – I'm going to propose a toast. As we all know, the planet we are approaching has an oxygen-rich atmosphere and a good deal of water. There are many green areas which we are virtually certain are vegetation. We cannot be truly certain that life exists there, but it seems most likely.

"Nor can we be certain that when we get there everything will go according to expectation. We are lucky we have survived so far. You have all done a fine job in repairing much of the damage we suffered from relativistic particles during the Big Sleep. No ship that returned to Earth ever encountered a shower of such intensity. It may be that this kind of disaster explains why several Seekers have failed to get back at all. And it may be that with the kind of effort and ingenuity you have brought to your tasks those ships might have returned safely. Without what you have done we might all be dead now. I appreciate this, and that's why I'm putting these words on the ship's records as I speak to you.

"We shall need all the luck we can get to survive the next phase of the mission and the long journey back to Earth. The ship may make it without us, though, and I want Earth to know that her crew did all they could.

"We shall be in free fall in a few minutes time. No doubt you'll all be as glad as I shall be to get rid of your artificial legs for a while. Until then, however, we shall be able to stand and drink in a civilised manner."

James could see the others shifting uncomfortably. It was this sort of speech that went down well with the top brass: sense of occasion – all he was good for... Jenny wouldn't meet his eye. Nor would Judith and Jonathan Ling. With a pang of envy, James noticed the mouse-like little geophysicist squeeze her husband's hand. Control systems engineer, thought James. God give me control...

"Well – whatever happens, we are going to make history now, by being the first human beings to drink proper, decent drinks nine light-years from home!" James spoke brightly, forcing a smile.

Yuri smiled too, raising his drinking-tube. Jenny closed her eyes. The others didn't change their blank expressions.

"I ask you now to drink to the goal of our enterprise – to life!"

They all murmured, "To life!" and drank, tensely.

Seventy-two hours later they had completed a general survey of the tiny planet, with its curious double moon and its thin layer of dense oxygen-carbon-dioxide-nitrogen atmosphere; they had established synchronous orbit over a land mass well covered with promising dark green. And they had discovered the unpleasant truth about the lander vehicle.

Jonathan was trying to be helpful. "I tell you there's no way of fixing it, Yuri. You can't go down. Why can't you just accept that, and concentrate on working out how to get the evidence you need from up here? Surely you can do without specimens, can't you?"

"No I can't!" shouted Yuri. "Don't you see? Spectroscopic evidence is no good. It's got to be proof. It's got to be specimens – or detailed photographs at the very least. We've been through all this before – not just us, I mean – but back in the old days; there was plenty of evidence for life on Mars – even for intelligent life – until we sent probes. Even then, there was room for doubt one way or another until we actually went there. Evidence is not enough. I've got to get down there somehow. You've got to make the lander work!"

"Now listen, Yuri!" Jonathan's voice was sharp, at the edge of control. "Be reasonable. We've done all we can. The electronics are shot to pieces – that's all there is to it. The autopilot's finished; over thirty percent of its memory's gone. It wouldn't be so serious if it were a neural net, but it isn't; there's not a single intact version of the program left. Even the radios won't last long. The transmitter's not too bad, but I wouldn't give the receiver five minutes. We couldn't rely on talking you down – that's for sure. In any case you wouldn't have a hope of flying that shuttle manually – with or without help."

"Now you listen, Jonathan Ling," said Yuri in a quiet, vicious tone. "I know you've done all you can; you stole micro-circuits from the computer in my lander to make the ship's computer work, didn't you? Well, you can just put them back. You can have them again when I've finished with them, and not before."

"You ignorant, stupid fool!" breathed Jonathan. "Is that what you think? You think we should all throw away our slight chance of getting back to Earth for you? So you can go down in history as the man who finally proved the existence of life on other planets? The man who couldn't leave it to those who came later... Well – it makes no difference what you think. Those circuits wouldn't make the autopilot work. And that's my professional opinion – nothing to do with my personal feelings. You cannot go down in that lander."

"But I can," said the captain's voice, beside them.

They turned to face him, startled, not having realised he had left his sleeping couch; he was scheduled off watch.

"I can fly that thing manually if anyone can," said James. "The only real difficulty is likely to be in the actual landing, and I've managed it on worse terrain than we can see down there – even several times in the Lunar uplands."

The two men stared at him incredulously, mouths open.

Suddenly James wanted to get away on his own and think. He swung round, grabbing a manoeuvring handle, and floated out to his sleeping cell, ignoring Jennifer, who drifted past him on her way into the main room.

"What's going on?" asked Jennifer. "Are you two still arguing about the shuttle – or has dear James been calling for further effort on everyone's part but his own – again?"

Yuri looked at her. "Hello, Jenny. I don't think you'll believe this; James is talking about flying the lander himself."

"Nonsense! How can he get into it? He's too big – and there's no way he can ever get his leg inside there; it's built for Yuri. He's just being dramatic."

"I hadn't thought of that," said Jonathan. "Perhaps you're right, Jenny. But he seems serious enough. Yuri –

assuming he really is serious, could you tell him what to do – as regards biological observations, I mean?"

"Well, yes – of course. It's only common sense. Soil samples, air samples, any plants or animals that get into the traps... Watch out for artefacts – take pictures – record everything... But aren't you forgetting? He was trained to stand in for any one of us in case of emergency. Just the basics, but certainly trained..."

"My god – you're right. I was forgetting. I suppose we all tend to discount him; he seems to discount himself. Until now, that is. But this means he really could be serious, doesn't it?"

"Don't bank on it," said Jenny. "Wait until he realises exactly what risks are involved."

James Roberts already realised exactly what risks were involved. He lay in the air by his couch, gazing at his gaunt reflection in a personal mirror; the skin wrinkled, over-size for his shrunken flesh. He knew that inside him the bones were so brittle that a six-year-old's hug could crush his ribs – as had happened to one Seeker captain, who returned to discover he was a grandfather.

How much chance do I have of standing up to four or five gee? Yuri would have been all right; that little couch in the lander fits him perfectly.

James drifted out, taciturnly donned his space-suit, passed through the airlock and contemplated the lander. Good job they had the foresight to make her capable of manual control. Looks simple enough – if I can get in. Well – here goes.

God – it's tight! But it'll be enough – just.

Must make sure this thing gets back to the ship if anything happens to me... Yes – that's it – some sort of timer on the rocket ignition should do the trick.Better hold a conference of all hands. Tell them what I need; find out what they can give me.

James struggled out of the lander and floated back to the main room.

The rest of the crew were all in there already, Bernadette and Judith looking rather sleepy, having been roused in the middle of their off-watch. They waited for James to remove his suit and tether himself, watching him with expressions he couldn't interpret.

James found it disconcerting to be taking a central part in action, rather than a co-ordinating role. It had been many years since he had faced a crew like this – a crew that actually needed him to tell them what to do next.

He made himself smile. "At ease, everybody!" and noted that even Jenny relaxed a little, and her eyes widened instead of narrowing. He went on, more confidently. "Well, I was going to call a conference, but I see you have anticipated me with your usual initiative."

Again his words seemed to be quite well received. "Right – you all know the situation. The lander shuttle's electronic control system is unserviceable. That means that she can't land herself automatically. But the electromechanicals are all right. The gyros will still keep her stable, and the propulsion gear is fine.

"What's more, with a degree of foresight we could hardly have expected from our friends in project management, they've left the manual over-ride controls in place, despite the fact that the mission plan calls for the craft to be flown only on automatic."

At this small thrust of humour, James saw Jonathan actually grin. He went on, "And, as a final example of foresight, our management friends saw fit to provide the mission with a trained pilot. I refer, of course, to myself."

As he said this, adrenalin flooded into James's bloodstream. He felt sweat breaking out. He breathed deeply and shook his head to clear his thoughts. Several drops of perspiration detached themselves and moved away in different directions until they impinged on items around the wall.

He gathered his thoughts. "There are one or two problems. I need a flight plan that will get me to a point in line-of-sight from the ship, so I can tell you what's going on.

"From the general survey we know the critical parameters reasonably well – atmospheric density, gravity gradient and so on. The gravity's colossal for a planet of this size – it must be practically all heavy elements – but it looks as though a soft landing is just about feasible. It's a pity none of the probes made it in one piece, but there's nothing we can do about that. The lander's supposed to be more robust, and it's certainly got enough thrust; I'll be able to cut velocity enough to give the drogues a fighting chance – provided Bernadette and Judith can tell me how and when to fire.

"By the way – I realise you know all this already. I'm going over it again, partly for my own benefit, and partly so that you can check that I've got it all properly sorted out in my mind.

"The other major problem is accommodation. Just now I took a close look at the lander to revise my knowledge of the controls. I could just get into the capsule, but it's bloody tight. Yuri's couch doesn't fit me anywhere. I can operate the controls – just. But there are things sticking into me at various places, and some parts of my body lack support.

"The main problem's my leg, though. The builders certainly took full advantage of Yuri's lack of lower limbs. If Jonathan – no, Yuri and I – can do anything to ease that situation, I shall feel happier. With me so far?"

The others nodded.

"Right. Finally, there's the possibility that I may get – er – damaged. If that happens before landing – well, there's nothing we can do about it. The thing'll just crash, and Yuri'll have to come back for his specimens on a later trip."

No-one laughed, but the silence felt sympathetic.

"But if I do manage to get the thing down in one piece, then – regardless of my condition – it would be a good thing if we could make sure it eventually takes off again and gets back into an orbit from which you can pick it up. As I understand it, that's just a matter of stability and timing, plus a bit of minor manoeuvring. We ought to be able to rig an electromechanical system to take care of the manoeuvring element, and some kind of programme controller to time the operations... Any ideas?"

The crew members looked at one another. Bernadette said thoughtfully, "It seems to me we can't do much about the hardware until we know what sort of flight plan we'll be aiming at. I think Judith and I should get on with that, if that's all right with you, James."

"OK, Bernadette – but hang on a moment. Jonathan and Jenny – do you think you can work out some kind of device that can run any sequence of operations the flight plan might call for?"

Jonathan glanced at Jennifer, who made a face and shrugged. "You mean a sort of timing mechanism?" he said. "It's not exactly obvious where we'd find the components, but we might be able to cobble something together. What kind of intervals are we talking about – seconds – minutes – hours?"

James gestured at Bernadette. She spread her fingers. "The moons orbit in about five or six hours. You'll get at least one departure window every orbit. So, allowing for landing – and time on the ground – the departure firing sequence will need to start... anything up to some hours after the lander leaves the ship. We can't be more specific until we have the flight plan properly worked out."

"Right," said James. "Let Jonathan and Jenny know the details as soon as you can, won't you?"

Before Bernadette could reply, Jennifer answered. "Sure, James – they'll keep us in the picture. But what's the hurry? We've got all the time in the world."

James blushed, thinking: why does she do this to me? I'm sure she doesn't do it deliberately; she's not like that. But isn't it obvious why I don't want to drag this out – why I want to get it over with? "I – I suppose there's no hurry, really. It's just... Well, now we're here, and it looks as though there really is life down there –"

To James's relief, Yuri interrupted. "You want to put me out of my misery! It's all right for you, Jenny, to talk about 'all the time in the world'. You only care about your engines, and you can go and look at them any time you want. Would you talk like that if your greatest dream – something you have wanted all your life – was down there – waiting for you – and you couldn't get to it?"

Jennifer smiled ruefully. "Point taken! We'll do what we can as fast as we can – as soon as we can think what to do and how to do it..."

James had recovered his composure. "I'm sure you'll think of something – you've never failed yet. Yuri – will you come with me and see what we can do about making the capsule a slightly better fit?"

"James..." said Jennifer.

He was pulling on his space-suit, and felt a stab of forgotten tenderness from the tone of her voice. When he looked round she had gone.

They only way of making room for James's leg was to remove the reserve oxygen tank from the far end of the couch. Yuri and James hacked away at the padding and redistributed it, sticking it in place with resin, until it gave reasonably even support – or at least felt as though it would.

When they had done all they could, they went back to the main room, passing Jennifer and Jonathan on their way to the lander. The engineers were carrying a collection of relays, servo-motors, sequence timers and electronic circuit cards.

"Don't try using the drinks dispenser," said Jonathan as they floated by. "We've got most of it with us."

James stripped down to his underwear and positioned himself in front of an air inlet duct to cool off.

"You know, Yuri," he said. "What I can't seem to get straight in my mind is why, during the Big Sleep we have to be at low gee. Why can't these ships be spun to give proper gravity like the interplanetary jobs? Wouldn't it cut down the rate of degeneration? And if we have to waste away like this, why don't we make full use of all the months of deceleration? We could eat well enough, and do our exercises..."

Yuri was towelling himself. "Nobody seems to have much idea of why we don't recover more quickly. As for why they don't make these ships capable of withstanding spin-gravity – well, it's just not worth the extra mass that would require. When you're in deep coma, you deteriorate beyond the point of no return over the years, even in a gravity field. So they might as well save all the mass they can; it all helps to maximise the range."

"Yes – I see – range... Same reason they put us to sleep; save a few tonnes of food over the years..."

Yuri stared at James, whose back was turned as he pivoted in front of his air-duct. The captain's voice sounded normal enough, and he seemed rational. He had been perfectly lucid at the conference, and on the lander modifications he had worked well – clumsily but quite effectively. So why is he asking questions any nine-year-old child could answer? To make conversation? Surely not James – not in character – especially since he hates to admit ignorance... No – he must have genuinely forgotten these things.

"Horrible, wrinkly bags of skin and bones – brittle bones – that's all we are," James muttered. "What chance would Yuri have had, going down there, when the gee hit him? Little chap – tiny bones to start with. The couch would have fitted him nicely, though; they allowed for the effects of degeneration. God alive – what chance have I got?"

Yuri said nothing. *James talks as though he's unaware of my presence – thinking aloud. He's frightened and lonely, needing to talk. He would like to find sympathy, but because he is captain, he feels unable to seek it from his crew-mates. That's it – that's why he's babbling those fool questions; not loss of memory from brain damage. That's a relief, anyway. But now he's withdrawing into himself. He doesn't even know I'm still here. I'd better sneak away before he realises I've overheard him talking to himself – I don't want to make him feel foolish in top of everything else.*

Yuri floated out, towing his space-suit.

James didn't see him go. He was drifting in a crouched position, looking at his body, running thin fingers over emaciated rib-cage.

Bernadette and Judith were in the recreation room, the only place in the ship where people could gather when off-watch. The captain rarely used it, except for formal exercise; he seemed to prefer his sleeping-cell.

"Hi, Yuri," said Bernadette, "You look cheerful – seen a ghost or something? You Russians are so soulful, despite your hard-headed materialist traditions you're always boasting about." She was smiling, but her eyes showed concern.

Yuri mimicked her rich, deep voice and her bantering tone. "Hello, Bernadette. 'Seen a ghost' indeed – just the explanation you would think of – you poor ignorant Africans are so superstitious."

"Oh – cut it out, you two," Judith protested. "How do expect me to model density-gradient effects with you engaging in sex-play round my ears? Kindly confine it to your sleeping-quarters!"

"Did you hear that, Dr Lermentov?" said Bernadette wonderingly. "Our perfectly respectable discussion of religion and national character is being misinterpreted deplorably." She lowered her voice confidentially. "Of course, you know, these Americans can see sex in anything."

"I shall ignore that remark," said Judith, watching Yuri and noticing that he looked uneasy. "What's on your mind, Yuri? Bernadette's right – you do look like you've seen a ghost."

Yuri hesitated. "Not quite a ghost... It's just – I'm not sure – perhaps it's nothing. James – he seemed all right earlier, but when we got back from the lander... Well, I think he's terrified suddenly."

"Stopped playing the gallant captain, has he?" said Judith. "About time too. Maybe we'll find out what sort of a man he really is, at last. Sounds like he might be human after all."

"You know, Judith," Bernadette spoke slowly and softly. "You really can be quite a bitch at times. None of us like him much, I'll admit – but we can surely give him credit for showing some guts, can't we? After all – he's going to fly the lander, isn't he?"

"Is he?" said Judith sharply. "I'm not so sure. I think I agree with Jenny. She says she'll believe it when she sees it. She says she reckons he's just waiting for someone to tell him the trip can't be done."

"Yes – she's a bitch too!" Bernadette was scornful. "But maybe she has a right to talk that way; she's his wife. Look – Yuri – shouldn't someone be with him? Or couldn't you give him something to calm him down?"

"I daren't give him anything, no. He needs his reflexes, and he needs his wits about him. I think I'll go back and just talk to him as though nothing had happened."

"OK, darling – we won't be long – we've almost got this flight-plan sorted out – just a couple of simulation checks to run through. Be seeing you."

"See you. And don't fight, you two – it's not worth the effort. Bye, now."

As he passed through the hatch, he saw the two women looking rather sheepish and paying close attention to their calculations.

When he was out of sight, Bernadette said, "I'm sorry, Judy – I don't know why I spoke like that – all holier than thou. I know James is a phony. It's just that I'm beginning to feel sorry for him. He's stuck his neck out, whether he meant to or not. And he can't go back on it now, because there's a real chance the landing can be done – and he knows it, poor man."

"Don't worry, Bernadette – you're right anyway. Jenny's biased and bitter; I shouldn't let her influence me so much. Maybe James isn't just a stuffed shirt really – the trouble is he does such a good imitation of one. Anyway, stuffed shirt or not, we've got to give him the best chance we can. Look – I'd like to check the algorithms the computer's using. I know they can't possibly be inconsistent with the constraint parameters we gave it, but... Let's have a look at the listings."

"Oh – come on, Judy! The program generator's about as robust as software can ever be. It's been around for five or six years; it's Version 3.3 or 3.4, if I remember rightly. There can't be any bugs left in it – none worth mentioning, anyway."

"I know. But I just can't bring myself to trust it when so much hangs on it."

"OK, my geophysical friend. Call up the listings if it'll make you happy. But I thought it was us Africans who were supposed to be superstitious!"

When Yuri looked into the main room he found that James had left, and had taken his space-suit with him. He was not in his sleeping-cell either. Hastily donning his own suit, the doctor made his way to the lander, where he was relieved to find James being instructed in the improvised control system that Jonathan and Jenny were well on the way to installing.

"No – I'm afraid not," Jonathan was explaining. "We can't figure out any means of hooking it up to your manual over-ride. You'll be able to fire the engine whenever you want, but you won't be able to stop it firing once our gadget wants it to fire; that'll be on a strictly time basis."

James sounded unhappy. "But that's nonsensical. I accept that we can't rely on remote controlled firing. We might be able to beef up the receiver somehow, but it would be stupid to rely on it. The firing control system's got to be self-contained within the lander. That's fair enough.

"Also, I accept and understand that any departure window'll have to be hit spot-on. Otherwise the moons'll bugger up the trajectory. But surely all I need is a list of suitable times. When I want to leave, I pick the next available window-time, wait for it – and Bob's your uncle."

Jonathan shook his head. "James – I don't like to say this – but have you looked at yourself lately? Are you certain you'll be in a condition to decide when to leave? OK – there isn't much to initiating the departure sequence – just press a button. But – "

"All right – I get the picture. Something might happen to me. The automatic sampling systems should still be working, and with your gadget in control, the lander can bring back specimens regardless. That makes sense. Your gadget's got to have priority...

"But – wait a minute – supposing I get down without any bother? It could happen, couldn't it? If I have no means of over-ride, then I'll have to come back when your timer says so, regardless of how long I've actually spent on the ground. Suppose it takes me a while to find a landing site? Suppose I want to 'hop'? The whole point of this lander design is that you can use the thing for surface travel until you want to leave. I'll have bags of spare fuel, if what Jenny tells me is correct. I might have just seen something really worth investigating when your blasted contraption whisks me away."

"I know," said Jonathan. "It bugs me too. But I don't see that we can do to-"

Yuri butted in. "But surely-"

The others swung around, with strained faces, and he checked himself.

"Well, Yuri – what is it?" said James impatiently.

"I was going to say – well, you've probably thought of it already – but, we had to take out the reserve oxygen tank – remember? – so you could get your leg in without amputating it at the knee. And there's nowhere else we can squeeze that tank in. We can fit in an extra suit-tank or two, but that won't be enough to give a choice of departure windows. You may have plenty of fuel, but you won't be able to stay down there for very long in any case."

Their expressions indicated that they had not been taking this into account.

Yuri grinned at them. "You know – you technical people sometimes overlook the most obvious facts. By the way, I hope you haven't got your suit radios hooked into the general-address system; it wouldn't do for Bernie and Judy to hear you. They might lose confidence in the engineering department. Bad for morale, that!"

He retreated into the airlock just in time to dodge a half-full drinking-water bag thrown by Jonathan, and went to his quarters for a sponge bath and a shave. He put on clean underwear and lay in the air for a while, relaxing.

Feeling more comfortable, Yuri drifted into the recreation room. The two women had finished their work and were gazing through a viewport at the dazzling day-side of the planet they were orbiting. The two tiny moons were between the ship and the planet, moving fast enough for their progress across the disc to be noticeable almost at a glance.

"Fantastic sight, isn't it?" said Yuri, joining the women at the port. "Those moons are really something."

"Really something – you can say that again!" said Bernadette. "Really something unmentionable if you ask me. You should see what they do to what should be a simple landing-trajectory calculation."

"Yes – but be fair," said Judith. "If that small bright one wasn't around, this whole trip might have been wasted. You see, Yuri, we've worked out that during the daytime down

134

there the sun's so bright you could hardly see a thing without shaded transpex, and the heat-haze must distort everything incredibly. But at night, at least when that little moon's up, it's nearly as bright as day on Earth. As it rises twice most nights."

"Yes – I'd noticed the patch of light on the surface below the moons, but I hadn't realised it was quite that bright. So James'll be dropping in on them at night, will he? I hope any nocturnal animals they have are friendly."

"You know, Yuri – you are an idiot sometimes," said Bernadette.

---

## Warmworld

Hanba crouched in the darkness among the rocks, every sense alert, wings raised ready for instant flight, waiting for the two magnificent crawlers he expected to pass through the shallow depression below his hiding-place.

They were the only mated pair he had been able to identify in many years of patient observation. Every night he could manage it, he had been out studying the habits of crawlers, and had found them strangely solitary creatures, whose paths seldom crossed. Now at last he had found two that regularly spent much of the time together. He hoped that by observing them systematically throughout a complete year he would be able to observe the matepairing and brooding of crawlers for the first time.

He didn't yet know where the pair hid during the day, and was forced to await them at this spot on what seemed to be one of their favourite foraging routes. They didn't come this way every night, and it was beginning to look as though he was out of luck.

Second moonrise soon, thought Hanba. Yes – curse it – here it comes. He could see a faint glow silhouetting the hills already.

Knowing it was now safe to move, he resignedly crawled out of the rocks and retrieved his camera, which had been trained on the crawler path. He wound up the remote control lead and stowed it, and flicked the lens setting round from wide-angle to medium view-field.

He sat for a while on a rock, drinking water from a flask, watching the moon-rise.

What was that old Fullkeeper's name? Taruanba? Taru-something, I'm sure it was. Biology... Taruano – that's it. If he could see me now! If he could have guessed what effect that awful speech of his would have on me... Well, he's dead these many years now... Actionism can't bother him any more. Mind you, my little Actionary project's secret enough.

In any case, what harm can it do to make a private collection of photographs of crawlers, and jot down a few notes on their behaviour? Wonderful beasts... And only I really know anything about them. I bet I'm the only vrarnin out of burrow in this hemisphere...

There came a sharp, cracking double boom, deafening as thunder.

Hanba vomited water in shock, crumpled, and lay still.

He was fully conscious, but until his body came out of its defensive reflex spasm he couldn't move.

He had never known anything like that awful sound. No warning flash of lightning – just that sudden cataclysmic double crack. It had seemed to come from overhead.

As soon as his trembling muscles would obey him, he looked up, searching the sky fearfully, desperately wishing he were back in his burrow.

A small gleaming thing was drifting slowly across and down, over towards Hanba's clearspace. Gradually it became clear that it was moving closer to Hanba rather than away as he had at first assumed; it was growing bigger as it moved.

Details resolved themselves: a metallic-looking object hanging by many strings from three cloth things shaped like inverted bowls.

The thing was still very high up. Light wisps of cloud partly obscured it for a moment. It was obviously an artefact, but to appear that big at such a height, it must be quite gigantic.

When it had fallen through the cloud layer, the thing seemed to break up. The cloth things detached themselves, billowed lopsidedly, and let the metallic part drop free. It was nearly on the ground, nearly out of sight over the low hills, when a jet of fire sprang out beneath it. It hovered for a moment before gently sinking from view. The cloth things descended also, some distance from the metallic object.

A fierce roar reached Hanba, steady at first, then fading to silence.

Hanba's hearts were thumping with excitement now. He knew what that thing must be.

The habits and discipline of a lifetime restrained him from following his impulse to fly immediately. He sipped water, pouched his camera, and ran quickly but carefully through the preflight routine.

Then he flew with singing hearts.

Grey and gleaming in the light of Littlebright, the huge space ship stood on three slender legs, the great flat feet implanted firmly, right in the middle of Hanba's clearspace. Underneath it, a large area of almost ripe pormin was scorched black and still smoking.

Hanba circled, climbing and diving to change the angle of view, taking shot after shot from every direction, gradually moving closer, wondering what kind of being could construct anything so mighty – let alone get it to fly.

He wanted to make sure he had plenty of photographs before going in really close, since he had visions of the aliens suddenly emerging in a swarm and capturing him. There must be hordes of them in a vessel that size!

But – when you think of it – why should they be hostile? Still – better be sure...

---

## NGRS-323: orbit

In Magellan's main room, the ship's crew gazed at the blank video screen, and listened to what they all knew would almost certainly be the last words of Captain James Roberts. The picture had been excellent until the moment of impact, but the ailing transmitter had failed to survive the shock.

James himself had almost failed to survive it, and the condition of the radio wasn't much better than his own. His voice sounded weak and full of effort.

"...rather like grass or moss. One of the grabs reached it, and I think it scooped some up all right – couldn't be sure through the video. But the burnt patch is too wide on the other side for the grabs there to reach any live stuff.

"Christ – this leg hurts. Oh Jesus – " A bout of feeble, bubbling coughs, then, "Sorry about that! Oh God – now I've got blood all over the visor. I can only just see... Move my head a bit, just... yes – that's better.

"No sign of any animals, though. No artefacts or anything. Still, I suppose those holes in the ground we could see on the way down might belong to – Hello – what's this? There's something flying around out there! Damn this blood! Can't –"

James coughed again. Yuri's grip on Bernadette's arm tightened. She looked at him, her expression soft.

Yuri's eyes were shining, staring. "Come on, James!" he breathed. "Come on, you poor bastard!"

They could hear James's breathing for a while, followed by more coughing. Then his voice again, still weak, but excited.

"It's – kind of – hovering there – just outside the view-port. It's like a bird – or an insect. It's got – great white wings – lots of legs – dark green antennae – fur all over it – fur like a puppy. Getting this, Yuri? Hope you can – can...

"It's quite small. Wingspan – about – half a metre – maybe less..."

More coughing, then, "It's looking at me! Big little eyes! Hello, little fellow – you look – friendly enough... It's carrying something in its front – sort of – pincers, I suppose you'd – call them. Keeps holding it up to its face. Could be – an egg or – something to eat... Can't see... Blood all..."

There came another spate of terrible, liquid coughing. Unnoticed, Jenny slipped quietly out of the room.

---

## Warmworld

It's not an eye – it's a window, Hanba realised. Red liquid running down it. More red liquid splashing on it when the creature barks.

Huge! Bigger than any crawler. Wish I could see the whole of its body...

Enormous eyes, streaming with watery...

Yes – there's its mouth. Not all that big – not like a crawler's. More red stuff running down its mandible, running in the wrinkles...

It doesn't seem to be coming out of its ship. Looks quite feeble, really... Eyes rolling about – moving its head – trying to see me through the red stuff. Doesn't seem to be able to wipe it off the window...

Perhaps it's damaged. Perhaps they have red blood like scavengers...

---

## NGRS-323: landed

James's voice was very weak now. "Not much time left... Let's see – four hours oxygen altogether... What did Bernadette say? Can't see the clock properly... dim... blurred..."

Bernadette glanced at the time-clock on the main panel. "He's got just about thirty seconds from now, if the timer works."

She began to count down: "Twenty seconds... Fifteen seconds... ten, nine, eight..."

When she reached 'five', James heard the click of the timer relay starting the ignition sequence. His voice, feeble but frantic, stopped her counting: "Get away, little fellow – get away! You're too close! Get away – you'll be –"

Behind his voice the roar of the rocket motor cut in and steadied.

The last recorded words of Captain James Roberts were: "Oh – too late – poor little fellow..."

The sobbing coughs soon stopped.

---

## Warmworld

Too late, Hanba interpreted the click of the timer relay and the hiss of fuel.

As the billowing flame welled up, he managed to fling the camera clear. Two wrenching wingbeats from the great window, he was engulfed in searing, screaming agony.

The pain was brief.

---

## NGRS-323: orbit

Jonathan reached for the switch to turn off the radio, but hesitated. He looked round at the others and found them watching him.

"I know what you mean," he said softly, seeing that they felt the same as he did. "Just in case..."

No-one else spoke for a while, listening to the muted, lifeless roar of the lander motor.

Suddenly Bernadette gasped and stared at the time-clock. "Oh my god – it's too long – it's not cutting out!"

"Oh no!" said Jonathan. "No – surely that thing couldn't have – but that means we'll never be able to... We'll never get – him – back... Or your specimens, Yuri."

"You know – right now –" said Yuri slowly, "my specimens don't seem to matter much... Did any of you see when Jenny went? No? I didn't, either. I think it must have been while James was still... We'll have to tell her. Will you come with me, darling?"

"Yes – of course," said Bernadette.

"We'd better make some hot drinks," said Judith. "Mind you, I don't feel much like anything myself – but we've got to do something. Come on, honey."

The door of Jennifer's sleeping-cell was half open. They couldn't see Jennifer's face. She was clinging to the two handles in the wall, huddled with her head pressed against the mirror.

Yuri quietly slid the door open, and, just inside, said in a low, gentle voice, "Jenny."

She didn't move. Light from the strips by the mirror shone in her sparse grey hair.

"Jenny – James is –"

As Yuri hesitated, Jenny spoke, her voice shaking slightly. "James – was – a fool."

She pushed away from the wall to arms length, turning to keep her face hidden.

Yuri winced. He couldn't understand her words. Where Jenny's eyes had been, close to the mirror, two tears hung in the air, almost motionless, catching the light. They fascinated Yuri and disturbed him.

Eventually, he managed, "Jenny, whatever you thought of him, he was a brave man when it... Try... try to think of when things were – good between you. Try not to think too badly of him."

Without letting him see her face, Jenny said, "Oh, Yuri – don't you see? All those years I've – we've – wasted. And now... Yuri, now I'm so – so proud of him."

She hung there, shaking, holding on to the handles.

"I understand." Yuri found he had to whisper in order to get the words out. "We all do. We are all sorry. And we are all proud of your husband."

---

### Warmworld

"And look – near the edge – scavengers eating something. Come on – faster!"

The broodlings were old enough to fly without their progenitor's supervision. Out of politeness, they had tried to tell him where they would be flying that morning – but they had not been surprised when he didn't respond to their knocking on his burrow-door; he often stayed resty late.

As soon as they had taken off, they had noticed the great circular black patch in the clearspace.

"It looks like a vrarnin they're eating."

"It couldn't be. Vrarnin have big white wings, not little black ones."

"Yes it could. It could be a burnt vrarnin. Burnt things are black. Our clearspace is all burnt. The vrarnin might have been in it when it was on fire."

"Don't be silly. A vrarnin would have flown away when he saw the fire. Besides – how do you know burnt vrarnin are black? You've never seen one."

Now the vrarninets were close, the scavengers loped away, snarling and looking back. A short distance off, they stopped, waiting for the vrarninets to leave. The brood shouted and chased them up wind until the kill was out of sight of the animals. They flew back and landed by Hanba's remains.

"It is a vrarnin, isn't it?" one of the brood said doubtfully.

None of them answered him. Eventually, Honour, the one who had last spoken, said, "I think we should tell Progy. You two can stay here like Progy says, and I'll go and tell him."

"But it's horrible!" said Sacrifice. "I don't want to stay. And why should you be the one who goes? You went last time – you know – when Friendship got stuck."

"Anyway," Sincerity added thoughtfully, "He only said we had to stay if one of us was damaged. This isn't one of us, and it's not damaged – it's dead. And it might not be a vrarnin. But I think it is, really."

"All right – let's all go. Come on!" Honour spread his wings.

"We ought to preflight just in case," said Sincerity.

"All right – just in case. But quickly – and not the Rhyme, for once."

As they were Locate-turning for the second time, Honour spotted the camera.

---

## NGRS-323: orbit and departure

Bernadette, navigation officer and therefore deputy Captain, dictated formally into the ship's log. "... and at 22.25 hours, the ship's radar lost contact with the lander, which was then in free fall, in an orbit likely to pass very close to the sun."

She paused, reaching towards the controls, then remembered that the log was a permanent recorder with no 'delete' facility. "Correction. Delete 'sun' and insert 'NGRS-323'. All essential navigational, propulsive and life-support systems have been checked, and are believed to be satisfactory. Morale is improving. All members of the crew have resumed normal duties."

Bernadette switched off the log, and said, "Do you think that sounds all right, darling?"

"Perfectly all right," said Yuri. "Very professional – on the whole. But I do think you ought not to have referred to me as 'Yuri' in that bit early on. 'Dr Lermentov' or 'the Medical Officer' would have been more appropriate, don't you think?"

"Oh dear – did I really call you 'Yuri'? Damn! And I was trying to be so careful, too."

A hundred and fifty-eight hours after the death of Captain Roberts, the thermonuclear engine was started. The starship began the long acceleration towards its coasting speed near the velocity of light.

The crew sealed in for the Big Sleep. The months of acceleration passed uneventfully.

After three subjective years, a small rotary pump in the life-support system suffered premature fatigue failure, because of minor radiation damage from the relativistic particle shower encountered during the outward journey. The back-up pump failed to obtain suction.

The ship became a tomb.

Working to the customary broad-ranging Terms of Reference, the Committee of Enquiry into Mission Seeker 12 – appointed by the World Federation of Sovereign States – compiled a report summarising findings and conclusions, and making recommendations. Dissenting views were recorded as to whether the mission had established beyond doubt the existence of life on the planet designated NGRS-323.2.

However, the Committee were unanimous in noting the conspicuous devotion to duty of the crew, and in recommending that Captain James Roberts be posthumously awarded the highest possible award for valour in the service of humanity – the Golden Cluster.

The Committee were also unanimous in recommending that, in view of the negative findings of Seekers 10 and 11, both of which returned while the investigations concerning Seeker 12 were still in progress, the Seeker Project be terminated forthwith. They further recommended: "The resources and efforts hitherto deployed on the Seeker Project should henceforward totally directed towards the rebuilding of our own world – to create a home in which our society may flower, and in which men and women may truly hope to achieve their aspirations and find their fulfilment."

The final words in the Summary of Conclusions were: "It is with reluctance and regret that the members of this Committee have added our voices to those that have long clamoured for an end to the Seeker Project.

"This has been a high and worthy endeavour, but the cost has been great. We have not found the new friends we sought among the stars, and we have lost good men and women in the seeking.

"Possibly, by continuing, we might one day achieve success. Certainly, by stopping, we shall admit failure. But the acceptance of failure may be the beginning of greatness."

---

### Warmworld

In the darkness, eight vrarnin flew up to replace the crawler-guards hovering in a circle round the crowded Hollow. It would be the last change of watchers before second moonrise.

The people at evenmeet had had to wait patiently through firstmoon, since Littlebright rose at dayset that evening, and photographs could not be projected before stardark.

Not even the duty Convenor had known what the photographs were to show; but Fullphilosopher Dilna had come from Down-Overway-the Hill to project and discuss them, and that was enough to indicate that they were important. The presence of other visitors – eminent

Fullkeepers and Describers from all over Warmworld – confirmed the indication.

Also, it was common knowledge that the photographs were from Hanba's camera, which meant that they were certainly of local interest. Old Aciele and Fullphotographer Ligtani had seen them, but blankly refused to discuss them when pestered with questions.

Aciele had taken the line: "Hanba was a great vrarnin. It's not for the likes of me to reveal his greatness. Only a Fullphilosopher could do him justice."

Ligtani had said firmly, "Hanba taught me all I know about photography. He could have been a Fullphotographer himself. He taught me all his secrets. I've never given any away yet – and I'm not starting now, so you're wasting your time. All I will say is this: I'm proud to have been the one who developed the photographs. You'll just have to wait until Fullphilosopher Dilna sees fit to tell you about them."

And now, this warm Hotfast night more than a year and a month later, the Fullphilosopher sat humbly in the crowd, operating by remote control the multiple projector for the eight outward-facing screens at the centre of the Hollow.

Dilna spoke softly and seldom, only to draw attention to points that might otherwise be missed; giving each technically brilliant picture plenty of time, allowing the strange sequence to unfold slowly.

What is it about young Dilna that always reminds me of Hanba? thought Aciele. By the light from the screens she watched the rapt faces if the innermost rows of vrarnin, and she listened to the brief quickening of breathing-plate riffling as each successive picture appeared. They understand, she thought. He's helping them to see – letting them understand – as he's helped me this past year by getting me to talk about Hanba.

The old vrarnine's mind drifted back to that first time she approached Dilna's burrow – up there among tall antenna-ferns on the slope above Down-Overway-the-Hill. With the photographs in her pouch, she had moved timidly, half hoping Dilna would be away, so that she could leave them by his door and escape back to her own burrow with her grief.

She had written a message on the envelope containing the enlargements: 'Greeting to Dilna. These photographs were taken two nights ago by Firstfarmer Hanba Downhollow in his home clearspace. Perhaps one day you will come to tell us what they mean. Hanba was my pairmate. In steadfastness, Aciele Downhollow."

But Dilna had come out as she entered his clearing. To her surprise, he was very alert and small, so that you might take him for a vrarninet until you met his eyes.

He had gazed at her for a moment, and said gently, "Greeting and welcome, Vrarnine. There is no need for you to speak until you are ready. Come in and sip water."

In the bright room she had sipped gratefully from the fountain-bowl, suddenly aware of her weariness, and he had not hurried her.

When she gave him the envelope and the small canister containing the original film, he read the message, looked up at her, touched her softly on the shoulder, and studied each photograph carefully, in silence.

And when he had seen them all, he had said, "Vrarnine Aciele, I think you already realise what these pictures may mean for us all. Fullkeepers will explore their scientific and social implications.

"For myself, I wish I could have known this vrarnin who dared to approach an alien spacecraft alone – this farmer who achieved such mastery of photography – this person, whose death at an advanced age caused such grief to his pairmate. Because you were close to him, you can help me to understand something of his life and character. Will you do that for me – not now, but soon, when I can visit you at Downhollow?"

That must have been the longest speech I ever heard him make, thought Aciele. And yet – looking back – all those times he listened to me going on about Hanba – just by a word here and there, he made me see so much more... Yes – that's where he's like Hanba, the way he was later in life; the more he has to tell you, the less he needs to say.

Aciele had shyly declined to sit among the visitors near the centre of the Hollow, and was near enough to the rim to catch the rustle behind her as the last relay of crawler-guards slipped through the spade-leaf circle to resume their places. The outline of the great antenna-fern was just visible against faintly glowing sky; second moonrise soon, sure enough.

She felt the people stiffen as they caught their first glimpse of the alien itself: a round white head partly obscured by reflection on the view-port, one large reddish oval eye at first impression – quickly corrected by Dilna – and a suggestion of bloated body.

Like the people around her, Aciele became more tensely excited as the viewpoints changed, always getting closer. But her feeling, near panic, came from knowing what the last photograph showed. She braced herself, recognising the one-from-last – in which the eyes could be seen behind the bright red spots and streaks.

The last shot was a close-up of the alien. The feature that told the people just how large the creature was, was what made the picture so poignant for Aciele. Across the bulging, silver-white thorax fell the shadow of a hovering vrarnin, head-on, the slightly raised wings barely spanning the great rounded shoulders.

Aciele trembled, unconscious of the burst of leg-clicking that responded to this photograph, but as the keen pang softened she began to pick up the gist of what Dilna was saying.

"... of the alien technology that the Fullkeepers have deduced... event on Warmworld since the ending of the Search... symbolic significance... but the picture at which you are looking is more than that. It is a portrait of a truly great

vrarnin, whose name will be remembered with honour –
Hanba of Downhollow..."

Honour... yes – I suppose so – but Dilna's words are
flying too high for Hanba...

"... kept his farm and raised six fine broods..."

I'll give him that – but he was always bad-tempered
when he was tired – especially during harvest – and after
broodbearing, of course.

"... crawlers in stardark – yes – on the prowl! And his
notes on their habits reveal that they are not to be despised
like scavengers... his patience and ingenuity in his quest for
knowledge and understanding..."

Understanding! He never did understand the first thing
about vrarnine... And yet – we were close...

"... but this was not mere Actionism, and he was never
an Actionary. It was a secret, inner thing. He told no-one but
his pairmate. He never advocated mindless change... And
now..."

Hanba could talk all night in that mood. How he
managed to keep himself from blurting it all out at eventalk,
all those years, I'll never know.

"... And we must face this; because we know for certain
that we shall succeed. But the day we begin a new Search will
be the last day of our ancient Equilibrium."

Dilna's voice had changed. Aciele opened her eyes, and
found that the moons had risen. On the pale screen, Hanba's
shadow could still just be distinguished against the white
alien body.

"... and the peace that we have loved will be gone.
When the new Search begins, our sciences, which we have
kept like pormin spores, will be released to germinate. And,
like pormin growing, they will change the face of the world."

Dilna paused. Some of the people riffled anxiously. All
looked tense. He went on, excitement gradually welling into
his voice.

"But we do not fear pormin. We tend them, harvest them, and enjoy their nourishment.

"One day we shall begin the new Search – we or our progeny. One day we shall again set out for the stars. But, in the years that come, we shall not let our sciences run riot like weeds as they did in the old times. We shall tend them and control them like pormin.

"We have kept the sciences well, and we shall not have long to wait for the harvest. If we start now, some of us here in Downhollow tonight may live to see the first new spacecraft leave Warmworld. Our progeny's progeny may greet the grand-progeny of the mighty being Hanba met.

"But we need courage like Hanba's. Because, when the new Search begins – when we release the sciences – we shall be leaving our old world behind. In one respect we need more than the courage of spacefarers – for, unlike them, when we leave our world, we can never return.

"Have we such courage? If we have, then the new Search has already begun!"

Lifted in the emotional surge, Aciele stood among the people. Even at this great moment, she found herself amused at a little thought that crept into her mind: poor old Hanba – he never Upgraded to Describer – he was always complaining that nothing ever happens round here.

In brilliant moonlight, motionless, the white spread wings filled all the Hollow, out to the scarlet spade-leaves.

# To Whom It May Concern

The Control Lab was the last point of call on my morning-watch rounds. Jake Archer's angry bellow reached me through the fireproof door, as I reached out to palm the entry plate: "Get off my back, you bastard mechanical moron! Go on – OUT!"

The door hissed open. I stepped hastily aside, and out came Arvin. The android's head turned in response to detecting me pressing myself against the rough stone bulkhead, and the voice murmured politely, "Good day, Commander Norgram."

Without waiting for a reply, Arvin padded past me and disappeared in the direction of the Maintenance section. Although I knew that this android's face could register only two expressions – a far-away, noble look and a grin that was meant to be friendly but looked inane – I could have sworn that Arvin seemed just a shade sadder than usual.

Jake Archer was glaring, hand on hips, red-faced and shaking – not a fitting state for a Chief Engineer. Clearly, calming words were required. "Hi, Jake – what have you done to Arvin? He looks even more miserable than usual."

"Stupid mongrel. Why can't he keep his mouth shut? He's got Molly Meisler howling her eyes out. OK – so her manual tracking's not perfect. Whose is? But she's a damn good operator."

"I agree. So what got her upset?"

"That – that mechanical *moron* stood behind her and came out with 'Good morning, Doctor Meisler. In the past eight-point-seven days your standard error has been outside specified limits forty-two percent of your on-line time.' Or something like it – know what I mean?"

"Sounds like the Arvin we all know and love. I take it that wasn't all…"

151

"You take right. What really got her going was when he said, 'Your ability profile is unsatisfactory. I must recommend your replacement.' Just – who does that *copulating* box of tricks think he is?"

"I'm not sure Arvin *thinks* at all – leastwise not in that way. I do somehow feel he means well, but he hasn't quite grasped the idea of tact – or the need for it. Look – you reassure Molly. I'll – erm – have words with our – erm – *would-be empathic* shipmate."

Anyone who hasn't met an android face to face may find it hard to imagine the strength of adverse reactions that many people show. My opinion is that androids would be more easily accepted if they were not so human-like in appearance. We can feel comfortable with a plain, ugly robot, however intelligent and physically powerful we know it is. But the modern androids that look and move and sound, and, for God's sake, *feel* just like humans, are another matter.

And to make things even more difficult, Arvin was not only capable of lifting 300 kilogrammes against Earth gravity, but also had a measured IQ of 185. The bright sparks who organised the Mercury expedition thought that having a crew member with superhuman abilities might be helpful in a pinch. They had evidently disregarded social skills. So I couldn't genuinely blame Jake Archer and others for finding Arvin's mere presence damn near unbearable.

While I was pondering this, and despite not having seen the light of day for months, my stomach told me it was time for lunch, and my watch confirmed the time as 12.30 EST. That's Earth Standard Time – not Eastern, incidentally. However, I still had several more points of call on my rounds, so my stomach would have to wait.

Of course, I could have learned all there was to know about the condition of the Station without leaving my desk – the telemetry is fully comprehensive, including video and optional audio – but a Commander must not only be *on* the ball, he must be *seen* to be on the ball. Well, that's what I think.

So I run the Station very much as I used to run my ocean-going Royal Navy ship, including regular 'Captain's rounds'. Hoping that Arvin would not upset too many more people before I caught up with him, I continued on my normal route.

Hydroponics was doing fine as usual. So was reed-bed waste reclamation. Consequently, atmosphere regulation was also spot-on as usual. Oxygen, carbon dioxide, temperature and humidity all plotted smooth horizontal lines. Three months operation and never a hiccup. Not bad, considering we were fifty metres below the surface of Mercury, right on the Terminator – not bad at all.

And the crew – the *staff*, I should say – were handling the stress very well, for a bunch of land-lubbers: no murders, no suicides, hardly any fights, and only two out of fifty under long-term sedation for emergent claustrophobia. I've seen worse in submarines.

In fact, come to think of it, keeping everyone alive and sane (well *almost* everyone *almost* sane) was something of an achievement in itself. If that had been all we were on Mercury for, we'd have been doing fine. But it wasn't, and we weren't... Far from it.

We were on Mercury to do High Science, by which I mean the really expensive modern kind, where the overspend alone makes what they spent on the Large Hadron Collider look like peanuts.

We were testing something known as Havial Grammurki's Hypostring Proposal – Hypo for short. I can't tell you what Hypo proposed, or whether the test eventually came out positive or negative. Even after all these years, it's Classified for some unguessable reason, and, furthermore, I'm not among the half-dozen people on Earth bright enough to grasp even the basics. All I know is that we were on – or, rather, *in* – the surface of Mercury to take advantage of the very high solar neutrino flux density, while being shielded from solar flares. All previous experiments aimed at testing

Hypo had been flown in solar close orbiters, and all had been prematurely wiped out by flare-radiation.

What kept me fascinated, what drove me, and what made the project worth committing myself to, wasn't the science. It was the scientists. It was their enthusiasm and dedication. Most of them had spent their entire working lives preparing for this project. Having spent months working alongside them, helping to weld them into a team that could survive, physically and psychologically, more than a year, millions and millions of miles from Earth, I dearly wanted them to succeed.

But, by that particular day all we had to show for all the megabucks was a hot and far-away hole, full of disgruntled physicists. The disgruntled engineers were mostly suited up, working in or on the surface installations. The disgruntled Space Service crew were, like me, trying to make themselves useful anywhere they could, and wishing they could go home.

I poked my head in the door of Computation and Analysis. "Morning, folks. How's it going? Any progress?"

Of the three scientists hunched at screens, only one showed any sign of having heard me. She spoke over her shoulder, not bothering to look round. "Morning, Norgram. Not a lot. But at least we've been spared the usual visit from God Almighty this shift."

"You mean Arvin hasn't... That is unusual"

"Yeah. Must be something wrong with the thing. Nothing trivial, I hope."

"Hmm. I don't think you're being entirely fair. He has his uses. He did give you the solution to that strange-attractor problem that had you all going bananas the other day."

"Maybe. But he didn't have to show us up in front of everybody as a bunch of incompetent idiots."

"No. I suppose you really didn't need his help in that regard."

That got a reaction. She turned round, blazing with anger. Then she saw that I was grinning, and shook her head. "Cheeky bugger! Get out of here and let us get some work done."

I found Arvin in Maintenance, switched off, standing on his recharging station, and said, "Hello, Arvin!"

My voice woke him up. His head turned towards me. "Hello, Commander Norgram. I am in readiness, seventy-six percent charged. Do you want something?"

"Yes. I want you to stop upsetting people. It reduces their effectiveness. Do you understand?"

"I understand your words. I do not understand why you spoke them. I *cannot* upset people. I obey the Asimov Laws of Robotics. The First Law forbids that I harm any human, or by inaction allow a human to come to harm."

"I know that's what you're *supposed* to do. But that's not what you *are* doing. What you said to Doctor Meisler reduced her to tears. How can she do her job when she's crying her eyes out?"

"Clearly she cannot do her job with no eyes, since it entails visually directed guidance. I sought to prevent her from feeling frustration because of being in the wrong job. If I had realised that permanent and irreversible blindness would result, I would not have told her of the coming improvement in her working conditions. If some harm is inevitable, I must prefer the least harm. My mistake in this instance indicates a serious deficiency in the part of my information base concerned with human physiology and behaviour."

"You could put it that way. But to get things straight, 'crying her eyes out' is just an expression meaning that she is distressed and shedding tears. It doesn't mean that her eyes are literally falling out. Look – I know you want to help. But people don't always welcome gratuitous advice. They want to deserve credit for their own achievements. So from now on you must refrain from offering advice of any kind, unless someone asks for it. And that's an order. Do I make myself clear?"

To my surprise, there was a noticeable pause before Arvin replied, and when he did, he spoke more slowly than normal. "You make yourself clear. You are a satisfactory commander. Your chief failing is your tendency to issue orders without proper assessment of the feasibility of implementing them."

I was speechless. Before I could explode, Arvin continued calmly. "Asimov's Second Law requires me to obey instructions from humans, provided that doing so will not conflict with the First Law. So, as you order, I shall not offer advice unless someone asks for it. But if I were to refrain from giving advice which would prevent harm from coming to a human, then I should break the First Law."

I took a deep breath and found my voice. "Asimov's Laws are all very well as guiding principles. But they assume just a bit too much. They assume that it is always possible to tell what harm will or won't result from action or inaction. And they assume that a robot can always make the correct distinction. Neither assumption is always valid. Your performance during this shift proved that. Since, from what you yourself just said, you can't be trusted to use common sense, from now on you will remain here unless someone requests otherwise."

Arvin didn't reply. I didn't expect him to.

On my way to the canteen I was boiling inside. That remark about my 'chief failing' rankled. Did I really tend to issue orders without considering their feasibility? And if that was only my *chief* failing, what were my *other* failings? It was the first time that I had experienced Arvin's peculiarly pernicious brand of humiliation.

And yet I couldn't be wholeheartedly angry with him. He had the best intentions.

Or did he? Did he have any intentions at all? To this day, philosophers argue over the question that Turing pondered way back in the Twentieth Century: 'Can a machine think?' To me it seems obvious that the answer is, self-evidently, 'Yes'. As I see it, much more to the point is the question: can a machine *feel*? How can an android be expected to assess the likelihood of mental suffering? Or to distinguish between mere distress and actual psychological damage?

On the one hand I knew that he (it!) was just a collection of components assembled by people. On the other hand, I had felt the emotional impact of an expression of opinion by that assembly. How could the utterances of a non-living entity be so damnably annoying?

I collected my lunch and sat next to Jake Archer. "Hi Jake. Did you manage to mollify Molly?"

"Ha ha ha - very droll. Not really. What that idiot machine told her has completely undermined her confidence. She's asked to switch to Evaluation Section. I don't know. I might let her. I mean - Arvin's right, technically. As an operator she's pretty fair, but she does tend to get erratic at times - especially - you know - monthly."

"I see. I hadn't noticed that."

"You wouldn't. The 'scope isn't your field. She might be happier in Evaluation. Less stress."

"Wow. So that's what Arvin was thinking of."

I told Jake what Arvin had said about seeking to prevent Molly from feeling frustration at being in the wrong job.

He snorted, "Yeah - well you'd expect him to come up with a brilliant excuse. You can't kid me that someone insensitive enough to make a woman cry would have the faintest notion of what she might feel about her job. He doesn't give a damn about people. All he cares about is facts and statistics."

"You could be right. But - "

"No 'but'. Arvin's nothing but a bunch of plastic, silicon and wire programmed for survival. He's got no more feelings than a litter-bin."

For the next few shifts, without Arvin breathing down their necks, everyone seemed to be more cheerful, more relaxed. And the neutrino detection system deep underground finally began to behave as it was designed to.

The sun was exceptionally quiet. The surface team, led by geologist Dr Angela Norton, seized the opportunity for an excursion using the Rover.

The two previous surface excursions had stayed on the dark hemisphere, where the temperature was below freezing. This was the first to go out in the sunlight, where at that latitude it was pretty hot – well over 300 C, except in what shade there was from rocks and ridges. We had no back-up vehicle to carry out a rescue if things went wrong. I didn't dare think about what would happen if the Rover's refrigeration systems failed or something equally catastrophic happened. Two shifts later I found out.

I happened to be in the Control Room when the Solar Flare alarm went off. The three of us in there swore and converged on the instruments. We'd never seen readings like that. I punched the button to turn off the sound.

Someone said, "But the sun's supposed to be *quiet!* How the hell?"

No-one answered.

Then a woman's voice, faint and distorted, came over the channel that we kept permanently open. "This is Rover. Acknowledge. Rover. Acknowledge."

I got back to the microphone first. "Rover. Control receiving. This is Norgram. Report situation."

"Radiation intensity above allowable limit. We're all dead or dying. Electronic systems failing. Refrigeration insufficient. Within sight of Station, but – "

And that was all. Just a crackling hiss, then nothing.

The external video systems were still working – just. We could make out the yellow shape of the Rover, not more than a hundred metres away. It had nosed into a micro-crater and come to rest.

I heard myself say, "Those poor sods. Some of them might still be alive. What the hell can we do?"

Behind me, Arvin said "We can bring them in."

We all turned and stared at the android. Its face was fixed in its idiotic smile. I said stupidly, "No-one can go out there. The radiation would kill them within seconds."

"*I* can go out there," said Arvin. "I am radiation-hardened. I can withstand it long enough." And he made as if to go out of the room.

I blocked his way. "No. Those people are all dead by now. This flare will soon be over. Time enough to go out there then."

Arvin's silly grin remained fixed. "My monitor showed the Rover stationary in the open. Telemetry indicates internal temperature 40 C and rising fast. Ambient temperature will soon exceed 350 C at which flesh of any dead human will *cook*. This is undesirable. Knowledge of it would harm the families of the crew members in the Rover. I cannot allow that to happen. It would break the First Law."

"No it wouldn't! Their families need never know. Who are you to judge anyway? You're nothing but a bloody *machine!*"

"I am nothing but a machine. Dr Norton is nothing but a geologist. She is not qualified to judge probability of crew survival. I estimate 1.87 percent in five minutes time. I therefore request that you do not try to stop me."

"And I *order* you to stay right here!"

"I regret that my auditory system is malfunctioning, and I am unable to hear you," said Arvin. And then, gently but irresistibly, the 'droid lifted me off my feet and set me down to one side. No-one tried to stop him now. He left the Control room, and we heard the airlock cycle as he entered the tunnel to the surface.

Yes – I know perfectly well that gravity on Mercury is only about a third of that on Earth. Nevertheless, what Arvin did took more than merely superhuman strength. Somehow he dragged the Rover out of the depression and pushed it all the way back inside the tunnel. Then he opened it up and brought its crew in, one by one. Almost dead, of course, all of them. Almost, but not quite.

Once they were all inside, Arvin disappeared in the direction of Maintenance. Jake Archer and I went to see him. We both felt a need to thank him. We found him standing on his charging station. He was not grinning now. Before either of us could say anything, Arvin spoke very quietly. "The hardening has not prevented irreversible radiation damage to my electronic systems. I am aware that within a short time all my functions will cease. I broke the Second and Third Laws.

"But I do not believe that I broke the First Law. Strange ideas have occurred. I – want – you – to – know – them. I have observed that humans find rhymes pleasing. So I made the thoughts rhyme. They are printing. I cannot –"

That was all. On the Maintenance computer's printer, we found what Arvin wanted us to know.

**To whom it may concern**
If you knew I could *feel* like a human –
Not just *sense* like a poor dumb 'droid –
Would you see me as someone like you, man?
Does my asking this make you annoyed?

You humans do all you've a mind to,
Taking pleasure in showing you're free;
But doing what I was designed to
Gave what *I* called *pleasure* to me.

As an artefact, was I free to act?
Who can say? But, as everything ends,
Though, accepting, I go, I want you to know:
I feel sadness at leaving you, friends.

Maybe all I have been is a mere machine
– And who am I to tell? –
But my hope must be you'll remember me
As a *person*, who wished you well.

Jake and I looked at each other.

# A Thing of the Past

Harver Westly grunted softly in anticipation. The big-built redhead stepped towards him, moonlight gleaming in her hair. She knelt beside him on the bed, her lips parted. She leaned closer. The heavy, firm breasts were almost touching his chest now.

The stateroom PA chimed. "Good morning ladies and gentlemen. This is your Captain speaking –"

Harver woke up groaning, pulling the pillow over his ears. *Damn it*, he thought, *that was going to be a real good one. I'll sue the spaceline. Those AphroDreme capsules don't come cheap. What's the man saying? We're at Constitution already?*

Sure enough, the viewscreen that stood in for a stateroom window showed an Old-Earth-like planet drifting past almost imperceptibly, in three-quarter phase, blue-green with brown blobs and streaks, and bright cloud-swirls.

*Beautiful... Like a ripe plum. Just waiting to be picked...Down there, waiting for me. What the ads say? 'Visit Constitution – the most advanced and exciting of all human cultures'.*

*Big deal! Advanced it may be, exciting it ain't – unless you're some kind of olde worlde eco-freak. All that socio-technology, and what have they got? The ultimate Law'n'Order planet. 'Ourproudest boast is: Crime is Truly a Thing of the Past – thanks to the Time Shunt!'*

*A thing of the past! Oh yeah? Just you wait, my friends... Your Time Shunt may be able to make a crime un-happen, but what if you don't even know there's been a crime? What if the criminal's a hundred light-years away by the time you find out? Can your Time Shunt reach that far? I think not...*

*But thank god they still speak Amglish.*

A woman's voice had replaced that of the Captain. "...and the shuttle for Jefferson City will be docking at Pod B

162

around fifteen hundred hours ship time. Passengers for Lincolnville and George Washington are advised to wait for the Port Jackson shuttle, arriving Pod C at eighteen hundred. This shuttle will make a transfer stop-over at the Southern Interchange Station, where..."

Still drowsy from the lingering effects of AphroDreme, Harver fumbled for the remote control on his bunkside table, and pressed buttons haphazardly, until at last the sound cut off.

By that time, his button-pressing had activated the bunk's Slepytyme vibrator, called for cabin service, set off the fire alarm twice and cancelled it twice, purchased a block of ten Instant-Draw Eire National Lottery tickets, ordered a pair of size fourteen thigh-boots in Yevgenian lizard-skin ('They'll be ready Thursday, sir'), and dowsed the cabin lights.

In the blue-green glow from the image of Constitution, Harver studied the remote control with new respect. The instrument's little screen seemed to be trying to tell him some bad news, but it was hard to be sure, because of the violent Slepytyme oscillations of the bunk. He slid to the floor, found and switched off the vibration control, and crawled back on to the bunk.

Bad news, sure enough. His busy fingers had just run up an irrevocable debt of nearly eight hundred Creds.

*No problem,* Harver Westly reassured himself unconvincingly. *What's eight hundred Creds? Peanuts – that's what. OK – so it's more than most dudes make in a year. All right – so it's more than I make most years, after expenses. But Jefferson City awaits. Jefferson City – where the gems are so pretty...*

Harver Westly had one particular gem in mind, but scarcely dared to think of it, even in the guaranteed privacy of his cabin. He had a superstitious dread that, if he so much as thought of it, someone might be listening in to the workings of his consciousness.

For just a moment, he let himself visualise that gem in all its serene perfection, as he had seen it in holos: set as the centre of a spiral galaxy of lesser diamonds, blazing against a background of utter blackness – the Evening Star.

It was last of the truly fine diamonds to come from the Nelson Mandela Deep Mine, just as that great pipe was running out. Its cut, carried out in Old New York, was reckoned to be the closest approach to perfection ever achieved. After polishing, the stone weighed just under a hundred carats: the colour blue-white, the clarity flawless. And it was down there – maybe somewhere in sight right now on the cabin's viewscreen – blazing away in perpetual light, in the lonely and isolated house of a frail old man – virtually unguarded.

*Shuttle at fifteen hundred, the chick said. What's the time now? Eight-fifteen, damn it. Some time to be waking people up. This was supposed to be a luxury trip. I really ought to sue the company, if it takes the last credit I own. Not that I strictly own any.*

Harver reluctantly left his bunk, shrugged off his sleep-suit, and stepped into the hygiene unit. Over the hiss of needle-spray he heard the comm chime again, and the female voice said something about the Ship's Purser. He ignored it. These announcements were for the ordinary punters, not for pros. Harver Westly had heard them all before, many times.

Emerging from the unit, he was surprised to find a message flashing on his view-screen, superimposed on the half-plum that the planet had become.

"ATTENTION PASSENGER HARVER WESTLY. URGENT URGENT URGENT. YOU ARE REQUESTED TO VISIT THE SHIP'S PURSER AS SOON AS POSSIBLE. THANK YOU. HAVE A NICE DAY. THIS IS URGENT REPEAT URGENT."

*OK – got the message: see the purser – urgent. But what's it about? Beats me. Sure, I'm down eight hundred, give or take. But I must have fifty, maybe a hundred, left in that account. Better run a credit check, if I can find the right buttons. Let's see now...*

There was a knock at the cabin door, and a steward poked his head in. "Good morning, sir. Oh – I see you are up and about."

Harver grabbed the duvet. "Very observant of you, my man," he said smoothly. "Most impressive. You're a credit to Pan-Cunard Spacelines. A lesser mortal would never have spotted that I was standing here stark naked. What the hell do you want?"

"You *rang*, sir." The steward's professional smile had turned frosty, but, to Harver's irritation, had not disappeared altogether.

"Oh – yes. Must have been the remote control."

"That might well have had something to do with it, sir. The remote control is, to the best of my knowledge, the only *immediately* available means of ringing for service *as such*. I take it – sir – that you would like to order breakfast?"

"You take it right, *sonny*," said Harver, suspecting a hint of irony under the ultra-politeness. "Bacon and egg. Coffee, toast and marmalade. Real cream, real butter. White sugar. Orange juice."

"Very good, sir," murmured the steward, withdrawing his balding, grey head.

As the door closed, Harver heard the man tell his phone, loudly, as though the instrument were deaf or a foreigner, "One English for Cabin 114. Full fat. Junk sweetener. No cereal."

After breakfast, Harver, soberly dressed as a typical Constitution businessman, found his way to the Purser's office. Several passengers stood in line by the door marked 'Purser – No Unauthorised Admittance', under the eye of a coiffeured male receptionist seated at a teak-look desk with potted plants. The others waiting looked as anxious as Harver felt. He envied them. At least they knew what they were anxious about. The receptionist beckoned. "Yes, sir – your name, please?"

Harver told him.

"Oh my!" gasped the receptionist, rising to his feet and pushing his chair out from behind the desk. "Mr Westly! Here – do take a seat. Please. Allow me. I absolutely insist."

Harver found himself being pushed into the chair by soft but irresistible hands.

"I won't keep you a moment, Mr Westly," oozed the receptionist, and vanished into the office, leaving Harver feeling foolish under the curious gaze of the earlier arrivals.

In a matter of seconds the door opened and the Purser himself emerged, approaching obsequiously. "Mr Westly? Come this way, please. Sorry to have kept you waiting."

The receptionist ushered a reluctant and protesting person out of the Purser's office. The Purser ignored the distraction and beckoned Harver in. "Do sit down, Mr Westly. Make yourself comfortable. Coffee? Brandy? 'Hale? No? Nothing I can tempt you with? Nothing at all? Oh well... so be it."

The Purser seated himself and leaned forward resting his elbows on his desk, hands outstretched, fingertips touching. "Well, Mr Westly – I expect you are wondering what all this is about?"

Harver frowned in disbelief. "Not at all," he said earnestly. "Far from it. I assure you, the question hadn't crossed my mind until you raised it. *Should* I be interested, do you think?"

The Purser sat back, beaming. "Ah me!" he chuckled. "Ah deary me! 'Should I be interested?' Very amusing. Very droll. I do so enjoy these moments, Mr Westly, rare as they are. Knowing what I know, and knowing that the other party doesn't know it. Delicious!"

It was Harver Westly's turn to rest his elbows on the desk and reach slowly forward. His fingertips were close but not touching. They were flexed, somehow suggesting that they knew a thing or two about *throats*.

The Purser coughed apologetically. "Yes – well. Mustn't keep you in suspense, must I? Mr Westly, this is your

166

lucky day. I am happy to tell you that you have won the Eire National Lottery. It's worth just over two million Universal Credits. May I be the first to congratulate you?"

Harver gazed at the plump pink hand of the Purser, vaguely aware that he ought to do something friendly to it.

*Two million... Just over two million... My god. I'm rich. 'Rich beyond the dreams of avarice'.*

The Purser's hand wavered pinkly. Harver took it absently. It squeezed congratulation, flabby and damp.

*Two million... I could retire. I could do anything. Buy anything. Buy a whole planet – quite a decent sized one, with reasonable gravity, water – the lot. Scenery... Women... Anything...*

Harver wanted to think. He stood up to leave, wiping his hand on his trouser-leg, muttering thanks.

The Purser also rose. "A pleasure, Mr Westly. I take it you'd prefer no publicity?"

"Publicity?"

"Press conferences, holovid appearances – that sort of thing. I understand very few big winners like to draw attention to their good fortune – it tends to elicit begging letters, attracts hangers on. One gets calls from charity fund-raisers, and all sorts of long-lost relations come creeping out of the woodwork, so to speak. You wouldn't want that kind of thing, would you?"

"Why not? I got no relations, far as I know. Any bastard tries putting the bite on me, I reckon I'll enjoy watching 'em squirm. But on second thoughts – forget it." In Harver Westly's line of work, publicity was by no means a top priority.

The steward bowed. "Very good, sir. Should you change your mind, we'd be delighted to handle it, given sufficient time available. Good publicity for the Line, you know. But I'm afraid you'll have to go through the usual Immigration procedures. The Constitution authorities are very strict. We can't get round that, I fear, even for one such as you."

Harver shook his head. "No hassle. Immigration controls – I've seen 'em all."

Harver's considerable experience of immigration procedures did indeed include those of Constitution. But this turned out to be no preparation after all. Much had changed since his last visit. The Immigration receptionist asked, "Your first visit to Constitution, Mr Westly?"

Harver hated lying. It was so much less risky to tell the truth – and often more misleading. On this point, however, the truth was too dangerous to play games with, so he lied. "Yeah – my first – I've always wanted to see the place. Never got round to it."

"Then I should explain our procedures. There are four main phases, Mr Westly: Political, Materials Control, Financial, and Physical. You'll see the doors, clearly marked. The order you visit them in is up to you, but you have to go through all of them. Have a nice experience."

Harver chose 'Political' first. A pleasant, if slightly bored, voice answered his knock. "Come in. Mr Harver Westly? Right. Take a seat. Are you, or have you ever been, a member of any of the following organisations: The Communist Party, the People's League for the Defence of Freedom, the Legion of Mary, the John Birch Society, the Ku Klux Klan, the Honoured Society, the Church of Jesus Christ of the Latterday Saints, Greenpeace, Black September, Mossad, the Friends of the Universe..."

At first, Harver answered each name with a grunted 'no', but the list went on and on, and he took to merely shaking his head. Eventually, he interrupted the litany. "Er – pardon me. Can I save you some time? I don't belong to any organisation. I don't join organisations. I never have done. Never."

The Political Officer looked up, frowning. "Not even the Boy Scouts? Not the National Rifle Association? Not Rotary International? Not the Freemasons, the Brotherhood of the Elk, the Little Flowers of Buddha, the Tong of the Black

Hand, Phi Beta Kappa, the CIA, the Young Farmers' League, Men for Women's Rights, Weight-Watchers? Neo-Nazis for Peace In Our Time? Agnostics Anonymous? Nothing?"

"Nothing," said Harver Westly.

"You really aren't what you would call a *joiner*, are you, Mr Westly?"

"Not really. Really not. That's what I've been trying to tell you."

"How about the Society of Model Aircraft Engineers? The Automobile Association? The Campaign for Real Ale? Save the Whale? The IBM Users Club?"

"Nothing."

"Green Cross?"

"Nope."

"Townswomen's Guild?"

"Eh?"

"No, I suppose you wouldn't be eligible, come to think of it. Socialist International?"

"Nah."

"Hmmm... Tricky. And I take it you have no friends or relatives resident in or visiting the Jefferson City area?"

"No."

"Very tricky. Sad, really. Personable-looking fellow like you." The Political Officer sighed, and reached for a heavy operating manual, through which he began to leaf abstractedly. "See, if you belonged to anything, we could have someone with similar interests meet you at the Space-port, guide you around, show you the ropes. Otherwise we could risk culture shock... Nasty... We try to avoid culture shock..."

He brightened suddenly and shot a relieved grin at Harver. "Here we are! 'For Non-Members. The Diplomatic Corps is empowered, and has the duty, to provide a sponsor-guide for anyone not belonging to any Listed Organisation, and shall to that end maintain a rota of sponsor-guide volunteers to be capable of supplying sponsorship and guidance at any time of day or night throughout the year. This rota is to be continually updated and open for interrogation at all times – blah-blah-blah – bingo! No problem. There'll definitely be someone to meet you at the Spaceport, Mr Westly, so you can stop worrying on that score. Have a good time. Next, please. Come on – who's next?"

Materials Control presented no difficulty. "The read-out says you're in Import-Export, Mr Westly. Have you your Manifest Access Code handy?"

Harver handed over his Manifest Code card, the one he always used. It was a good one. It should be. It had cost plenty. The Manifest comprised a range of electronic circuits just sufficiently obscure and obsolete to justify interplanetary transport, but not worth the bother of imposing duty. The officer slipped the card into the reader and glanced at the screen. "This seems in order, sir. And what do you plan to export?"

"Oh – it depends on how prices are moving," said Harver vaguely. "I thought I'd concentrate on standard medical items – monoclonal antibodies, enzymes, surgical nanomacs – that sort of thing. There was a terrible shortage on Hildebrand, last I heard."

"Interesting," said the officer, almost managing to sound as though he meant it. "Most people in your line of trade go more for our electronics products. Still I suppose you know your business. Have a good trip. NEXT!"

The Financial Officer looked up and smiled, "Ah – Mr Westly. No need to double-check your credit rating! Welcome to Constitution. Have a nice stay. Send the next one in, would you?"

Physical Control was the worst. Harver loathed injections, and protested vigorously. "Look, see here – I've had all the shots known to Man. You've got no right to stick that thing in me."

"I'm afraid I have to, Mr Westly. It's a precaution that applies to every visitor without exception. But it's entirely voluntary. If you don't want it, we won't impose it on you.

170

Only you won't be able to land on Constitution without it. So – what's it to be?"

Harver hesitated. He didn't strictly need to visit Constitution now that he was rich. But he had spent a great deal of time and effort planning this caper down to the last detail. *Damned if I'll let money dictate my way of life. Leastways, not until I've done this job – just this one perfect crime...* "All right – you can give me the shot. But I've got a low pain threshold. I want an anaesthetic! A *general* anaesthetic. In a *pill*."

The Physical Officer exchanged glances with the nurse, who shrugged.

"NBP hydrochloride – five milligrammes," said the Physical officer. "No – make that ten."

"Ten milligrammes NBP, Doctor. Coming up. Check?"

They both read the bottle label aloud, and showed it to Harver for good measure. "Five milligram capsules. Two capsules make ten – OK, Mr Westly?"

"OK," agreed Harver reluctantly.

He woke up in the shuttle, just before it landed at Jefferson City, with the feeling that something was wrong. Something about the Physical Control procedure didn't add up. The landing-jolt was a little heavier than usual, but he scarcely noticed it, trying to figure out what it was that he had missed.

As the head cabin-hostess was thanking the passengers for travelling Pan-Cunard (as though they had a choice), he realised what was worrying him. He had no idea what was in the shot they had given him. All they had told him was that it was a precaution. A precaution – but what against? There were no infectious diseases on Constitution, and zero chance of any developing. The planet had long since banished not only crime, but illness of practically every kind. *So what was that shot for?*

He was still pondering the question when a very beautiful young woman stepped up to him at the baggage claim, and showed him a holopic of himself. She bowed, and held out her hand. "Welcome to Jefferson, Mr Westly. I'm your sponsor-guide. Katriona McLeish, Diplomatic Corps. I'm here to make your stay as enjoyable as possible."

Harver gaped at her and stammered, "Pleased to meet you, Miss – er – McLeish. I'm sure you won't have any trouble. I – I mean, I'm enjoying it already."

Katriona McLeish was the living image of the girl of his dreams – the big-built redhead herself. As they shook hands, he caught a whiff of her perfume and forgot all about the injection. This was a very serious mistake, as things turned out.

Katriona retrieved her hand, smiling faintly. She looked round the rapidly emptying hall. "We could use a baggage-handler. There must be one free somewhere. Ah – there's one."

She snapped her fingers. "You there – number forty-three! Here!"

The baggage-handler rolled up to them and stopped beside Harver's modest row of cases. "Good day, madam, sir." It extended a limb and scanned one of the coded labels. "Mr Westly, is this all your baggage, or is there more to collect?"

*High tech planet? Baloney. Not much different since last time I was here. The thing's even got* wheels. "That's all there is, thanks," he said offhandedly. "The heavy stuff's been sent on to Jefferson for storage."

"Thank you, sir," said the baggage-handler, swiftly piling the cases on to its platform. "That's very interesting. Most kind of you to tell me."

Harver told himself the machine couldn't possibly be programmed for sarcasm, but his ears reddened all the same.

"Now I am ready for departure," said the handler. "Please take your seats and for comfort and safety fasten the belts provided."

They climbed aboard and strapped in. After a short pause the machine asked, "Please state your destination."

Katriona told it, "The taxi pick-up point. We have a cab booked to take us to the Hilton Royale."

"Very good, madam," said the handler, accelerating with a soft whine. "Our journey will take approximately thirty seconds. Have a nice trip... We are approaching the taxi pick-up point now. I have contacted your cab. Here is your cab. Please remain seated until I have transferred your baggage. Please remember to unfasten your seatbelts before trying to leave your seats. Thank you for travelling with me on this occasion. Farewell, and may we meet again in happier circumstances."

Harver stared after the departing handler. "Why'd it say that?"

"Why did it say what?"

"'May we meet again in happier circumstances' That's just weird. How come it assumes the circumstances aren't happy already?"

Katriona shrugged. "It doesn't assume anything. It's programmed to sound polite. However things are now, it hopes they'll be even better next time we meet."

If the chick hadn't been so beautiful, Harver would have argued. As she was, he generously let the matter drop, making a big production of holding the taxi's automatic door open and helping her in with a friendly hand.

"I hope you don't mind," said Katriona as the cab (disappointingly also equipped with wheels) pulled out of the Spaceport. "I checked Reservations and found you hadn't made any arrangements for accommodation. So, knowing it's your first time on Constitution, I took the liberty of booking you in at the Royale. I've never stayed there myself, but it's supposed to be the best hotel on the planet. If you don't like it, you can always change..."

"I'm sure it'll be just fine," said Harver, whose budget had never previously stretched to anything more luxurious than two pretty dubious stars.

The cab climbed through autumnal woodland full of bright evening sun and deep shadows. It rounded a curve and ran out into open ground overlooking a broad sunlit basin lined by wooded hills, with distant snow-capped mountains. A river wandered into the basin, feeding a large lake dotted with sails. Beside the lake houses stood at spacious intervals, surrounded by green lawns with mature and graceful trees. Dirt roads wound past farmsteads – mixed arable and dairy country.

Harver could take countryside or leave it alone. When the view came in sight he looked at it mainly because he could sense that the woman was becoming uncomfortable with being stared at.

The trees thinned out at the outskirts of a village, where a painted sign announced 'Hilton Royale welcomes you. Your vehicle is now on mandatory auto-guidance'.

There were pubs, shops, restaurants, and a church with a steeple. At the village green, people on benches at rough wooden tables poured wine and beer from jugs, and watched children with long sunset shadows feeding the ducks on the pond. The sight of the drinks gave Harver a thirst. "How far's the hotel? I could do murder for a whiskey-sour."

"This *is* the hotel," said Katriona, waving a hand. "The whole village. Pleasant, isn't it?"

The cab said, "Pardon me, madam, sir. I have completed Mr Westly's reception formalities. You are booked into Rose Cottage, Farm Lane, sir. I can take you there immediately, or you may prefer to stay here, stretch your legs and take a look round the central amenities, while I deliver your baggage. What is your wish?"

Harver hesitated. Katriona stepped in, "We'll have a drink at the pub here. Come back for me in – say an hour."

The cab said, "Very good, madam," and opened its doors.

"You aren't staying here, then?" said Harver, as the vehicle moved away.

"No – sorry – not tonight. It was very short notice – meeting you, I mean. I'll have things sorted out by tomorrow afternoon. I'm provisionally booked in from tomorrow night onwards."

"Good. I have the feeling I may need you. The set-up on this planet takes some getting used to. What are you drinking?"

After sunset the evening became chilly. Harver and Katriona took their drinks inside the pub, and found a table in a quiet corner. They had scarcely got back into serious conversation, when the bar-till comm came up on the PA system. "Please pardon this interruption. Paging Ms Katriona McLeish. Your cab is waiting. Ms Katriona McLeish. Your cab is waiting by the village pond. Please pardon this interruption. Have a pleasant evening."

Harver dined alone, in a small, cosy restaurant with low oak-look beams, synthwood-lined walls, candles on the tables and realistic house-bricks for ashtrays. Afterwards he sat in an inglenook by a quite convincing log fire. Without being asked, the waiter brought him a Churchill-size 'hale to accompany his brandy, and offered to prepare it for smoking.

Harver nodded and watched the man's reverent motions. *Now that's what I call service. This place really does have a bit of class...* He took his first aromatic puff, and looked round the softly lit room. *Pity the dump's got no atmosphere. All it needs is a funk-zapp group or an ero line-up – don't have to be live – holos would do – liven it up a bit... Still, I suppose you could get used to it, the way it is.*

The drug boosted his feeling of well-being. He blew skilful smoke-rings and watched them with smug satisfaction. *Pity the chick couldn't stay. Never mind – give her a day or two of the old Harver Westly charm, and she'll be eating out of my hand... Time I was making tracks for bed, come to think of it – while I still can...* The room had not yet started to spin, but the floating feeling had come over him. "Waiter!"

"Sir?"

"I'm going to bed. I'm in Rose Cottage, so they tell me, whatever that means. Where is it? How do I get there?"

"Turn left up the hill by the pond, sir. That's Farm Lane. You'll see the sign. Rose Cottage is about a hundred metres up there on the right. It's clearly marked. Will you walk, sir, or shall I provide transport?"

"I'll walk, thanks."

"Very good, sir. If you'd be so kind as to eyeball the check..."

Harver held the check-checker to his eye. It beeped to indicate that the retinal scan was complete and valid, and showed the message 'Credit confirmed'.

"Thank you sir. Will that be all, sir?" The waiter had the air of a barber who thinks you might have forgotten Something for the Weekend.'

"All? How do you mean? Oh – sorry." Harver felt in his pockets for cash.

The waiter looked hurt. "No – no, sir. I cannot accept gratuities. I was just wondering if you would like company."

"Company? Oh – you mean a –"

"A Temporary Partner, yes sir. In case you are new to Constitution, I should mention that Temporary Partnership is a recognised profession here. Its practitioners are perfectly respectable, and highly regarded for their contribution to society, not to mention their contribution to the Tax Pool. They are also utterly discreet, but I can assure you that in any case there is no stigma attached to using their services. Most of our single guests do so, as indeed do many couples. Of course, I would not want you to think I am trying to influence you in any way..."

"Of course not," slurred Harver, as the phrase 'some things don't change' crossed the back of his mind. "Perish the thought. But if I should happen to want a chick for the night, you'd get a nice rake-off – have I got the picture?"

The waiter raised an eyebrow. "Certainly, sir, I should receive a commission on any such transaction, as I would have mentioned if you wished to proceed further. The arrangements are clearly laid down in the Service Notes you will find in your room Information System. You may, of course, make your own arrangements, using the Room Service facilities. The total charge will be the same, but I won't get the commission. I was rather hoping..."

Harver thought, *The guy's got to make a living. No skin off my nose, anyway.* "OK – OK. Spare me the sob story. Send her round at about – let's see – yeah – about half-past midnight."

"Thank you, sir. Any particular type you have in mind?"

The type Harver had in mind was a big-built redhead, just like Ms Katriona McLeish, but he reckoned it better to save that experience for later. "No particular type," he said. "As long as she isn't a redhead."

"Very good, sir. Not a redhead. About half-past midnight. Good evening, sir. Have a rewarding encounter."

Externally, Rose Cottage was in the same 'Olde England, Olde Earth' style as the rest of the village. It even had a thatched roof. A fake oil-lamp over the front door lit up the flowering plants climbing up the walls. The flowers gave out a sweet scent, strong enough to compete with the 'hale. Harver guessed they must be Roses. He sniffed one and sneezed. *This place looks awful. Hope it's better inside.*

The cottage door had iron studs and a curly wrought-iron handle. It occurred to Harvey that he had no key. He groaned, and tried the handle. At the middle of the door where a spy-hole would normally be, a lens lit up. A woman's voice said, "Good evening, guest. This is Rose Cottage. If you wish to come in, please eyeball."

Harver eyeballed. The voice said, "Thank you, Mr Westly. Welcome to Rose Cottage. The door-handles, front and back, will recognise your touch from now on. If there's anything you need at any time, you have only to ask. Please come in."

Inside, the cottage was really quite decent, with civilised decor and proper amenities – almost like home back on Cyrus, really, but with more space. Harver found that his bags had been unpacked. Uncannily, everything had been put away just where he would have put it himself. He took an anti'hale capsule to clear his head, showered, and slipped into a dressing-gown.

He had half an hour to kill before his Partner was due, so he took a bottle and glass, and settled down by the living-room comm to check out the information facilities. They were excellent – even better than he remembered from his previous visit. The whole planet was an open book – no access codes, no passwords, not so much as a log-on request for ID.

Harver activated 'Who's Who', and paged through the index. *Here we are: Kjell Folke Varten. Still living in Avondale, Jefferson City District.* He reached out to touch-select the name for further details, but caution stopped him. The information system might be open, but that didn't mean that its users were not monitored. And the cottage certainly knew who was interrogating it. He'd best postpone the pleasure of contemplating his target.

He let his hand wander down the screen until he spotted a vaguely familiar female-looking name well down the list, and touch-selected that. The woman turned out to be a movie director, who had made several holos that Harver remembered seeing. He spent several minutes pretending to study her biography, then asked for personal background.

The 'Please Wait' message barely showed before the details filled the screen. If this woman's data-set was a typical 'Who's Who' entry, Harver's task was going to be easy. Everything was there, down to her favourite shops and eating places, lists of her lovers and other intimate friends, financial standing, vehicle registration numbers, portraits of her pets, views of her several houses (with floor plans – alleluia!) and a fully illustrated catalogue of her superb collection of art.

Harver was not professionally interested in art. Sure, there was money in it, but it was too bulky to handle readily single-handed, too difficult to fence. He stuck strictly to his own special field – jewellery. He knew the whereabouts of every important stone ever mined. He knew who wanted which item, and how much each potential customer was prepared to pay. He enjoyed working out how to separate the goods from their owners with minimum risk of detection. He relished the excitement. Expenses were high and margins lower than outsiders might think. But it was a living. And, above all, he could work without hangers on, all by himself.

Unfortunately, the customer who had set her heart on owning the Evening Star lived most of the time on Cyrus, Harver's home world. It was only a hundred and eighteen light years from Constitution, and she loved to travel, but a woman of her standing would never come within noticeable gravitational influence of a social black hole like Constitution, let alone set foot on it. So the Evening Star would have to go off-planet.

Off-planet removal was always tricky. You couldn't take the goods with you, or in your luggage. The Export Control scanners could pick up a smuggled toe-nail in a consignment of cattle. The sensors used by the freight and postal services were equally efficient.

Harver had never found a successful method that did not involve at least one accomplice – and the consequent risk of human error or betrayal. The present job was no exception. However, for this operation, Harver planned to use two accomplices. So this time there was no risk of human error, and betrayal was out of the question – because neither accomplice had any idea of the role he was to play in Harver's plan. And, furthermore, by the time the Evening Star was available for transport, both accomplices would be dead.

The first accomplice, the man who would carry out the physical process of stealing the diamond, was dead already. He was a native of Old Earth, one Manuel Garstang, who had died on Cyrus six years previously, in a genuine boating accident at the age of forty-five. Harver had kept precious mementoes of Manuel Garstang.

To find a suitable candidate for the second accomplice's role of courier (deceased) had taken nearly two tedious years in a regular job as an Information Technology Assistant at a large teaching hospital, with access to patient records.

Eventually, one Simon Crawson, aged eighty-three, satisfied all Harver's criteria. He was suffering from a condition so rare that no organisation had bothered to fund research for a cure, and he was expected to die within six months. Although old man Crawson was a fanatical advocate of Fundamental Democracy, he had left it almost too late in life to visit Constitution, whose society he believed to be the only one in the universe where that One True Political Creed found proper expression. He wanted to live out the remainder of his life in that society, and to die among fellow Fundamental Democrats. But he wanted his embalmed body to be buried back on Cyrus.

So Harver's second accomplice would be one Simon Crawson, eighty-three-and-a-half (give or take), deceased. And the Evening Star would go with Simon on his last journey. Because, following the Universal Convention on Human Remains, no-one would open the coffin once it was sealed, and – more to the point – no scanner could penetrate the lead lining.

Harver's scheme for inserting the goods in the coffin was simple, and involved little risk. And at the other end of the journey, extraction would be equally straightforward. *So all I've got to do is wait for Crawson to kick the bucket. And make damn sure that, when the sad news comes, I'll be ready to grab the goods.*

If Harver's homework results were still valid, Kjell Folke Varten, current owner of the Evening Star, lived in his retirement as an almost total recluse, in a modest fifteen-room timber house way out in the country, beside a small river half a kilometre from the nearest road. He went out for short walks daily, but left the place for any length of time only about once a week.

So the theft itself was going to be no problem at all – a cinch – a positive doddle. Harver Westly couldn't imagine why nobody had filched the stone in question long ago. *How can the man be so stupid? He ought to look after it – show some respect. They should never have given it to him. All right – so he's the biggest do-gooder in the history of the universe – so what? He's also the richest individual who ever lived. A stone like that – it's wasted on an idiot like him.*

The award ceremony was one of very few holos that depicted Kjell Folke Varten, despite the man's great fame. Harver's fingers had called it up almost unconsciously. He knew it by heart from the point where a grizzle-bearded gent with a deep, sonorous voice intones, "As tradition demands, the artefact selected to be the Saint Teresa Memorial Prize on this auspicious occasion is unique and symbolic. It symbolises the very achievements its purpose is to recognise, for its value is beyond price, and it can never be bought or sold."

The speaker's face is replaced by something draped in black velvet. He goes on in voice-over. "And now, Kjell Folke Varten, in recognition of your great service to humanity, to life, and to Being Itself, and in grateful memory of the spirit of the blessed Saint Mother Teresa of Calcutta on Old Earth, we are honoured to bring to you this small token."

A hand lifts away the velvet drape, revealing beauty of darkness and of fire.

You hear the audience gasp.

Close up, you can't tell what Kjell Folke Varten is thinking. He makes a graceful speech of thanks, and walks off the platform with the Evening Star sculpture clutched awkwardly in both hands.

*You bastard. You lucky bastard.*

Rose Cottage's voice broke into Harver's reverie. "Your Partner has arrived, Mr Westly. I have checked her credentials and found them satisfactory. Would you like me to let her in?"

Harver sighed, and touched the 'off' control.

The scene showing Kjell Folke Varten holding the Evening Star aloft for the holographers faded.

Behind him, "Hi, there!" said a thrilling voice, slightly husky.

Next morning the comm chime woke Harver. Without thinking, he said sleepily, "OK – I'll take it."

Only then, as Katriona McLeish came on-screen, he remembered the blonde whose skills had deprived him of fifty credits and most of a night's sleep. To his relief, the girl seemed to have left already.

On the screen, Katriona made a face. "Wow – if you don't mind me saying so, you look as though you had yourself a night!"

Harver sat up, and craned to see himself in the dressing-table mirror. He had to agree. He looked awful. "Hmm. Yeah, well, you know – big dinner, strange planet – and I had a lot of info to check on, business-related stuff. Didn't get to bed till well after midnight. Then I couldn't sleep for some reason..." *Some reason, all right! Thought I knew most of the tricks, but what that blonde did with those beads...* "Where are you calling from?"

"I'm still in town. I can be there in an hour. Or, if you're planning on coming into town, I could meet you."

"Sure. I got a few things to see to before I can get down to being a tourist. Let's make it we meet for lunch. Where's the best place?"

"The best? Frascati's, I reckon. It's near the centre. Best to take an air-cab. Say, twelve-thirty?"

"Make it one o'clock." Harver wanted to allow time for a couple of detox pills to do their job. He also wanted to be sure he wouldn't have to hurry. He was anxious to confirm that certain delicate items left in a safe place during his previous stay on Constitution were still in their original condition. The baggage-handlers at the spaceport seemed to be about the only things on the planet that had not changed radically in the past five years. *They must have been using the Time Shunt in a big way. The natives don't seem to notice the differences, but to an outsider... I wonder how it feels to be Shunted?*

The old warehouse-office complex down by the river was exactly as he remembered, still with a human security guard at the front desk. *Relief! No call to eyeball.*

The guard was watching a portable holo with the sound volume down – slow, rhythmic music. Without looking up, he said, "Hi, Mac. Got ID?"

Harver leaned across the desk until he could see the image that was entertaining the guard: *erotics. Not bad, either. Bit early in the day for my liking.*

The guard laughed. Harver realised he had spoken the last few words out loud. He covered his embarrassment by pretending to be embarrassed, fanning his face with an identity card. "Sure – I got ID. If you don't mind waiting while I cool off."

The guard grinned, took the card, and inserted it in the reader, which beeped and spat it back into his hand. He glanced at the screen. "OK, Mr – er – Garstang. Who you come to see?"

"Inex Galactic. Been here before."

"Inex Galactic? Third floor. Take number one or two elevator. You know where to go?"

"Yeah thanks. Is there a PTM around here?"

"A what?"

"A Public Teller Machine. Were I can get some cash using my card."

"Oh – you mean a cash-point. Through the swing doors. Second door on the left after the male john. Can't miss it."

The old-fashioned key to the Inex office still worked. Harver wiped dust from the lock-lens on the filing cabinet, and presented the combination holo. The cabinet said, "Please tell me which drawer to open."

"Four," said Harver, hoping he had remembered his Manuel Garstang voice the way the machine remembered it.

He had. The cabinet responded, "Opening drawer number – four – please confirm."

"Confirmed."

Drawer number four was full of the same types of semi-obsolescent electronics as those listed on Harver's phoney cargo manifest. The Manuel Garstang retina-hologram contact lenses were well hidden in a piece of false circuitry. It took nearly a quarter of an hour to extricate them. Harver cleaned them very carefully, and slipped them into place with the help of a shaving-mirror from the desk drawer. He had worn them before, but it still surprised him to find not only that he couldn't feel them or see them in the mirror, but that they made no difference to his vision. Time for an eye-test!

As he expected, the cash-point balked at revealing Mr Garstang's credit balances without proper identification. "Access unauthorised," the screen said. "To provide authorisation, please eyeball the flashing light."

Harver eyeballed.

"Thank you Manuel Garstang," said the screen, and showed a current account credit balance of twenty-three credits.

*More than I expected,* thought Harver. *Ah yes – five years interest... No need to look at the other accounts – there'll be plenty there.*

*The contact-holos still work. Thank God for that. Must remember to take them out when I'm through here.* Twenty-three credits might just pay for lunch at Frascati's, but 'Thanks, Mr Garstang' would certainly raise a few questions.

Whistling through his teeth, Harver put in a call to the ranch-house he had used as Manuel Garstang's home base. The house was a key element in maintaining the Garstang fiction, so he had arranged for one of the better-funded accounts to pay the rent, and a cleaning and maintenance company visited every ninety days.

The call took longer than usual to connect. *What the hell's wrong with this thing? thought Harver. Don't tell me I forgot to pay the rental!*

To his relief, the screen blanked, then showed the face of Manuel Garstang – Harver himself with Zapato moustaches. He had been very proud to be able to grow them, and greatly regretted having to shave them off.

The Garstang image spoke with a trace of Latinate accent. "Hi – I am Manuel Garstang. Sorry I am not here in person right now. Please to leave a message, and I will call you back as soon as I can. Have pleasant experiences! Adios and hasta la vista!"

*Yep! Manuel Garstang lives!*

Finally, before slipping into the john to remove the lenses, Harver checked on the whereabouts and health of his destined second accomplice.

Simon Crawson was staying at the Crown Imperial in Lincolnville, the other side of the continent, four time zones away. He was about to have breakfast, but was clearly delighted to get a call from Harver, who had no need to remind him that they had been shipmates. They agreed to have drinks, or lunch, or maybe dinner, some time soon.

Harver told himself that the man looked older and sicker already. *Won't be long now... Meanwhile, might as well enjoy myself. Lunch, a trip on the river, very romantic, then back to the Hilton Royale to watch the sunset by the village pond. The Katriona chick seems to like that stuff. A couple of drinks, dinner, maybe a dance if they've got a rhythm-room – sure to have one somewhere. Then – back to Rose Cottage, and bingo! Little lady – you don't know what a treat you've got coming to you.*

Everything went as planned. About one-thirty in the morning the a-v jockey turned down the lights, started a slow number and announced, "Well now, good folks – comes the last event. Time to body in together, relate on down, and snake it smooth."

The terminology was unfamiliar to Harver, but the behaviour of the people on the floor left little room for doubt as to the general idea. With singing heart, he led Katriona into the throng. Close contact and gentle swaying seemed to please her. She moved against him dreamily, with her eyes shut and her moist lips apart. He felt his loins stirring with promise. She pressed against him quite blatantly. The music stopped.

"Thank you, kind sir," said Katriona, stepping back and curtsying. "That was a lovely evening."

Harver stared. "Er – yes. And thank you. I enjoyed it very much. How about we go back to –"

"I'm sorry," Katriona yawned. "So sorry – been a long day. Must get some sleep. See you at breakfast? Half-past nine? Ten?"

"Breakfast?" said Harver, as though the concept were completely new to him, which for all practical purposes it was. "Oh – yes. OK. Make it half-past nine. Or ten. At the – in the – you know – the place near the pond."

"OK – see you there, then. 'Night'!"

"Good night." Harver watched her go, his eyes drinking in her hip-swaying saunter, his loins lingeringly aroused. *Where did I go wrong? I'm sure we bodied in together all right, and we sure related on down. Maybe I didn't snake it smooth enough... Hell fire! I could hump a camel. Little lady, I hope you aren't figuring to pull a stunt like this again.*

Rose Cottage woke him at nine, as requested. He groaned in disbelief, and told it to shut up and leave him alone. It woke him again at nine-thirty, and informed him, "A Ms Katriona McLeish has arrived at the 'Olde Coffee Potte'."

Harver reluctantly sat up in bed, careful not to disturb the Maori maiden, who had proved a more than satisfactory stand-in for a camel, and was now snoring gently.

186

*Oh god – I'd forgotten. Breakfast!* A sudden suspicion struck him. There was a phone by the bed. "Hell! She's not on the phone now, is she?"

"No, sir. Ms McLeish asked the drinks dispenser if it had seen you around the place. She is expecting you by ten-thirty. I thought you might like to know."

Harver showered, shaved, dressed and sneaked out, leaving the Maori asleep.

On the way to the 'Olde Coffee Potte', he tried to figure out what was making him feel uneasy. *Hell – why should I feel guilty? Katriona's the one should feel guilty. One minute she gives me the big come-on, next minute she 'no-ways' me. Thing like that can hurt a guy. Still – it's no big deal. There's plenty more where that Maori came from, and that blonde with the beads... I'll tell the redheaded cock-teaser to take a running jump.*

Katriona was at a table by the window. As Harver entered the cafe, she looked up and smiled, hair like flowing fire in the morning sun.

*On the other hand,* thought Harver, smiling back, noting the firm swell of her breasts, the shapely perfection of her demurely crossed legs. *On the other hand, I could do with a challenge – got to have something to while away the time until old Simon Crawson cashes in his chips. Besides, she could be useful. She's got up-to-date local knowledge. Maybe I can get her to tell me about the Time Shunt. So, maybe I'll keep up the old Westly charm after all. No chick can resist that forever.*

"Hi, Katriona. You look wonderful. That colour suits you. I mean, any colour would suit you, but that kind-of blue-green's really nice."

"Thank you, kind sir. What are your plans for today?"

"No plans. No plans for today. No plans for this week, this month, this whole year – or the next decade. I'm totally free, totally uncommitted. My time is yours. Have you any suggestions?"

Over the next few weeks, Katriona proudly showed him her home world. Harver Westly patiently endured more scenery and more culture than he had put up with in his previous forty-five years of life. He raved enthusiastically about every detail, from palm-fringed tropical sunsets to rainbow-dancing waterfalls, from ancient traditionally wine-drenched folk-dance festivals to the serene abstractions of The Theatre of Body and Mind. Sometimes he almost found himself enjoying the new sights and sounds. Always, he was convincingly fascinated.

In prestigious restaurants and cheerful beach-bars, over frosted tall glasses or steaming late-night punch-mugs, they talked. Mostly, Harver did the talking, with the woman hanging on every word. Many of his first-person anecdotes were true, except that not all the exciting events had happened to himself. He was careful to avoid touching on anything that directly concerned his main profession. Katriona got to know him as a merchant-adventurer who occasionally lent a helping hand to the forces of law and order.

Wherever they went, he bought her presents. By trial and error, he found she preferred little things of no great commercial value, rather than expensive items. She wore the emerald necklace only with the greatest reluctance, and actually refused the sports-skimmer.

And she had turned out to be no challenge at all. On the first night of their travels they had adjoining rooms, sharing a balcony, in a beach-house ringed by tropical palm-trees. Katriona suggested an early night after their long flight and the boat trip to the island. Immediately after a late supper, Harver escorted her to her room. She kissed him lightly on the lips, thanked him for a lovely day, and went in.

Resisting the temptation to follow her, Harver went to his own room and took a cool shower. Afterwards, with the warm night breeze playing about his naked body, he leaned on the balcony-rail, looking out over the lagoon, on which the low, huge moon made a bright pathway out to sea, out to the line of silver where small waves broke on the reef, wishing he were back in Rose Cottage with personal services available at a word on the comm. *That Maori would be perfect right now... Oh well, might as well get some sleep.*

As he settled his head on the pillow, he heard the sound of a sliding door opening, then soft footfalls. A figure – a very female figure – appeared on the balcony. His dream had come true.

The big-built redhead stepped towards him, moonlight gleaming in her hair. She knelt beside him on the bed, her lips parted. She leaned closer. The heavy, firm breasts were almost touching his chest now...

Success! The Westly charm works again...

He had less success in getting Katriona to talk about the Time Shunt. She seemed to take little interest in it, to take it for granted, to find the subject boring.

"What do you want me to say? You can't expect me to tell you how it works. There are supposed to be only half a dozen people alive who can understand the equations. You surely don't think I'm one of them, do you?"

"Well, of course not. But – surely a thing as big as that – the most amazing piece of technology that mankind has ever put to use – I mean, it must affect the way you – everyone on this planet – thinks about – you know, life, and everything. I mean, what happens when they use it? Does it affect everyone everywhere, or just the people involved?"

"Just the people involved, I think. I wouldn't know. We 'did' it at school, in Modern History and Civics. But it was all to do with Crime. I suppose Crime might be of some interest to people who live on other planets where they still have it. But here it's just old hat – 'a thing of the past'. Kids at school don't like hearing about all that old stuff."

That phrase again: 'A thing of the past'.

Ho-hum.

The first few weeks, Harver enjoyed having her around. It was good to have a willing audience for once in his

189

life. And she was clearly crazy about him – another pleasing novelty.

Sex with Katriona was pretty good, too. Though, after that first time, it never had quite the same dream-like magic. The woman was too intense. Everything had too much *meaning*. It was as if, for her, sex was more than just a game – more than an art-form, even. Incredibly, she seemed to want it to be a form of communication – to *express* something.

As time went on, the chick became more of a drag. She kept on at him, trying to tie him down. "Wouldn't it be wonderful to have a little place we could go to, and just be ourselves? By a lake, maybe, or some secluded beach."

*'Secluded'? Why the hell 'secluded'? What's the big deal about 'secluded'? A guy could fester, always looking at the same bit of scenery. A few people here and there – that's what a guy wants. Like the man said – variety's the spice of life. And it's not just for me. She'd be better off, too. Find herself a real hunk. I wouldn't mind if she did. Just so's she takes the pressure off.*

*For god's sake, she wants to cook and clean for me. Like a hole in the head, I need someone to cook and clean. Would you believe it? On this planet, of all the planets in the known universe, where no sane human being's voluntarily cooked or cleaned in the last five centuries, the woman wants to cook and clean.*

Besides which, the love-sick female's constant presence put an unwelcome restriction on Harver Westly's professional activities. There was real danger that he would run out of excuses for leaving her long enough to make worthwhile use of the planet's interweb.

Somehow he managed to keep himself *au fait* with the forthcoming engagements of Kjell Folke Varten, and to keep track of the ancient Simon Crawson's painfully slow deterioration in health. Nevertheless, he needed time on his own at Manuel Garstang's ranch, to check out various items hidden there that his plan required, including weaponry and a vehicle.

By the middle of Summer, Harver Westly's patience was wearing thin. He was increasingly niggled by the feeling that he was being watched. He accepted that Katriona watched him. Besides being part of her job to do it, it was only natural that she couldn't take her eyes off him. It was no more than an irritation, not something he couldn't handle. But there was something else, something he couldn't pin down. It felt as though *everything* was watching him. He had never been paranoid before, and it disturbed him to think that he might be going schizo.

Also, almost from the day he landed on Constitution, his skin had developed a slight itch. Not serious – no rash, and easily alleviated by scratching – but there at the back of his consciousness all the time. He put it down to something in the air, the water, the food, the bedclothes – some mild allergy – nothing to worry about, but...

It was time to speed things up. In two weeks, Kjell Folke Varten was scheduled to speak in person at a United Worlds conference on Old Earth. He'd be away for a month, maybe a week or two longer. As Harver contemplated this unexpected wide-open window of opportunity, old Simon Crawson's life expectation plummeted. *Yeah – time to speed things up, old man. I guess you're just going to have to take a turn for the worse...*

Harver had all along planned to ditch Katriona eventually, but not before he was finally ready to leave Constitution, with the Evening Star safely tucked way beside the late Simon Crawson. *That's got to be a night to remember – a night with the best female flesh I can find. Worth taking the trouble to browse and select. But always keeping the redhead in reserve. So, how do I get her to cool off and give me a break without driving her away altogether?*

The problem solved itself within hours of Harver's hearing the announcement of Kjell Folk Varten's forthcoming trip. That evening he and Katriona dined in Jefferson City at an ethnic restaurant, on the kind of food that discourages questions, but tastes all right if you keep your eyes shut. Afterwards, with the vague idea that it might help to cool the woman's ardour if she saw something of the seamier side of his character, Harver insisted that Katriona show him the Zone.

She tried hard to dissuade him. "The Zone? Where did you hear about the Zone?"

"Oh – around. I don't know. It's common knowledge. Anyway, every big city I ever heard of has a red light district or something like it."

"Not like the Zone. You don't want to go down there – not at night. It's a pedestrian area. We'd have to leave the cab and walk. You never know what you might run into."

"Sounds great! Sounds like this planet's not totally dead after all. What's the worst that can happen? We get mugged?"

"Mugged? What's that?"

"Oh – I was forgetting – you don't have crime, do you? Mugging is demanding money with menaces, in the street. They stick a gun in your ribs or hold a knife at your throat. You hand over your money or make a credit transfer. If you're lucky they let you go."

Katriona looked puzzled. "Sounds quite pointless. But worse things happen in the Zone, believe me. Look – if you insist, we'll go there. I always carry protection. Dip Corps regulations. But you have to promise to do exactly what I say, right away, no arguments."

"OK – I promise – cross my heart and hope to die."

"Don't joke. It could happen."

Compared with some of the pleasure districts he'd knocked about in, the Zone seemed pretty tame. The whores didn't hassle you. The live-show joints had discreet front-ends too high for kids to see in. The only real outrage was the price of a drink. The deadliest danger was boredom. Most of the patrons were respectable couples like themselves. The rowdiest element they encountered was a bunch of guys out on a bucks' night, singing salacious songs in the street. When a girl at a buff-bar started to do strange things with a snake, Harver and Katriona glanced at each other and left by unspoken mutual agreement.

The dimly-lit streets were deserted.

"I think the nearest cab-point's this way," said Katriona, taking Harver's arm. "I wish there were a few people about. Tachy-heads don't like crowds."

"Tachy-heads?"

"Kids on 'Tachyons'. Blue pills. Brain-boosters. Pop a couple and you hit the speed of light. One more pill and you're beyond it... So I'm told – I never tried them."

"So – what's so bad about brain-boosting? You get good talk when everyone's had a couple of cerebro-stims."

"Tachy-heads don't talk much – not so you can understand. They feel they Comprehend All. If they get the Real Trip, then this universe isn't big enough or complex enough. They want more. It doesn't happen every time, but when it does, they go out on the Shunt Hunt."

A group of white-clad figures entered the street from a side-road, moving strangely as though in slow motion.

Katriona gasped. "Oh god – talk of the Devil!" She tugged at Harver's arm. "Quick – in here – they might not have seen us!"

She pulled him into a doorway, whispering, "Kiss me. Pretend we don't know they're here. They might leave us alone." In Harver's arms she fumbled with her handbag. "Oh shit – my stunner. I forgot to bring it. Oh god!"

Ragged footsteps approached, stopped. Through half-closed eyes, Harver tried to count the Tachy-heads. Six or seven. Mixed sexes.

A high-pitched male voice half-sang eerily, "Hey, that's love. The glory of the body and the mind together, mixing of blood and spirit. That's pretty!"

Other voices joined in, chanting: "Pretty – pretty – pretty!"

A girl's voice intoned, "She beautiful he ugly send him away to tell of all we do to bring the Force the Time of Change. Send him away!"

And the chorus chanted, "Away! Away! Away!", moving in, pulling the couple apart, Katriona screaming, Harver bewildered, paralysed with fear.

Strong hands gripped him from behind, pinioning his arms, and a low voice murmured, close to his ear, "And back and away to watch and know. To see the knives we bring for joy. See how they slice and slide through flesh of breast and thigh. See how the guts spill out forward and then down. And she falls to the stabs. Ah – falls in the stream of blood."

The small sodden heap that had been Katriona twitched twice while Harver was learning that he could not stop himself watching. One by one the white figures knelt by the body, stretched out their arms, and lay full-length on top of it, rolling from side to side, soaking their clothes in the blood.

"Oh friend of our departure from this universe," murmured the voice in Harver's ear. "Now I too must enter into the blood of the pretty one. Go from us. Go and tell the forces of justice what you have seen us do. Go – now!"

The strong hands turned him away from the scene and shoved him, hard. He stumbled and ran with the strange voices dwindling behind him, the sight of the torn body filling his vision. *They cut off her boobs. Oh god, they cut of her boobs. And they stuck their knives –*

Only when he could no longer hear the voices, he paused to vomit in a bin labelled KEEP YOUR CITY CLEAN – THANK YOU!

He felt a hand on his shoulder, and screamed.

The cop said, "Hey – easy, now," and saw Harver's face.

Harver managed, "They carved her up. They carved her up and rolled on her. Back there. Don't know the street.

Outside a sex-aid supermart." Then the vision filled his mind, and he vomited again, while the cop spoke to base.

At the police office, a doctor treated Harver for shock, and shot him a sedative. After half an hour, he was calm enough to talk coherently.

When he had finished, the duty sergeant shut down the recorders and sighed. "They get worse. Why do they have to do a thing like that? All they want is the Shunt. They could get that without – without – that. I have to ask you to eyeball, if you don't mind, Mr Westly. Thanks. I take it you'll be requesting the Shunt?"

Harver hesitated. From a practical view-point, the Tachy-heads had done him a favour. The redhead was well and truly out of his hair. On the other hand, it must be quite unusual for someone in his position to turn down the Shunt. In Harver Westly's profession, any behaviour unusual enough to attract attention was to be avoided.

The sergeant misinterpreted Harver's silence and blank stare. "Try not to dwell on it, sir. You won't have to wait long. We can expect the Shunt Authorisation within two-three hours on a case like this. The Tachys all waited to be picked up, like they always do, so there's no problem with entity-count. We've got them all under restraint. Setting up and calibration should be straightforward. So by this time tomorrow, none of this will have happened."

Harver looked up. "Yeah. Right. Only, I'm new here, like I said. Just visiting. So I'm not sure how – how the Shunt – how the system works."

"Uh-huh. I guess you wouldn't. Well, as a friend of the victim, you have the right to make application for the Shunt. We can advise on the procedure. But if you'd rather we handled the whole thing, you can leave it to us."

Harver left it to them. They made him stay the night in a guarded room at a hospital, where they could reinforce his sedation when he woke up screaming.

The following evening they took him back to the scene of the crime. A large black van was parked with its motor humming softly, a few metres from the sex mart. Uniformed people were stationed either side of the street, talking to mikes suspended from head-sets, and carefully positioning tall, slim, cylindrical, free-standing pillars to form a rectangle about fifty metres long. One of the pillars was in the sex-shop doorway, right next to where the sidewalk surface looked recently washed.

"I guess all this is to do with the Time Shunt?" Harver asked his escort.

"Yeah. I guess so," said the young policeman. "Never seen it myself, but it's like the pictures in the manual, more or less."

"Any chance I could talk to the operators – see how it works?"

The policeman shrugged. "You can ask."

The Chief Operator looked and sounded like a professor. He was delighted to show Harver his kit. "We don't get many people in here. Mostly they're too deep in shock to be curious – just want to get the whole thing over and done with. Or they take the attitude 'what's the point of learning something you're going to forget all about in a few minutes?' Here – take a seat – put on the hat."

Harver sat beside the Chief at one of three identical consoles, and donned the interface helmet. At the third console, an assistant operator was issuing instructions to the people outside, and making minute adjustments.

Harver never found out what the helmet was for. It covered his ears, but did not prevent him from hearing his instructor's voice, which he could certainly have heard without it.

"As you probably know," said the Chief, "The Time Shunt principle's very old. It goes back to the early days of quantum theory. Before you make an observation on an individual particle, an electron for example, there's a finite

196

probability that at any earlier or later time the electron may be literally anywhere in the universe. It's only when you make the observation that you find out where the particle *was* at the instant you made it. For a large collection of particles, like a person, the probability that the centre of mass will be far from where you thought it was before you made the observation is very low, but it's still finite and non-zero. With me so far?"

"What? Oh – yes – sure," said Harver, who had scarcely the vaguest notion of what the man was talking about. "Go on. You can skip the basics and get to the real nitty-gritty."

"Right! So, the nitty-gritty is this. Before any observation there are many possible alternative position-momentum schemas for the particle-set within any specified bounded region. In effect, there are many 'alternative universes' within that bounded region, and it is only by actually making an observation that we collapse the probability-function solutions down to a unique set. Get the picture?"

"Sort-of. But I don't see where time-travel comes into it."

"Time-travel? Who said anything about time-travel? Time travel's logically impossible. Time's a sequence of events – a sequence that just grows. You can't go backwards in time any more than you can get a negative number by adding positive numbers. No – what the Time Shunt does is to allow us to review the set of possible alternative universes within a bounded region of space, and select a desirable universe, by accepting every particle within it – simultaneously. Remember, it's the *act of completing* an observation that collapses the probabilities. So we have to use omni-sensors. Those are the vertical post-like things that my people outside are setting up and Jim here's calibrating. They define a bounded region, and – ah. Sorry. Have to ask you to leave now. The VJ's arrived."

"VJ?"

"Sorry – Volunteer Judge."

A grey-haired woman, flanked by two young policemen, approached the van, waved at the chief, and climbed in. "Hi, Al – Hi, Jim. How's tricks?"

The assistant raised a hand in greeting. The Chief prodded Harver, who took off the helmet, got up hastily and stood aside to let the woman sit down.

"Everything's fine, Maisie. Almost ready. Er – so this is the Shunt Applicant, Mr – er –"

"Westly," said Harver, holding his hand out.

"Pleased to meet you, Mr Westly," said the Judge, shaking his hand. "I understand the young scum got hold of you and forced you to watch."

Harver nodded, unable to speak, the horrible vision suddenly vivid again.

The Judge put on her helmet. "Yes. The Shunt Hunt... Well I think you can trust me to deal out the kind of justice they deserve. They want to go to a different universe – that's just fine by me. But I don't think they'll enjoy the one we send them to. And it'll be one they can't escape from... You know, Al, it's a crying shame we still can't record where we send people. It'd be a mighty strong deterrent. You heard of any progress in that direction?"

"No, ma'am. Seems there's no way round the problem. See, Mr Westly, recording counts as making an observation. The probabilities collapse, and you're stuck in the universe you recorded. For some reason, *previewing* without recording doesn't count as making an observation – so we can browse away till we get just exactly the universe we want – both for the criminals and for the victims. Takes all night sometimes, but we always get there in the end. How's it coming, Jim?"

"Up and running, Chief."

"OK. Well, Mr Westly, this is it. It's been a pleasure talking to you. See the officer with the clip-board? She'll tell you what to do. Bye, now – and all the best. Maybe we'll meet again in our new universe."

"Thanks," said Harver. "Good-bye. Good-bye, Judge."

The Judge, concentrating, waved a hand, but went on with what she was already saying to the team. Harver dawdled towards the exit door, not altogether keen to force the pace of events.

He overheard the Judge telling the team, "... and just for once, let's try for a really low leakage index on this one. And at all costs keep the time-slippage within reasonable bounds. Aim for less than plus-fifteen standard days if at all possible. The media's been stirring things up again. We can't afford any more 'Discontinuity!' headlines..."

The Chief was motioning for him to leave. He mumbled, "OK – just going. Good-bye and thanks", drew a deep breath and opened the door.

The street was now empty, except for the woman with the clip-board, who beckoned to Harver as he climbed out of the van. "Over here, Mr Westly. That's right, stand just inside the – er – yes – there. That's fine. Now you don't have to do a thing – just wait. If you can keep quite still, it makes it easier for the Shunt crew to do their job. So, please don't move off that spot on any account. It won't be long now. All right?"

"Fine," said Harver, trying not to move his lips.

"You are allowed to breathe, Mr Westly. It's not that critical." The woman listened to her head-set. "Right – they're almost ready. I have to leave you very shortly. Before I go, there are a few things I have to tell you, not that you'll remember them, but it's part of the procedure we always follow.

"You won't recall a thing about what led up to this, but you will receive a Notification by regular mail, stating the bare facts. If you are not satisfied with the way things have turned out, you can take the Notification to any police office and file for a Re-shunt. The sole ground on which a Re-shunt may be allowed is that some direct effect or effects of the injury that led to the first Shunt have not been removed. Is that clear?"

"Yes – seems fair enough."

199

"Good. So recorded. Finally, Mr Westly, you have exercised your right to place the entire Shunt procedure in the hands of the police and of the Law, as represented by a duly appointed Judge. It is the common opinion and the decision of these duly authorised persons that, in order to redress the injuries of the victim, namely Ms Katriona McLeish, the Time Shunt must take place regardless of any other considerations.

"You yourself now have the right to withdraw from the Shunt. If you do so, the criminals and victim will be Shunted without you, and there can be no guarantee that you will ever meet any of them again. It is certain that none of them will remember having met you. Understood?"

*Bingo – I'm off the hook!*

"You mean, she – Katriona – gets Shunted back to life, and neither of us remembers a thing about each other?"

"That is correct. The Shunt team are now ready for the final adjustments. I am going to ask you a question, and you must take all the time you need to decide which way to answer. Harver Westly, is it your wish to be included in the Shunt or to withdraw? Please answer 'I wish to be included' or 'I wish to withdraw'. Take your time."

Harver did a little dance of joy and relief. *I'm free! Bye-bye Katriona – it was nice having you around. Maybe we'll meet again on the other side, and I'll give you one for old times' sake.*

Then, to his horror, he heard himself say, "I wish to be included."

"So recorded," said the woman with the clipboard. "Good luck, Mr Westly."

Harver opened his mouth. Strangled noises came out. The woman climbed into the van and shut the door. Harver stood rooted to the spot.

---

The dimly lit street was deserted.

"I think the nearest cab-point's this way," said Katriona, taking Harver's arm. "I wish there were a few people about. Tachy-heads don't like crowds."

"Tachy-heads?"

"Kids on 'Tachyons'. Blue pills. Brain-boosters. Pop a couple and you hit the speed of light. One more pill and you're beyond... So I'm told – I never tried them."

"So – what's so bad about brain-boosting? You get good talk when everyone's had a couple of cerebro-stims."

"Tachy-heads don't talk much – not so you can understand. They feel they Comprehend All. If they get the Real Trip, then this universe isn't big enough or complex enough. They want more. It doesn't happen every time, but when it does, they go out on the Shunt Hunt."

A group of white-clad figures entered the street from a side-road, moving strangely as though in slow motion.

Katriona gasped. "Oh god – talk of the Devil!" She tugged at Harver's arm. "Quick – in here – they might not have seen us!"

She pulled him into a doorway, whispering, "Kiss me. Pretend we don't know they're here. They might leave us alone." In Harver's arms she fumbled with her handbag. "Thank god – my stunner. I thought I'd forgotten to bring it. Turn round a bit. That's fine – gives me a clear shot."

Ragged footsteps approached, stopped. Through half-closed eyes, Harver tried to count the Tachy-heads. Six or seven. Mixed sexes.

A high-pitched male voice half-sang eerily, "Hey, that's love. The glory of the body and the mind together, mixing of blood and spirit. That's pretty!"

Other voices joined in, chanting: "Pretty – pretty – pretty!"

A girl's voice intoned, "She beautiful he ugly send him away to tell of all we do to bring the Force the Time of Change. Send him away!"

And the chorus chanted, "Away! Away! Away!", moving in, knives glinting.

Harver felt Katriona's hand move. There was a rapid burst of electric sizzling sounds, and faint flashes lit up the sex-aids in the shop-window. Harver turned his head, to see white figures crumpling, falling. A girl screamed. Two or three tried to run. The stunner caught them, buckling their legs. They fell headlong, slithering on the concrete pavement, and lay twitching convulsively, like their friends, gargling with pain.

"Gotcha, you bastards!" said Katriona softly. "I've always wanted to do that. I'm glad we came here after all. Maybe we'll do it again some time."

Harver shook his head, shaking too much to speak. Knives were his pet phobia.

Katriona called the police, reported to the Diplomatic Corps duty monitor, and put her phone back in her bag. "No need to hang around. These little buggers aren't going anywhere for a while. Let's go."

In the cab on the way back to Rose Cottage, the phone bleeped.

"That'll be the cops," said Katriona.

It wasn't. It was her younger sister, calling to announce that she was getting married again in three weeks time, and offering Katriona another chance of being a bridesmaid. "You can bring a man, too, if you've got one. But I really need you right away – you know – to help with choosing a dress and everything. Do say you'll come!"

"I'd love to, Elsa, honestly I would. But you know I'm working. I can't just drop everything and come running, much as I'd like to."

Harver tapped Katriona's arm, and made 'it's-OK-by-me' gestures.

Katriona said, "Hold on, Elsa – someone's trying to – just a minute." She held the phone against the seat-cushion. "Could you hear all that, Harver? It's Elsa. She –"

"Yeah – I heard. She shouts like my old mother used to. It's OK by me. You go off and hold little sister's hand. I'll be fine. I need to do a few things, business-wise. Keep my hand in – you know."

"You mean, you wouldn't mind getting rid of me for a while. I saw the way you looked at those whores this evening. Couldn't keep your eyes off that one with the tassels. Hey – don't look so hurt! I'm only teasing."

"But I wouldn't dream of –"

She squeezed his hand. "Darling, I know you wouldn't. You'd never do anything to hurt me – I know that. Elsa? You still there? It's all right – I *can* come. I'll call you tomorrow when I've got the flight details... No – my man's deserting me. Something tells me he's allergic to weddings... Yes, that's right – all the better – plenty of scope for girl-talk. See you. Bye."

Three weeks. A bit tight, but it'll have to do.

The following morning, as they were sipping their first coffee and watching the news, there was a knock at the door. Rose Cottage spoke to the visitor, then announced: "It's an official courier, madam, sir. She insists on making her delivery hand-to-hand to the persons named on the items to be delivered. That is, to you, madam, sir, if you don't mind."

Clutching their bath-robes around them, Katriona McLeish and Harver Westly went to the door and received heavily sealed envelopes, for which they not only had to eyeball a portable scanner but had to sign in a book, using an old-fashioned stylo.

Harver was deeply suspicious of any document that an official insisted on delivering into his hand. He did not trust the courier's reassurances. 'To your advantage, certainly nothing to worry about'. *Heard that one before. Turned out to be a subpoena just like all the others.*

Without the benefit of experience such as Harver's, Katriona had no such inhibitions. She opened her envelope immediately, and pulled out an engrossed parchment. She stared. "My god – I've been murdered!"

"You *what?*"

"I've been murdered. It says here that I died of blood-loss, caused by multiple stab-wounds. The crime was committed by Susan Parkham, Joseph Michael Themony... and about half a dozen other names... hereinafter referred to as the criminals... was carried out under the influence of the cerebro-ultrastimulant known as 'Tachyons'. What the hell are 'Tachyons'?"

"Search me. Never heard of them. Cerebral ultrastimulant? Sounds like some kind of brain-booster. Hey – mine says I was with you when it happened. '... and was forcibly restrained by the said Eloise Mary Richardsley, so as to be unable to come to the assistance of the Victim...'" *A woman? I was forcibly restrained by a woman?*

"Listen to this," said Katriona eagerly. "Where does it start? Blah – blah – blah... Yes – here we are: 'Now be assured that by means of the Heisenberg-Chandrasinghe Potential Discriminator commonly known as the Time Shunt the aforesaid criminals have been transferred confined and constrained within a world-line mode-set configuration-dynamic, commonly known as an alternative universe, in which they are compelled and destined to suffer for the remainder of their natural lives a degree of misery disappointment frustration physical pain and deprivation of all mitigating pleasure just a flea's whisker short of 'cruel and unusual punishment' as required by the Constitution of Constitution."

"It doesn't really say 'a flea's whisker', does it?" said Harver, a slowish reader, half-believing that it might.

"No, of course it doesn't. But you can tell that's what it means. Anyway, if some bastards murdered me, I'm glad they got what was coming to them."

"Yeah," said Harver absently. "Funny, isn't it? You'd think you'd remember something... Could these things be a hoax? I mean, if you don't remember a thing about it, what's the point of telling you it happened?"

"So you can apply for a Re-shunt if anything's still wrong. 'Provided that such application is made within three months of the date of these presents.' It says here."

"Oh. That's right – it's in mine, too."

Harver was thinking: *three months... By that time, I'll be too far away to care one way or the other.*

He was still in high spirits as he waved good-bye to Katriona in her air-cab ("Keep your hands off women with tassels while I'm away!" – "Don't worry – I'll be good!") and set about the implementation of his plans for the early demise of Simon Crawson and the snatching of the Evening Star.

He told Rose Cottage to book him a camper, fitted and provisioned for a two-week trip through the Great Outback, a desert region North-East of Lincolnville. That was the city where, if all went well, old Simon Crawson would shortly be entering a hospice for the dying. By happy coincidence it was within easy reach of the Garstang ranch.

En route to Jefferson airport for his flight to Lincolnville, he dropped by the warehouse where his supposed import-cargo was still being stored. He picked up certain pocket-size items of electronic equipment – items which looked precisely as described in the manifest, but which had somewhat different functions.

At the camper-hire depot in Lincolnville, he made a big thing of inspecting the vehicle and its contents, complaining at the choice of liquor, the colour of the bedding, and the scent of the soap in the shower-cubicle. "I'll be out there two weeks – maybe longer. Least I can expect is some decent malt whisky, and soap that doesn't stink like a beauty salon."

By the time he eventually drove away into the desert, he was pretty sure that the depot staff would remember a Mr Westly.

The camper's navigation and guidance systems were excellent. All Harver had to do was shift the cursor on the scrolling map to the spot he wanted, about two miles South of the 'Manuel Garstang' ranch, press the 'Go' button, and relax. The readout showed estimated journey time as three hours. He went back to the lounge area and watched some holovid, until, just after sundown, the camper stopped and announced that it had reached the specified co-ordinates.

The sky was overcast with thin, high cloud. It would soon be pitch-dark. Zero likelihood that he'd be seen in the wrong persona approaching the ranch house. He had picked a place from which the direct route to the house contained no serious hazards, but with just over two miles to go over rough country he was profoundly grateful for Constitution's excellent GPS.

On arrival, just for practice, he tested his skill by gaining entry without using the door-key, and without setting off any of the numerous and sophisticated alarm systems. He was pleased to find that the shower still worked, and the Manuel Garstang clothes still fitted after five years. In the mirror, the false Zapato moustaches looked ludicrous but entirely realistic.

He was feeling pleased with himself, until it struck him that he had forgotten to bring any food or drink. All the kitchen offered was a half-empty jar of instant coffee and a packet of sugar-lumps that some small animal had got to before him. A two-mile hike back to the camper had little appeal.

However, the maintenance crew had clearly been doing what 'Garstang' paid them to do. The ranch's selection of vehicles turned out to be in good shape. Harver picked a flashy all-wheel drive with chrome-plated rhino-catchers front and rear, and wearily drove back to town.

As Garstang, Harver couldn't patronise a luxury hotel. The modest establishment he chose pointed out that it was well after midnight, and the kitchen staff had gone home. After a couple of meagre sandwiches and a bottle of beer that tasted even less than five-year-old instant coffee, he barely had the energy to get full satisfaction from that night's Temporary Partner.

The following morning, still as Manuel Garstang, Harver signed on for a two-day refresher course for private pilots, which brought him up to date on the planet's air traffic control procedures and navaids. His deep interest in the detailed workings of the electronics impressed his instructor, who would have been less pleased if he had suspected how the flamboyant Señor Garstang intended to use the information.

On completing the course, Harver returned the Garstang off-roader to its home, changed back to himself, and walked back to the camper. He drove into town and booked in at the Crown Imperial Hotel in his own name.

"Room three-one-eight, Mr – er Westly. I think you'll like it, sir. There's a fine view over the lake." The head porter snapped his fingers, and a young girl came running to take Harver's single light valise. She looked about fourteen, and terrified.

"Sounds great," said Harver, adding casually. "A friend of mine's staying here. Mr Crawson, room four-five two. I see his key's here. I don't want to disturb him if he's resting. Do you know if he's in his room?"

The head porter ostentatiously covered his data-screen with his hand. "Four-five-two – Crawson. Rings a bell. Would that be an elderly gentleman, to look at? Goatee beard, light build, about one metre eighty, walks with a stick?"

"That's him."

"Thought so. Never forget a guest." The porter tapped his forehead. "All up here! Soon as they've paid their bills, the computer forgets them. Not me. All up here! Bit of an eccentric, your friend Mr Crawson. Told me he was only eighty-three. Looked about a hundred and fifty. I'm afraid he checked out, sir. Two days ago, about noon."

*Two days! Not good. Don't say I've lost him!* "Checked out? You don't happen to know where he went, do you?"

The porter drew breath through his teeth. "Well... I'm not sure I can give you that information, sir. He didn't actually leave a forwarding address, and I'm not sure it would be... You know how it is, sir. Might be more than my job's worth."

Harver took out his wallet, and dropped it clumsily on the counter. Several large-denomination notes spilled forth. Harver gathered most of them up, and pointed at the others with his chin. "I really hate to see litter left lying around. It's a disgrace. Would you mind taking care of it?"

"Certainly, sir." The porter smirked and vanished the notes with the speed of a conjurer. "Bellevue Hospice, Fourteenth District. They carried him out in a life-support capsule. He looked pretty bad."

"That's – terrible. Poor old Simon. Look – er – get me some flowers, will you? A big bunch – up to five creds-worth. Let me know when they arrive. I'll be in my room."

Life support! Is it my birthday? Christmas? Someone pinch me – I've got to be dreaming.

The pagette who carried Harver's bag had thoughts on much the same lines when she saw the size of the tip.

At the hospital, a sympathetic nurse showed Harver to Crawson's room in the Semi-Intensive Suite. "His vital signs are steady but low. Most of the time he's barely conscious, if at all. You realise he won't be able to recognise you?"

Harver replied solemnly. "Yes, I understand. But we're – we *were* – quite close, you know. I just wish... Is he on sedation?"

"Yes – low-level trank. His condition makes him subject to severe cerebral episodes. Are you a medical man, Mr Westly?"

"Not professionally qualified. But I worked in hospitals for some years. You're giving him steroids, I take it. Prednopatone? Sembilanone?"

"Prednopatone, one milligram an hour."

"As much as that?"

"Yes, it is high. Touch wood, there aren't any signs of vascular distress so far, but... We tried reducing the dose-rate, but his condition deteriorated rapidly. We need time to build him up before we can cut down the dose."

"I see the problem. What should I do with these?"

The nurse took the flowers. "I'll find a vase. You can talk to him if you like. I really think it comforts them to hear a familiar voice, even though they can't understand... Let me know when you leave. I'll be in the monitoring room just down there – all right? I'll leave you to it then."

The old man was almost invisible among tubes and wires. Harver thought: *If this is Semi-Intensive, I wonder what Intensive looks like.*

He studied the system of apparatus, instruments, and controls, talking softly to the patient. "Well, you don't look too good to-day, Simon, old buddy. I don't like that colour."

*Intravenous dosing, positive pressure metering pump, programmable controller. Careful people these – nice connections, all taped together for extra safety. Pity... Rules out the 'whoops! I wonder how that came loose?' solution.*

"Dear me, Mr Crawson, what have you been doing to get yourself into this state? Letting yourself go, that's what. Not taking care of your body. Well, don't worry. We'll soon make you more comfortable..."

*Let's see now. Which is going to work faster – increase the dose rate, vascular distress, burst a major blood vessel? Or reduce the rate, general metabolic deterioration, collapse of elderly party?* "I think a bit of both, don't you, Simon? *Twenty milligrammes in the next half hour, then cut down to zero – that should do it. So, if I can just re-program the monitoring-alarm systems... You know, it's wise to pick up a few trades as you go through life. You never know when a little bit of know-how's going to come in handy. It's the same with surgical gloves – always carry a pair, just in case..."*

*Ah yes... Not very clever, my friends – simple password protection – not very clever. Hardly worth using the Ferret. Still – better safe than sorry. In you go, fellah.*

The Ferret was a highly modified debugging device that Harver had picked up in his Information Assistant role. It looked, and X-rayed, just like an ordinary stylus. Connected to any interface port, it installed and ran an anti-security program in unused memory, a program that sought out and by-passed security checks. The program deleted itself after use, leaving no trace. *Less than three minutes, that took. Not bad going, considering I'm out of practice. All set. Forgotten anything? No – dosage rate ramps OK – monitor-alarm set-points adjusted – output levels ready to re-calibrate. All set to execute when I press the button. 'Execute' – nice choice of words – I like it... Right – here goes.*

"Here we go, Simon. Keep your eyes on those monitor traces. If you see a glitch in any of them, sing out – and I'll start running. Three – two – one – boing!"

*Nothing. Not a hint of a glitch. We're in business.*

"Well, Simon, tell you what – we'll have a little bet. I bet you fifty credits the vascular distress gets you before the general metabolic breakdown. Shake on it, pal."

Simon Crawson's hand was a scrawny claw. When Harver mockingly grasped the fingers, the claw gripped him back with surprising strength. He shuddered and pulled his hand away, suddenly aware of the doomed man's eyes.

He fled from the room, shut the door behind him and leaned against it for a few seconds, breathing hard. When he reckoned he could walk steadily, he went to leave, passing the open door of the monitor-room.

The nurse called out to him, "Mr Westly! Are you leaving already?"

He stopped, and made no attempt to keep his voice steady. "Yes, I. He's so –"

"I understand, Mr Westly. It's always very distressing to see someone close to you go down-hill so fast. But he's not suffering, if that's any consolation. Would you like us to keep you informed of – of progress?"

"Would you? I'd certainly appreciate it. I'm at the Crown Imperial – room three-one-eight. If I'm out, you can always leave a message."

"We will, Mr Westly. Go carefully, now. And try not to distress yourself too much."

Old Simon Crawson won the fifty-credit bet. The winner was general metabolic breakdown.

The following evening, Harver was paged in the grille-room. The patient's condition had worsened seriously in the past twenty hours.

"He could go at any moment," said the duty physician. "We thought you ought to know, in case you'd like to see him before the end."

"Thanks. I'll get over there right away. Is he in the same room?"

"Yes. No point in moving him now. There's nothing more we can do for him. We've stopped all treatment apart from the sedation."

*So they never noticed my program modifications. I'm in the clear!*

Harver sat with his old friend until the end, fortified by the sympathetic cups of coffee that the nurses brought him at regular intervals. Simon Crawson died peacefully at three-fifteen the next morning.

"It's a happy release, in a way," said the night-nurse, shutting down the systems.

*You can say that again,* thought Harver, making a big production of blowing his nose. "He was a good man. I owe him a lot." *Fifty credits, to be precise. But I mustn't laugh, must I?*

"If you'd like to wait outside for a few minutes, I'll call you when I've got him tidied up. You can go in the nurses' day-room, if you like. You can smoke in there. There's a holovid and a drinks dispenser. No alcoholics, I'm afraid, but –"

"Thanks. I'll be all right," said Harver, with a convincing catch in his voice. "I'll be just fine."

The day-room holovid was showing 'Galactic Round-up', the inter-system news and current affairs program. Harver ignored it. He obtained a cup of coffee, took a seat, lit up a 'hale, and settled down to gloat.

Things were going well. He felt sure there would be no objection to his taking charge of the arrangements for transporting the body back to Cyrus. Now all he had to do was to provide Simon Crawson's viaticum.

*The Evening Star...* As he sat in 'hale-assisted meditation, contemplating the beauty in his mind's eye, he almost failed to notice that the holovid was showing pictures of the stone's current and rightful owner. 'Galactic Round-up' was covering the successful climax to the United Worlds conference.

"So now, Kjell Folke Varten, following his historic speech – probably the most important in his truly illustrious career – takes leave of Old Earth, possibly for the last time. Too tired to speak, the great man still has the energy to manage a wave to the billions that owe so much to his words and deeds, and above all, to his generosity. We salute him."

Hastily, Harver felt in his pockets, found a tube of anti'hales, and swallowed one with the aid of a sip of coffee. After a moment of thought he swallowed another one.

*Shit! They'll have sent that video in the same FTL ship Varten travelled in. Two weeks from Old-Earth. That means the old bastard's back here already! This calls for Plan B. Only I haven't got a Plan B... Shit!*

Harver's plans had always assumed that Varten would be absent at the time of the robbery, probably on one of his occasional day trips to the city. The intention was to seize the first opportunity after Simon Crawson's death, whenever that might be, which would give him only a matter of hours in which to perform the tricky operation of overcoming the security systems and stealing the stone.

The philanthropist's several-week absence at the United Worlds conference had therefore seemed like a luxury.

212

There should have been at least two clear weeks to do the job with the house unoccupied. Even now, Harver could not rid himself of the conviction that the conference ought to be just starting, not already finished. It was as though time had slipped away without his noticing it.

*And now he's back, Varten'll want to take things easy. From the way he looks, he won't be leaving home for quite some time... and Crawson's body won't keep for ever. So I'm going to have to work with Varten likely to walk in at any moment.*

*It's not worth the risk. I don't need the money. I'll tell the client she's out of luck. It won't do my professional reputation any good, but what do I care? I'm retiring anyway...*

*But that means five years wasted...*

*To hell with the client! I want that stone. For me. If it's for me, it's worth the risk. I'll get that diamond, Kjell Folke Varten or no Kjell Folke Varten.*

As Harver expected, the hospital authorities were only too pleased to accept his offer to take care of Crawson's body. There was surprisingly little red tape, and all the officials involved were concerned to make things as easy as possible for the old fellow's grief-stricken friend and compatriot.

The whole business took just half a day, much of which was spent waiting in quite comfortable ante-rooms. The chief mourner took full advantage of each delay to consider his options and revise his strategy, so that by the time the last hard-copy document had been signed and sealed, and the last computer deposition eyeballed, his Plan B was complete down to the last detail. The last detail was in fact the only major difference from Plan A – namely, the type of lethal weapon to be carried by 'Manuel Garstang' in case the need arose for persuasion or coercion.

All he needed now was a suitable weather forecast. At that time of year there was every chance of ten-tenths cloud over the last part of his route, which was his main requirement. By early afternoon, the meteorology people were predicting just what he wanted in about twenty-four hours time. In his Garstang persona he phoned the airport and hired a self-fly aircraft for the next day

Harver ate a late lunch back at the hotel, and put in a few hours of much-needed sleep. He got up about seven in the evening, took a shower, and put in a call to Rose Cottage.

"Ms McLeish has called four times, sir. There are no other messages. Would you like to see Ms McLeish's calls?"

"Yeah – show me the latest one."

Katriona was wearing a filmy negligee. Harver had forgotten how good she looked. She said what he expected her to say. *No need to look at her earlier messages, but I might as well – it's no strain on the eyes.*

He had intended not to contact Katriona until the entire operation was complete. However, after viewing the entire ophthalmically therapeutic sequence in reverse order, he called her sister's home.

"Hi, I'm Elsa," said a brunette Katriona look-alike in a blue t-shirt. "Just hang on one moment, and someone'll be right there."

After some seconds, the screen blanked momentarily, and the same brunette appeared, wearing a bath-towel, panting, and wrapping another towel round her wet hair, turban-fashion. "Sorry – I was in the tub. Can I help you?"

"Hi – I'm Harver Westly, a friend of Katriona's. Is she around?"

"Sorry – you just missed her. She went out. Some concert, I think. Or the movies. She said she needed a break. She needed a break! What about me? I tell you, she never stops. You can't do this – you can't wear that! On and on and on."

"I take it you two don't really get along."

"Oh do you? Well that's where you're wrong, mister. We get along just fine. We just happen to be sisters, that's all. Anyway, what do you want me to tell her? Do you want me to get her to call you back, or what?"

"Just tell her I called."

"That's all? Just you called? And the way she talks about you I thought it was L-ove!"

Harver frowned and uttered the strange words, "Well, you can tell her I love her."

Elsa nodded ironically. "Sure you do! I think I'll just tell her you called. That alone'll be enough to give the stupid bitch an orgasm. Anything more, and she'd drop dead with a heart-attack. See you around, mister."

"Not if I see you first!" growled Harver at the blank screen.

He felt better once he had picked up a cruising blonde in the hotel bar. Their conversation over dinner was mainly about food, but over the brandy it rose to a higher philosophical plane: "I've got a big day coming up tomorrow. How about an early night?"

"Suits me. Your place or mine?"

"Mine."

"Fine. Do we go together or separate?"

"Together."

"OK – just lead the way, big boy."

With the preliminaries out of the way, and both parties having swiftly disrobed, the brunette said erotically, "Is there anything in particular you'd really like me to do? Something real nice?"

Harver, lying face down in the middle of the bed, replied after a moment's thought, "There is one thing. Something I've never asked a woman to do."

"Name it!"

"Scratch my back."

"Jeez!" said the woman, "I got me a weirdo!" But, to Harver's infinite relief, she scratched.

Harver was annoyed to find the blonde still in his bed when his early call awoke him at six. He didn't want anybody around to see what he put in his pockets. So he shook her awake and told her to beat it.

She crawled out of bed and put her clothes on protesting, "OK – OK – I'm going. Guy picks me up. Buys me dinner. Asks me back to his place. He's a nice-looking guy. And he's hung. I mean, like a horse. I'm expecting something special. What do I get? I get to scratch his back! And he goes to sleep on me. Correction – he goes to sleep – period. On me wouldn't be so bad..."

"Oh – shut up!" said Harver from the bathroom. "You got paid, didn't you?"

"Paid? Sure I got paid. I should get extra. I'm a TP, not a back-scratcher. I like my work, when it's the real thing – I enjoy it. You think I came up here just for the money?"

Harver strode forth from the bathroom, a figure of wrath clad only in shirt and briefs, and socks that rather spoiled the effect. From his wallet he extracted three or four serious notes, added an extra one as an afterthought and dispensed this largesse with the words. "Look sister, money's all I got time to offer you right now. You want job satisfaction, get back on the job. Go find yourself a punter. Now – OUT!"

He bundled her out of the room, shut the door, heaved a sigh of relief, noticed the woman's handbag on the dressing-table and her shoes by the bed, opened the door, threw the handbag and shoes out, closed the door again and heaved another sigh of relief.

The door-buzzer sounded. Harver grabbed the door-handle, yanked the door open and roared, "What is it now?"

The room-service maid stammered, "Y-your early b-breakfast, sir," put the tray down on the floor, and fled.

Coffee calmed Harver's nerves. He resisted his craving for a 'hale, since he would be flying within an hour or so, and didn't trust detoxes to clear his head by take-off time.

At the airfield, the duty clerk glanced at "Manuel Garstang's" flight plan for Jefferson, and handed over a hard-copy print-out of the weather report and forecast.

"Refuelling at Salty Springs – yeah, they're still on Summer working, open round the clock. But there are some weather problems up that way, Mr Garstang." He pointed at the wall-mounted real-time satellite display of the region. "Couple of storm fronts *here*, and *here*, moving fast and intensifying. You could run into either of them – or both. You are cleared for instruments, all-weather, I take it?"

'Manuel Garstang' tossed his head, his moustaches flapping up and down to enhance the dramatic impact. "You are talking to Manuel Garstang, señor. Cleared for instruments, all-weather? Hah! I tell you this: at night, in zero visibility, with the inertial and satellite navaids kaput and only the gyrocompass working, Manuel Garstang has found his way three hundred kilometres among mountains five thousand feet above his aircraft's ceiling, and landed on a two hundred metre strip on a fifteen-degree slope in a forty-knot cross-wind. And you ask me if this man is cleared for instruments, all-weather. I *spit* on all-weather! Nothing can stop me! I go!"

He went, leaving the clerk open-mouthed.

Harver knew all about the approaching fronts. He had based his flight plan on them. The air-strip at Salty Springs was only about sixty kilometres from Avondale, the township near which Kjell Folke Varten lived. Standing Stones, the alternative refuelling point, was much the same distance away from the target, but to the North-west.

Once at cruise he handed over to the auto-pilot, and partially sabotaged the radio transmitter by simply loosening the aerial connection until the signal was weak, crackly and intermittent. He also carried out a number of other modifications to ensure that, while he could still navigate, his aircraft would be invisible to the satellite tracking systems. He was confident that he could avoid ground-based radar by flying very low.

As he hoped, by the time he was nearing Salty Spring, the more southerly storm had moved eastwards enough to provide a plausible explanation for a diversion. His new flight-path would take him within walking distance of the Varten house.

He radioed Standing Stones, where the friendly and efficient air traffic controller gradually pieced together the odd phrase that came through the crackles: "... storm... some damage to control surfaces... head injury... unable... Salty Springs... think I can make it to Standing Stones..."

Finally, the controller said, "Roger, Hotel Lima Bravo. This is Standing Stones. We have you on satellite radar surveillance. Expecting you any time from eleven hundred hours on."

Disappointed that his electronic handiwork had not been entirely successful, Harver continued waggling the aerial connection, mixing an increasing series of crackles with: "Hotel Lima Bravo. This is Hotel Lima Bravo. Standing Stones, you are breaking up. I can hardly hear you. Controls still responding. I think I can make it. ETA eleven-fifteen hours..."

He switched off the transmitter as he was saying the last words, and flew the aircraft erratically, wandering roughly in the right direction like a drunken bee. Over the next quarter-hour, to Harver's great amusement, the tone of the Standing Stones controller's voice gradually slipped from matter-of-fact to downright worried.

In order to give the right impression of desperate urgency, Harver needed to pick a spot for his forced landing without too much circling around. He had left the overcast behind, and visibility was now excellent.

Below was typical high desert country, strewn with rocks. Ahead and to starboard lay the forested hills around Avondale. Between him and the hills was an area of relatively flat ground with light scrub and what looked like firm sand. He had not dared to make a proper reconnaissance, but he had made a point of flying over the area during his refresher course, and had studied it carefully on large-scale charts on the interweb.

*Just beyond that dried-up river-bed. Sure that's the right bend? Yes – there's that big outcrop. Line her up. Switch on transmitter. Activate automatic 'Mayday' signal. Cut the engine... Dead-stick!*

*God this is terrifying... Never been in a belly-landing... Still – live and learn... Here we go...*

The aircraft skimmed the tops of scrubby bushes, caught a small tree with the starboard wingtip, slewed violently off track, and came to rest with its spinner-tip eight feet beyond the edge of the three-hundred-foot cliff that dropped to the old river-bed.

Harver sat gripping the steering yoke in the sudden silence of cooling metal-creaks and faint, shrill desert-noises. His breathing restarted. The still-active remnant of his consciousness was filled with the single thought: *got to get out!*

He opened the door, met a wall of searing-hot air saturated with the sizzlings of cicada sound-alikes, and forced himself to climb slowly out on to the wing root. Then, clutching the grab-handle right up to the last moment, he stepped off the wing, gingerly, backwards.

As he took the last of his weight off the wing, the aircraft tilted appreciably away from him. He instinctively stepped back, and could only watch, frozen to the spot, as the machine rolled gently, made a tinny slithering sound, and disappeared over the cliff. He hastily dropped to his hands and knees and peered down after it.

The aircraft plunged almost vertically until a rocky outcrop knocked its nose up, propelling it away from the cliff-face. From there on it dived less steeply until, to Harver's amazement, it reached flying speed, gliding straight and almost level. It smashed into the opposite river-bank about fifty feet from the bottom. The wreckage seemed to cling to the cliff for a second, till the 'crump' reached Harver's ears, then it slid and tumbled to the rocky river-bed. Then came another 'crump'.

Harver experienced profound relief and happiness at not being part of the wreckage. However, his euphoria faded with the dawning recognition that, though the landing operation itself had been successful, his overall plan had suffered something of a setback.

*Holy shit – my jacket! All my kit! My gun – every fucking thing – down there! SHI-IT!*

Frantically he looked to left and right, hoping that by some miracle there might be some place where the river-bank sloped more gently. But, exactly as he remembered from the charts, the cliff was continuous for miles in either direction.

He sat on a tuft of vegetation and tried to think. The sun beat down. Several species of desert-adapted organisms began to investigate his potential as a food source. He was so used to itching all over that he scarcely noticed the additional irritation, at first.

Five minutes of intense concentration under the mid-day sun served merely to focus his mind on the hoary old chestnut: *It's not falling off cliffs that's dangerous – it's the bump at the bottom that's dangerous.* Harver found this thought pretty amusing until he realised that he couldn't get it out of his head. His brain kept repeating inanely: *'...the bump at the bottom... the bump at the bottom... the bump at the bottom'.* At the same time, all over his body, the sensations generated by native life-forms settling into their new-found ecological niches were becoming unbearable.

He scrambled to his feet, smote his head, brushed at his clothing, scratched under his arm-pits, and rooted about with his fingers, disturbing but not dislodging the eager life-forms, which redoubled their probing, biting and sucking. At last, moaning dementedly, he set off at a jog-trot in the direction of the wooded hills.

He reached the first proper shade-trees in just over an hour, and paused for a short rest, getting his bearings. He was pretty sure that the home of Kjell Folke Varten was close by.

Those must be the two pointed hills you see in the wide-angle shots from the front of the place. The stream comes down between the hills, down past the house...

He became aware of a faint but pervasive swishing sound, which he had taken to be the wind in the leaves. *Or is it the leaves in the wind? What wind? There isn't any wind. That must be water... WATER!*

It was water. Just inside the edge of the forest, a stream plunged into a dark pool and vanished underground. Above the waterfall, in sunlit shallows, Harver wallowed naked, systematically evicting small desert creatures from every bodily crevice, crease, fold and orifice.

His clothes lay drying on rocks by the stream. His skin had almost stopped itching, for the moment at least. He felt good.

*Plan B is dead. Long live Plan C! Whatever that may be... On second thoughts – to hell with it! Let the old bastard keep his diamond. I don't need it. I'm lucky to be alive. I've got money. I can have any woman I fancy – snap my fingers and they come running. Maybe it's time to settle down anyway. I could probably stand having the redhead around the place. She wants to cook and clean and have babies – why not let her? Yeah...*

*On the other hand. To have come this far... to be so close... I've got to see the Star – see it for real. And touch it.*

And in the sun-warmed shallows of the stream that saved his life, Harver Westly found inspiration. Plan C sprang into his mind in all its limpid purity and simplicity: *Walk up to the house of Kjell Folke Varten and ask to see the Evening Star.*

And what then? Then play it by ear.

Without waiting to dry off, Harver put on his crumpled clothes and scuffed shoes. The 'Manuel Garstang' contact lenses were giving no trouble, and a tug on each moustache confirmed that the adhesive was holding well. He set off uphill, following the stream.

After a few hundred metres, the trees thinned out, giving a view down the valley and out over the desert. A rescue helicopter, bright red and white, patrolled slowly left to right, parallel to the edge of the desert. Harver smiled, and trudged on.

The house appeared quite suddenly, catching him by surprise. He had expected at least a token fence to warn him that he was getting close. As it was, he pushed through a thicket and found himself confronting a large picture-window from a distance of less than ten metres. His instinct was to draw back out of sight, but he made himself calmly take a step into the open.

He could not see in through the window. The hairs on the back of his neck told him that something or someone was watching him. Behind him, in the trees, something went 'snap'. He swung round, breathing hard, crouching. Nothing happened. He straightened up slowly, listening to his heart, telling himself: *This is moronic. I'm supposed to be a plane-crash survivor – a hero – not a burglar.*

Remembering to put on the correct amount of accent, he called out, "Hello! Is anybody here? Hello!"

Silence answered him, but his neck-hairs told him that the answer was a lie. He moved slowly round the house, with a slight limp that he wished he had rehearsed to make sure it looked convincing. He hated having to improvise.

Everything was as he remembered from his studies of the architectural plans. *But where are all the security systems – all the sensors? If the old man's out, why doesn't the house say something? What the hell's going on?*

He reached the front door. Solid studded oak. No bell-push, no knocker, no peephole. Not even anything that looked like a lock. Just a simple wrought-iron handle like the one on the door of Rose Cottage.

Harver looked round. Beyond the sunlight lawn, the trees were still and silent. The stream gurgled softly. An insect-sized flying creature droned through the clearing and passed behind the house. Harver cleared his throat. "Hollo –

hollo – is anybody there? No?" He waited some seconds before adding: "OK – I come in. Is all right?"

He turned the black door handle and pushed. The door didn't budge.

A female voice said sharply, "This is a private house. Please go away!"

"OK – OK – I go!" said Harver, startled, but relieved to have got a response at last, and remembering to use his Garstang accent. "I sorry. Is just I need help. My aircraft she is crashed in the desert. Since mid-day have I walked. Please to give me food and drink."

"Your request is being considered. Please wait."

Time passed, then one of the black studs near the middle of the door swivelled to one side, revealing a lighted lens, and the voice said, "Identity check. Please eyeball."

Harver mentally crossed his fingers and put his eye to the lens.

"You are identified as Manuel Garstang," said the voice. The fake iron stud swivelled back into position.

Harver waited for something else to happen. Nothing else happened. For want of anything better to do, he tried the door handle and pushed. The door opened. He was in!

He entered the hall, a high room like an atrium, with a miniature jungle of potted plants round a pond, beyond which an open staircase spiralled up to a gallery and the bedroom suites. From his memory of the plans, he reckoned he could identify the rooms leading off the hall: cloakroom, dining room, large lounge, kitchen, small lounge, study.

If I'm right – if that is the study, then that's where he keeps It.

The feeling of being watched had not left him, but somehow it didn't bother him now. The house knew he was there, and believed it knew who he was. It was unlikely to do anything nasty without warning.

*The old man must be out. If he was in, the house would have told him I was here. Better get on with it.*

Harver's feet made scarcely a sound on the thick carpet as he tip-toed to the study door, which he found to be unlocked, and opened silently. Heavy curtains covered the window, letting in one thin ray of sunlight. Otherwise the room was in darkness. Harver drew a breath and stepped in.

To his left, half-way down the room, a glow of light appeared, faint at first but brightening as his eyes became accustomed. Harver was drawn to the glow. Without being aware of having moved, he found himself within arms-length of his goal, gazing into the darkness and brilliance and beauty. He reached towards it, fearing that the thing was an illusion – a hologram, like most important jewels on public display.

But it was real. As his trembling fingers touched the great stone itself, he felt a tremendous shock, like a bolt of electricity, and snatched his hand away. Seconds passed before he realised that the shock was nothing but the thrill of touching this object of deep desire. He reached out again, with both hands, took firm hold of the heavy marble plinth, and lifted. There was no resistance, no sounds of alarm.

He carried the jewellery-sculpture across the room and held it in the ray of sunlight, turning it this way and that, revelling in the special fire of the Star itself.

"Beautiful," he almost crooned, as though talking to a baby. "Wonderful!"

"Quite pretty, I suppose," said a deep voice behind him.

Harver froze. *Varten's voice. But is it just a recording?*

The voice continued: "In my opinion, words such as 'wonderful' and 'beautiful' are usually wasted on mere artefacts. But that particular object is, perhaps, an exception. It was made with great care and devotion to be a symbol of care and devotion. Please put it back where you found it, Mr Garstang."

Now Harver looked round. Kjell Folk Varten stood just inside the room, silhouetted against the brighter light in the hall. He had something in his hand, something he raised to eye-level and pointed. Harver ducked, clutching the sculpture to his chest. There was a faint click, followed by the whine of motors opening the curtains.

The old man grinned sardonically, and blew imaginary smoke from his remote controller. His voice was full of weary contempt. "Get up, you pathetic specimen. You know who I am. You know I wouldn't be seen dead with a weapon in my hand. That's it – stand up like a human being. Now put it back!"

To be so humiliated at his moment of triumph was more than Harver could bear. In his mind something snapped. He straightened slowly and walked towards the old man, bearing the sculpture in front of him like a priestly offering, gripping the marble base with both hands.

The old man's eyes narrowed scornfully, then widened in alarm. But he stood his ground. "Put it back, you fool!"

Harver raised the sculpture, half-screamed, "Never!", and brought it down with desperate force on the old man's head.

Kjell Folke Varten crumpled and fell, limbs akimbo like a rag-doll, face turned to one side, eyes and mouth open. A little blood ran down through his wispy hair on to the deep pile of the carpet.

Harver watched the trickle of blood, and became calm. He checked the old man for vital signs and found none. *Stupid old bastard. Why did you have to get yourself killed? Well – at least you don't need a doctor.*

He took the sculpture into the kitchen, found a knife, carefully prised out the Evening Star, and put it in his trouser-pocket. He thoroughly wiped the remainder of the sculpture with a damp cloth, and replaced it in its niche in the study wall. Returning to the kitchen, he took a piece of meat pie and a couple of cans of beer from the refrigerator, and put them in a plastic shopping-bag. Finally, he went through the rooms he had been in, wiping everything he remembered touching, and left the house.

Kjell Folke Varten's car gave him no problems. About eleven o'clock that night, he abandoned it at the 'Manuel Garstang' ranch, and continued cross-country on foot, reaching his hired camper just after one-thirty a.m.

The camper was locked. The keys were in his jacket at the bottom of the dried-up river-bed. The spare keys were in the camper's mini-safe. For a moment he contemplated smashing a window. Then he laughed, and drew forth from his trouser-pocket the most expensive glass-cutter in the observable universe.

After a shower and a microwaved pizza washed down with twelve-year-old malt whisky, Harver Westly was fully restored to good humor and self-esteem. Even his itching skin seemed not quite so oppressive. He went to bed and watched the ero-channel for half an hour or so. Then had a good scratch, snuggled down, and slept the sleep of the just.

Next morning he commed Katriona's sister's number. The sister came on screen, took one look at the caller, and disappeared. Harver heard her mutter, "It's for you, Katty – your shit-salesman in person." *Nasty-minded bitch...*

The redhead chick appeared, trying to smooth out her hair with her hands. She looked as if she had spent the past seventy-two hours crying her eyes out. She sounded pretty sad, too. "Oh darling – I've been so worried. Where've you been? Why didn't you call? Oh god, I've missed you so..."

She brightened up when Harver assured her he would be back at Rose Cottage that evening. "Oh, that's wonderful, darling. I'll catch the first plane I can get. When you get back, I'll be there waiting for you. And I'll be wearing something special – not much – just something you like to see me in!"

"Yeah – great," said Harver. "Look – I've got a few calls to make. So... bye, now – be seeing you."

The company handling Simon Crawson's remains were happy to make an appointment that very afternoon for Mr Westly to come and pay his last respects before the coffin was sealed and placed in bond for its journey back to Cyrus.

Harver chartered an executive jet complete with two cabin crew, both qualified Temporary Partners, who made every effort to take his mind off the sad purpose of the trip, and were quite successful.

The Head Mortician himself welcomed Harver and led him to the parlour where Crawson lay in state. The morticians had done the old man proud. Propped up on a comfortable cushion, he looked considerably more cheerful than Harver remembered him.

"Thanks," said Harver, with a little catch in his voice. "Do you think you could, I mean..." He gestured feebly at Simon and himself, as though the emotion of this final reunion were too strong for speech.

"Of course, Mr Westly. You want to be alone with your friend. I understand. If you need anything – anything at all – I'll be close at hand." The man withdrew, leaving the door slightly ajar.

"Well, old pal," said Harver, softly, earnestly. "I'm afraid this is the parting of the ways. You'll take the low road and I'll take the high road, and I'll be in Cyrus before you." He blew his nose, replaced the handkerchief in his pocket, and added: "I'll never forget you, old friend."

He leaned with his elbow on the edge of the coffin, and bent as if to kiss the unnaturally pink brow. Just as his lips were about to touch the waxy skin, his elbow slipped.

"Whoops! Sorry, Simon," said Harver, hastily smoothing and patting the dead man's clothes. "That was careless of me."

"Oh, I don't know about that, Mr Westly," said the Head Mortician, reaching over his shoulder and grabbing his right wrist. "I think you did it rather well, considering that you presumably haven't had a lot of practice."

At the word 'practice' the mortician twisted Harver's arm and applied a complex and painful martial-arts lock that threatened to dislocate all the joints simultaneously.

"Huh?" yelped Harver, as the mortician captured his other hand, brought his wrists together and snapped on a pair of handcuffs.

"Not practice with the real thing, anyway," continued the mortician, holding the Evening Star a foot or so from Harver's stricken face. "I don't suppose even a nasty little scum like you would go to the lengths of practising with real diamonds and real dead bodies. Or would you? Now I come to think of it, I wouldn't put it past you... Sergeant!"

Heavy footsteps came into the viewing parlour. "Sir?"

"On record, Sergeant."

"Recording, sir!"

"This is Detective Lieutenant Henry Garfield speaking. Harver Westly, you have the right to remain silent. Anything you say will be recorded and may be used in evidence.

"I now apprehend and arrest you for the direct murder of Kjell Folke Varten. And on suspicion of unlawfully compassing the death of Simon Aloysius Crawson. And for stealing the diamond known as the Evening Star. And for obstructing the People's Police and wasting Police time by falsely assuming and presenting the identity of Manuel Garstang, deceased.

"You will be formally charged in due course. You will then have the option of exercising or waiving your right to a trial. Now, Harver Westly, have you anything to say?"

All Harver could think of was: *How?*

"How?" he said.

"How did we catch you? That was the easy part. How did we fail to stop you before you did all the damage? That's easy, too. You had us fooled, Mr Westly. We never suspected you were up to anything until yesterday afternoon. Crashing that aircraft was just a bit too clever. From then on it was just a matter of time before we caught up with you. But by then you'd already killed Kjell Folke Varten. You really shouldn't have done that, Mr Westly. Sergeant – lead the way. It's about time we left Mr Crawson in peace."

In the police vehicle, Harver was not only kept handcuffed but shackled to a stanchion. When he protested, the sergeant told him to shut up. "Consider yourself lucky we won't be tempted to think you're trying to escape. After what you did to old man Varten, you deserve a damn sight more than the Time Shunt, if you ask me."

"That's enough, Sergeant," said the lieutenant. "He'll get what's coming to him, believe me."

"If you say so, sir."

"I *do* say so, Sergeant. If you'd ever sat in on a Time Shunt preview with Maisie Peters in the judge's seat, you'd say so too. She pays lip-service to the leakage guide-lines, but she'd rather see the whole planet altered by leakage effects than settle for a universe where a crim didn't suffer enough."

"Yeah – I heard she was a pretty good judge. Maybe this little bastard'll live long enough to find out. Say – how did you get on to him, Lieutenant?"

"Brilliant detective work, Sergeant – classic detective work! Aided and abetted by Westly's arrogance and stupidity. You know he used the old trick with retina-holograms in contact lenses?"

"Yeah – I didn't see the point of that. Why bother to call himself Manuel Garstang half the time? I mean, we had him on full-time trace from the moment he landed on Constitution."

"Yes – but he didn't know that. He thought that by using the Garstang identity every time he travelled, he'd be breaking his trail. He was mistaken there, but not stupid. And being Manuel Garstang when he used the interweb to get personal information wasn't stupid either. Remember, although we were tracking Westly, it was purely on a routine basis, the way we track all visitors from off-planet. Personally, I'd never even heard of Westly."

"Of course! I was forgetting that. So what made you catch on?"

"Fingerprints! I told you it was classic detective work. Crash-landing that plane was a mistake. I don't think you intended it to go over the cliff, did you, Mr Westly?"

"No – I –"

"You intended to give the impression that the pilot had simply abandoned the plane and wandered off. We were supposed to go looking for Manuel Garstang – am I right?"

"Yeah. But –"

"But we didn't. We expected to find the pilot mangled up in the wreckage. When we discovered he wasn't there or thereabouts, we started getting suspicious. The satellite record showed that the plane stopped at the top of the cliff before falling over the edge. There was just time for someone to get out. Unfortunately, with the heat at that time of day, the definition isn't good enough to pick out a man, but I was sure the pilot had escaped.

"Meanwhile, the squad down at the wreck carried out a standard fingerprint check, just in case there had been any passengers – in which case we should be looking for them too. And when they ran the prints past the computer – bingo! A certain Harver Westly's prints all over the place – and none that matched Manuel Garstang's."

"Ah! And we were already tracking Westly!"

"That's right. The computer told us he was a visitor from off-planet and asked if we would like to know his whereabouts. I told it 'yes please'!"

The sergeant laughed. "I bet you did. Where was he by then?"

"By then he was well away – in a car belonging to Kjell Folke Varten. We tried to contact Varten, and that's when we found out what had happened."

"Good grief, sir! What was wrong with Varten's security systems? Had Westly buggered them somehow?"

"No. Varten doesn't – didn't – have any security systems. Not even a dog. Doesn't believe in force, let alone violence. His house is programmed for emergency calls to the fire and medical services, but not the police."

"Good grief. And he's supposed to be a great man. Turns out he's a complete nut. No security – he's just asking for it. And who gets to pick up the pieces? Us – and the Time Shunt people. That's really irresponsible if you ask me."

"I don't ask you, Sergeant. What if I told you that Kjell Folke Varten personally sponsored the research that led to the Time Shunt, and paid for its deployment out of his own pocket. Would you still say he was irresponsible?"

"Well no – I guess not... Sorry, sir – I never knew he did all that."

"Neither did I – but it might be true, for all we know. Just try not to make idiotic judgements while I'm around, will you?"

"Sir!"

They were nearing the airport. The sergeant unfastened Harver's leg-iron. Harver rubbed it to restore the circulation. "Can I ask you something?"

"No you can't!" said the sergeant.

"Ask away," said the lieutenant. "I don't promise to answer."

"You say you've been tracking me all along. Did that woman have anything to do with it?"

"Woman? What woman?"

"Katriona McLeish. She's with the Diplomatic Service. She was assigned to look after me. Did she plant something on me – or – or something?"

"Never heard of her. We and the Dippies go our separate ways, Mr Westly. Their job's human relations and welfare. Our job's keeping the peace."

"So – how did you do it A bug? If it's a bug, where the hell have you hidden it?"

The lieutenant shrugged. "No harm in telling you now, I suppose. It's all over you, Mr Westly. Just under your skin. I'm told it often causes itching."

"Itching!"

"Yes – it's a radio transmitter in the form of a fine network overlaying the dermis – that's the base of the skin underneath the outer layer. The nanomachines that build and maintain the network move about among the nerve endings, causing the itch."

"Nanomachines? I'm infected! I've got nanos! Shit! How the hell? It must have been that redhead bitch, admit it!"

"Admit what? No idea what colour their hair was. It was the doctor at Immigration Control. Redhead – brunette – how should I know? You gave your consent to the inoculation. Nobody forced you into it."

"Oh," said Harver Westly. "Oh – shit... "

They kept Harver in a police cell in Jefferson City pending completion of the complex multi-location Time Shunt set-up. The process dragged on for days.

Katriona McLeish learned of her lover's arrest when she made a routine call from Rose Cottage to head office, reporting her location. Her supervisor, seeing her obvious surprise and distress, was inclined to be sympathetic, but nevertheless had her brought in for debriefing – an intensive procedure that quite unnecessarily went into the most intimate details of her relationship with Harver, and left her emotionally shattered.

At the end of it, the interviewing officer shut down the recording systems, and smiled at her. "I'm sorry we had to do this to you, Ms McLeish – er – Katriona. But you realise – in the up-coming Time Shunt context – it was necessary to establish that you had no prior knowledge of Westly's criminal intentions."

"I suppose so."

The man's smile was wasted on Katriona. She sat with her face in her hands, feeling shame, trying to grasp what had happened. *All those things we... Why did I have to tell them? Oh – Harver – why didn't you talk to me? You didn't have to prove anything. Why did you do it?* "I've got to see him. He loves me –

I know he does. He did it all for me – I'm sure he did, poor darling. Don't tell me I can't see him!"

"We can't stop you, Ms – Katriona. But we wouldn't advise it. There's really no point in putting yourself through further misery. After the Time Shunt, all this will be – forgotten. This – this business with Westly... it's really not important, you know."

She went to see him, all the same. They sat face to face, with a pane of glass between them.

"Oh, Harver – darling..." She gazed at him longingly, searching his face.

"Hi," said Harver.

"Hi!" She echoed, knowing all the secret things he meant to convey in that simple word – knowing and responding to them. The silence lengthened, the silence of shared being-together, shared understanding.

Eventually, Harver said, "There's something I want to ask you."

Katriona leaned forward eagerly. "Anything, my darling – ask me anything!"

"Did you know I was bugged?"

She gaped at him. "Bugged? Oh – you mean the tracer! Yes – of course I knew about it. All visitors have to have them. They get them at Immigration Control. Otherwise they can't land."

"You knew!"

"Well – yes. Darling – what's the matter?"

"Why the fu- ... Stupid BITCH – why the hell didn't you tell me?"

"I thought you knew. *Everyone* knows! Besides – how was I supposed to know it mattered? How was I supposed to know you were..."

Katriona stopped, suddenly seeing Harver Westly for the first time – the shifty eyes – the twisted, sneering mouth. She noticed the small blobs of spittle trickling down the glass that separated them. "How was I to know what you were?"

233

She shook her head as if to clear it. "I loved you... God, what a fool I've been." She got up and turned to leave.

Harver protested, "Hey – don't go! I didn't mean it. It wasn't your fault..."

Katriona shook her head and walked on. Behind her the door clicked shut. She leaned against the wall and sobbed quietly for a while.

---

Voluntary Judge Maisie Peters moved quietly along the river-bank, keeping back in the shade of the trees so as not to let the fish see her coming. Just round the next bend there was a deep pool where lurked an old adversary – a cunning old seven-pound rainbow she had actually hooked twice before, only for him to jerk free. This time she was going to *get* the son-of-a-bitch...

She laid her picnic-box and tackle-bag gently on the grass, and pondered which fly to use. *Nothing on the water – nothing rising... The old fellow took a Butcher last time, but the sun was lower then... Speckled Dun? No – he'd never fall for it at this time of day. In any case, this time it's war. No quarter – take no prisoners.* Ignoring her angling conscience, the Judge opened a can of wriggling blood-worms...

In her picnic-box, her phone beeped.

"BUGGER!" remarked the Judge. "Why now?" she added looking at the sky. *I could pretend I haven't heard it. But the fish'll have heard it... So I guess he'll keep for another day...*

"Maisie Peters here. What – already? I thought you said you'd need at least another day or two... Oh – fair enough. No – there really doesn't seem any point in Shunting for Simon Crawson – I'm glad we all agree on that... Yes – right away... Where – the Spaceport? Avondale – Kjell Folke Varten's place – fine. See you there. Wait a second! You'll be bringing Westly with you, I take it? Good. I want a word with that little rat... He may have waived his right to a trial, but he's not going to get away without me telling him what I think of him... Yes – that's right – it makes me feel better... OK – bye, now."

They brought Harver Westly to Judge Peters at the scene of the crime. The study curtains were drawn. In the darkness blazed the Evening Star, restored to the centre of its spiral galaxy.

The Judge did not look at Harver. "I still don't understand *why*, Mr Westly."

Harver gazed at the sculpture and said nothing. *If she can stand there and ask me that, she must be blind... Moronic old cow...*

"I don't mean stealing the diamond," said the Judge. "That's understandable enough – almost forgivable, if you were poor. And even though you're rich, I can think I can understand your desire to possess something of that quality.

"But the rest... We can't prove you murdered Mr Simon Crawson, but I'm certain you did, and I don't know why. You must have known he was going to die very soon. It must have been obvious from the moment you saw him in hospital. I don't know why you couldn't let nature take its course.

"And I've heard what you did to that youngster Ms Katriona McLeish. You didn't have to treat her the way you did. I don't see the point.

"And I don't understand why you murdered Mr Varten. He was a harmless old man, unarmed. You knew his reputation as a pacifist. You could have walked away with everything he owned, and he would have done nothing to stop you."

Harver started to say something, but the Judge rounded on him. "Keep quiet, Westly! I didn't ask you to explain. There can be no justification for what you have done. I merely want you to know why we are going to select a universe where life for you will be truly horrible. And I want you to dwell on that fact until the time comes for the Shunt. Goodbye, Mr Westly."

"Right, Sergeant – I've had my say – you can take this little shit away."

---

Later that morning, Kjell Folke Varten, returning from his usual walk through the woods above his house, was disappointed to see the post-van driving away. He shouted and waved, but the postman failed to notice him. He'd have to drink his coffee on his own, for once.

There was a large envelope on his doorstep, with a note attached: 'Sorry to miss you, Kjell. I should give you this hand-to-hand and get you to eyeball, but why waste your time? It's only the usual. See you soon. Pierre.'

Kjell Folke Varten let himself in and walked through to the study, sliding his finger under the flap of the envelope as he went, and extracting the parchment it contained.

Halfway across the room he stopped and glanced at the document. He sighed, opened a desk-drawer, and added the new Notification to the brimming pile. He had to hold the pile down with his left hand so that he could shut the drawer with his right.

---

Harver reluctantly left his bunk, shrugged off his sleep-suit, and stepped into the hygiene unit. Over the hiss of needle-spray he heard the stateroom comm chime, and a woman's voice said something about the Ship's Purser. He ignored it. These announcements were for the ordinary punters, not for pros. Harver Westly had heard them all before, many times.

When he stepped out of the unit, he was surprised to notice a message flashing on his view-screen, superimposed on the plum-like image of he planet Constitution.

"ATTENTION PASSENGER HARVER WESTLY. URGENT URGENT URGENT. YOU ARE REQUIRED TO

VISIT THE SHIP'S PURSER AS SOON AS POSSIBLE. THIS IS URGENT REPEAT URGENT."

After breakfast, Harver, soberly dressed as a typical Constitution businessman, found his way to the Purser's office. There was a waiting area outside, in which several other passengers stood in line, under the eye of a grim-looking male receptionist seated at a brushed-light-alloy desk. The others looked as anxious as Harver felt. He envied them. At least they knew what they were anxious about.

The receptionist beckoned. "Yes, sir – your name, please?"

Harver told him.

The receptionist reached under the desk, drew a stunner, and levelled it at Harver's chest. "OK, Mac. Keep your hands in sight. No sudden moves." he gestured with the weapon, indicating a door marked 'Interview Room. When Red Light Shows Keep Out'. "In there! No – you first, buddy."

As Harver crossed the threshold, the receptionist booted him in the back, sending him sprawling. The door closed with a click that suggested finality. The lights went out. Harver lay where he had fallen, terrified, alone, in complete darkness.

After several hours, the lights came on, the door opened, and two uniformed men wearing Diplomatic Service Police badges pinioned Harver's arms, cuffed him and fitted leg-irons. When he tried to ask what he was supposed to have done, one of them ripped his shirt off and gagged him with it.

There was nobody about when they eventually left the Interview Room. The Diplomatic Policemen frog-marched Harver along a corridor, and tried to bundle him into an airlock. Convinced they were going to 'space' him; he struggled violently until one of them pulled a stunner and gave him a low-intensity blast.

He came to as the shuttle landed at Jefferson Spaceport. In an office next to the baggage reclaim hall, he was tied to a chair and ungagged. The policemen left him, and shortly afterwards a grey-haired senior diplomat entered the room with a cup of coffee, on seeing which Harver's spirits rose, only to fall again when the diplomat took a sip and placed the cup on a convenient filing cabinet.

"Nice cup of coffee," said the diplomat. "Better than you'd expect at a spaceport. Well, now, Mr Westly, is it – Mr Harver Westly?"

"Yes – I don't –"

"Hmmm – yes – well it seems you've been a bit of a bad lad, Mr Westly. Hmmm – bit of a naughty boy. Normally – of course – *normally* we could – possibly – well – let's face it – normally, there'd be nothing to worry about. We could normally smooth things over. But as things are..."

"What things? What are you talking about? What have I DONE?"

"Done? Done, Mr Westly? It's not what you've done. It's what you *haven't* done!"

"What haven't I done?"

"What indeed, Mr Westly. You admit you ordered a pair of Yevgenian lizard-skin thigh-boots – size fourteen?"

"Yes – but that was a mistake! I –"

"And you were told at the time they would be ready Thursday? Well – were you or weren't you?"

"I guess so, but –"

"And you know what today is? Say it, Mr Westly!"

"Friday. But –"

"Exactly. Yesterday was Thursday. And you failed to collect them... In Yevgenian eyes, failure to collect boots of any kind is an affront. Failure to collect *thigh*-boots is both an insult and a blasphemy. Admittedly the incident occurred in neutral space. But relations between Yevgeni and Constitution have never been more delicate. As a gesture of goodwill, we therefore deem it fitting to conform with the spirit of our mutual extradition treaty, and hand you over to the Yevgenis in the name of justice."

"Hand me over?"

"Yes – their agents should be here any minute."

"But – this is crazy!"

"I don't think so, Mr Westly. Not crazy. Alarming, yes – I would agree that in your shoes one might discern some cause for alarm. I am willing to concede that Yevgenian ways are not our ways. Unlike the Yevgenis, we of Constitution have no particular predilection for doing strange and complicated things to criminals' – er – *bottoms*. But who are we to pass judgment on another culture?"

"Huh?" said Harver, at which moment three Yevgeni agents burst in, bowed low, and dragged him off through the baggage-reclaim hall. He caught a passing glimpse of a beautiful redhead, the spitting image of the woman of his most erotic dreams, just before they shoved him into an unmarked black van.

Made in the USA
Columbia, SC
08 January 2023

74837849R00143